THE OTHER GIRLFRIEND

ALEX STONE

Boldwood

First published in Great Britain in 2022 by Boldwood Books Ltd.

Copyright © Alex Stone, 2022

Cover Design by Head Design

Cover Photography: Shutterstock

Every effort has been made to obtain the necessary permissions with reference to copyright material, both illustrative and quoted. We apologise for any omissions in this respect and will be pleased to make the appropriate acknowledgements in any future edition.

A CIP catalogue record for this book is available from the British Library.

Paperback ISBN 978-1-80280-321-1

Large Print ISBN 978-1-80280-322-8

Hardback ISBN 978-1-80280-320-4

Ebook ISBN 978-1-80280-324-2

Kindle ISBN 978-1-80280-323-5

Audio CD ISBN 978-1-80280-315-0

MP3 CD ISBN 978-1-80280-316-7

Digital audio download ISBN 978-1-80280-318-1

Boldwood Books Ltd
23 Bowerdean Street
London SW6 3TN
www.boldwoodbooks.com

For all those who encouraged me to never give up.

1

NOW

I froze. The mug of coffee I held in my hand was instantly forgotten, leaving it poised just centimetres from my lips, as the doorbell chimed for a second time.

Who would be visiting me? I glanced across my kitchen table at Kate. The only unscheduled visitor I ever got was already here.

At least, the only welcome one.

My stomach churned as panic started to well up inside me.

Who could it be? The grocery delivery had already arrived and my parents would always call first.

I remained totally still. Was it fear that paralysed me, or a desperate hope that if I didn't move, maybe they would leave?

The doorbell rang again.

They weren't leaving.

Kate started to stand. 'Do you want me to get—'

'No.' I sprang to my feet. My fear of opening the door was outweighed only by my fear of Kate seeing through the façade of normality that I had created around me. 'I'll get it.' I had to. I was expected to. It was what normal people did. They didn't cower and hide any time their doorbell rang.

But then, there were a lot of things normal people did that were somehow just a little out of my reach.

I turned towards the hall and took a deep breath as I tried to restore the outward appearance of calm that I worked so hard to portray. I coaxed my feet forward, frowning at the intrusion, vaguely aware I was still holding my coffee.

As I lifted my hand to the catch I hesitated for a moment. My home was my sanctuary from the outside world. Unscheduled visitors were a disruption to the peace that I only ever managed to find here.

With a deep breath I summoned the courage to pull the door open, a polite smile fixed in place despite my apprehension. 'Hi, can I...' My words fell away as my eyes met his. I felt the mug start to slip from my fingers and I jolted it upwards, splashing the hot liquid over my hand. But I barely even noticed.

I stared at the man before me, transfixed, unsure if I could trust what my eyes were seeing.

'T-T-Tom?' I stuttered over the once familiar name, which now felt strange and alien on my tongue.

Bile rose in my throat, leaving a bitter taste in my dry mouth.

No one can know.

Tom's last words to me echoed in my ears.

He'd been right of course. Tom was always right.

He smiled at me. 'Hi Lizzie, it's been a while,' he said, his voice full of energy and excitement.

The hairs on the back of my neck stood on end at the sound of that name and I gripped the door tightly. No one called me that any more.

Lizzie had gone. She was my past. My failing. My nightmare.

Just like Tom.

'Lizzie?' Kate's questioning voice from the hallway behind me made me flinch.

'Hi, there,' Tom said as he peered around me. 'I'm Tom, an old friend of Lizzie's.'

An image of a younger Tom grinning at me flashed in my mind. He and I had been inseparable as kids. He was my best friend.

Or, at least, he had been.

* * *

Tom and I took our final bows as our parents clapped furiously. His younger brother, Harry, dropped the torch he had been using as a spotlight, flicked the lights on and rushed to pull the cord to draw the curtains in my parents' living room. Tom and I stepped back, trying not to get caught in the curtains, and giggled as we squeezed up against the window behind us. The bay window really wasn't big enough for a stage, but we always made it work. Just about.

'Encore!' Dad shouted, and he was echoed by everyone else.

Tom stuck his head through the gap in the curtains. 'You really want us to repeat it?'

Laughter erupted from our audience.

'It was great, son, but everything's better in moderation,' Tom's dad told him.

'The key,' Dad added, 'is to always leave your audience wanting more.'

'Oh, okay.' I heard the disappointment in Tom's voice, before he shook it off. 'I mean, thank goodness for that, because I'm too tired to do it all again.'

I gave Tom a playful shove and we stepped out from our hiding place, as laughter filled the room again. But I knew he wasn't tired at all. Tom could act all night if they let him.

'I don't know where you two come up with all these ideas for such clever plays,' Mum said as she started collecting the empty tea mugs.

'It's Lizzie, she writes all our scripts,' Tom announced proudly.

Heat rushed to my face. 'But you bring them to life,' I told him, deflecting the praise. While I loved to be in the background, taking things I'd seen or done and turning them into stories, Tom was the one who insisted we perform them for our families.

'He certainly does that,' Tom's dad agreed. 'Tom'll either be an actor or a politician when he grows up. He can convince people to do anything.'

'Hmm,' Mum murmured. 'I'm not sure that's always an ideal skill to possess.'

* * *

Tom reached his hand out towards Kate, leaving me no choice but to step out of the way.

The past and the present were colliding in my own home, and I was trapped in the middle, unable to prevent it.

'I'm Kate,' she said as she walked forwards and shook Tom's hand. 'A neighbour,' she added, jerking her head to the left towards her house.

'And a friend by the looks of it,' Tom said, nodding at the coffee mug in her hand.

'Of course,' Kate turned to me and smiled. '*Lizzie* and I are good friends.'

I noted the emphasis she placed on that name and knew there would be questions later.

Many questions.

My shoulders slumped at the thought of it. Kate was right, we were good friends. But there were some things even good friends shouldn't know.

'Am I missing something?' Tom asked, glancing back and forth between Kate and I.

I tried to shrug. 'No one calls me Lizzie any more. I go by Beth now.'

Even as I said it, I regretted it. As strange as it had been to hear him call me Lizzie after all these years, it felt even more disconcerting to share my new name with Tom. The two didn't go together.

Beth was who I'd become when I'd reinvented myself. She was my way of distancing myself from the past and the bad memories I still carried. It was the only way I could live with them. They belonged to Lizzie, not Beth.

'Beth,' Tom repeated, tipping his head to the side as if assessing whether my new name fitted. 'Really?'

I could tell by his tone that his conclusion was no.

'I guess you'll always be Lizzie to me.'

I stared at him silently, unable to think of a reply. It was true. When Tom was around I would always be Lizzie.

The trouble was, that wasn't a good thing.

'Well, Lizzie or Beth, I don't recall her ever mentioning a Tom before...' Kate's curiosity broke through the strained silence.

'Ah, we grew up together,' Tom said. 'But sadly, we kind of lost touch when I moved away.'

Part of me wanted to correct him. We'd lost touch years before he moved to London. It wasn't the distance that had separated us.

It was me.

He may have been the one to cut me off. But I was the reason.

'Well, in that case,' Kate took a large swig of her coffee, before thrusting the mug towards me, 'I should get out of the way and let you two catch up.'

'No, you d—' I started to protest despite instinctively taking the mug, but Kate was already out the door.

I watched as she veered off the driveway and cut across my front lawn to her house in the warm afternoon sun, while I stood in my hallway with two coffee mugs in my hands, feeling helpless and abandoned.

'I'd love a coffee, if you're offering.'

My gaze fell back to Tom, still standing on my doorstep, staring at me expectantly.

I nodded automatically while common sense screamed at me to say no. But then I'd never listened to common sense. Not when it came to Tom.

I expected him to step straight through the open door, seizing the moment before I changed my mind. It was how he usually worked. But instead, he turned to his left and reached out his hand.

I leaned to the side, curiosity overriding the realisation that there was still time to slam the door shut on both Tom and the past.

My eyes widened as he pulled a wheelie case towards him. I watched it, transfixed, as he stepped into the hall and strode towards the kitchen, dragging the case behind him, the wheels rumbling along the tiled floor.

A familiar queasiness stirred in my stomach and I swallowed, hoping to push it away.

Tom was back in my life, with baggage.

2

ELEVEN YEARS AGO

I squealed as I read the email on my phone and shot up in bed. I automatically opened the contacts list and selected Tom's name. My thumb hovered over the call button, but I hesitated. What if he hadn't heard yet? Or worse still, what if he had and it was bad news? Everything hinged on us doing this together. Like we always did.

My phone rang.

'Did you hear?' Tom asked.

'I got in,' we said in unison.

We laughed. 'I can't believe it,' I said, struggling to speak through my laughter. 'We did it.'

'Told you we would. With you by my side I can't fail.'

I rolled my eyes. 'That's 'cause you're the optimistic one.'

'And you're the pessimist.'

'No,' I corrected. 'I'm just the cautious one.'

Tom chuckled. 'You always make things sound better.'

I beamed with pride. 'Have you told your parents yet?' I asked, deflecting the attention.

'No, you were the first person I wanted to tell.'

'*Same here.*' *A warm glow enveloped me. I was important enough to be the first to know.*

'*Told your parents what?*' *Mum asked, peering round my bedroom door.*

A flash of frustration tore through me for a second, before the excitement of my news bubbled back to the surface. '*We both got into Arts University Bournemouth.*' *There was no need to define the* '*we*' *I was talking about. Mum would know it was Tom. It was always Tom.*

'*That's fantastic. But I'm sure other unis will be in touch soon too,*' *Mum said as she picked up the pair of jeans I'd left on the floor where I'd kicked them off last night.*

I sucked in a breath through my gritted teeth. '*We talked about this, Mum.*'

'*I better let you go,*' *Tom said.* '*Good luck.*'

'*Thanks, talk to you later.*'

We hung up and I turned back to Mum as she placed my neatly folded jeans on the stool by my dressing table. '*You know AUB is my first choice.*'

'*But it wasn't originally. What happened to your plans to go to one of the bigger institutions somewhere a little further away?*'

'*Tom considered it, but he wants to stay here.*'

'*That doesn't mean you have to.*'

'*I thought you'd be pleased I want to stay in Bournemouth.*'

'*I am. Of course I am. But this is the time in your life when you should be spreading your wings a little and having adventures.*'

I shook my head. '*We can't afford adventures, and neither can Tom.*'

'*Your dad and I would find a way—*'

'*But you don't need to,*' *I interrupted. We'd been through this before. Mum never listened to what Tom and I wanted.* '*If I stay locally we can save on the cost of accommodation. And besides, you know AUB has both of the courses that Tom and I want. Between my creative writing degree* and his events management degree we both get to follow our dreams and stay close together.'

'There must be other universities that offer both courses, and if not...' She shrugged. 'Would it be the worst thing for you two to spend a little time apart?'

'Mum! Tom's my best friend.'

'I know, Lizzie, but you're so dependent on him: his timescale, his plans, even his approval.'

'I am not.' I bristled. 'You make it sound so one-sided.' Why couldn't she see what Tom and I had together? Why couldn't she accept that we wanted to be together?

I needed us to be together.

'Isn't it one-sided?'

'No, we make time for each other. We encourage each other and support each other. Like friends and family should.'

Mum drew back and I knew my comment had stung, but I didn't care. She'd always been disapproving of Tom. She'd never really given him a chance. He hadn't even done anything wrong. He was always polite and friendly towards her. And yet, for some reason she just didn't like him.

Or perhaps, more accurately, she didn't trust him.

He was too confident for her liking. Too sure of himself. Of his goals. His ambitions. He never let anyone hold him back. Not that anyone tried. Apart from Mum, of course. For some reason, she was the only person he'd never been able to win over.

She just didn't know him like I did. She didn't see how supportive he was. Or how interested he was, asking questions about my day, my feelings. Always encouraging me with my writing. Always helping me to improve. To be more than I was.

Not many people cared enough to devote their time and attention to someone else. To me.

But Tom did.

3

NOW

I followed Tom to the kitchen, a thousand questions racing through my brain.

Why was he here? Back in my life? My home?

After ten years, I should be nothing more than a faded memory. At least to him. He'd always meant more to me than I had to him. But I'd accepted that. Even a little of Tom's attention was somehow superior and more significant than the full attention of someone else. He had a way about him. He made me bolder. Better.

Without him...

I took a deep breath. It had taken a long time to pick up the pieces. To start over. To rebuild my life. Myself.

But was that the result of his absence? Or my mistake?

Even now I knew I wasn't the same. Somehow the pieces no longer fit quite like they once had. There were gaps. Weaknesses.

Life was a precarious balancing act that I still hadn't mastered. After all this time I was barely hanging on by my fingertips. Not that anyone knew.

Despite all my failures, there was one thing I had excelled at in the last ten years; I'd learnt how to fake it.

No one knew the real me.

Maybe not even myself.

My life was an act, an illusion of being fine; being normal; being in control.

I emptied the coffee mugs into the sink and lined them up neatly in the dishwasher. My hand trembled slightly as I refilled the kettle and I set it back on its stand quickly.

I'm just making coffee for an old friend, I reminded myself as I flicked the switch. It was just the same as making coffee for Kate.

Except it wasn't.

The air was charged with nervous energy now. Curiosity battled with fear. Tom shouldn't be here. I knew that. It was too risky. Too dangerous.

'The old place looks good,' Tom said as he peered out of the kitchen window at the small back garden.

'Thanks,' I replied. It looked almost the same as the last time he'd been here. That was part of its charm. Its safety. Its necessity.

I nibbled the inside of my cheek. And part of its trap too.

My gaze drifted to the buds that were just starting to poke their way up in the borders. The first signs of spring.

I glanced back at Tom, wondering what he was a sign of.

'A lot of good memories here,' he said, turning to face me.

I nodded. 'I think you spent more time here when we were kids than you did in your own home.'

Tom chuckled. 'True, but it wasn't the house that kept me here.'

My cheeks flushed and I turned away, picked up the dishcloth and wiped the already pristine worktop. 'How did you know I still lived here?'

Tom shrugged. 'I figured it was a good place to start.'

I nodded. It made sense.

'Your parents aren't here?' His voice held no hint of nervousness at the possibility of seeing them, even though he must have known he wouldn't receive a warm welcome.

'No,' I told him. 'I bought the house off them when they retired to Spain.' I smiled as his shoulders relaxed. 'They're off having adventures in the sunshine.'

'And you're still here.'

There was a flatness to his tone that made me shrink inside. Tom was right. I was still here. I'd never moved away. Never gone anywhere. Never done any of the things I'd planned to.

From the outside, my life must look to Tom as though I'd given up. He didn't know what it took to even have this.

I glanced back at him, studying his movements, his expressions, his body language, searching for any clue to his motives.

Surely there couldn't be a good reason for his surprise visit. Not for me. Not given what he knew.

I should ask him to leave. I could tell him I had somewhere I needed to be. I could tell him anything. It didn't matter, as long as he was gone.

And yet I knew that I wouldn't.

He was Tom.

I'd never been able to say no to Tom.

He moved about my kitchen, his vibrant blue eyes taking in every detail.

He'd always been good looking, and the years had only enhanced his attractiveness. He was more muscular now, and there was a maturity to him, which added to his existing confidence. He moved purposefully. Calmly. Everything was done with intention and commitment.

There had never been any half measures with Tom.

My kitchen felt different with him in it. Somehow the room seemed to shrink with his presence, making it feel claustrophobic. Had he always had that effect?

I tried to recall, but it felt like a lifetime since I'd last seen him. But then, in a way, it was. I wasn't the same person I used to be and despite appearances, I knew that thanks to me, he couldn't be either.

Don't think about it.

I nodded slightly, even though I knew it was impossible to forget.

I had tried.

And I'd failed.

I spooned coffee granules into fresh mugs and poured in the boiling water, stirring methodically. I focused on the swirling movement, hoping the rhythm would calm the swelling panic I felt inside. I could do this. I had the strength to stay in control. At least that was what the therapist had repeatedly told me.

Tom opened the door to the fridge and handed me the milk.

I mustered a smile, but something withered inside me. Who was I kidding? Now Tom was back, I wasn't in control of anything.

I never had been.

I took a sip of the hot coffee, hoping it would help settle the queasiness in my stomach, and winced as it scalded my tongue.

'Careful,' he cautioned, even though it was too late.

I set the coffee back down on the worktop and tried to regain my composure, aware that Tom looked more relaxed in my home than I did.

'W-why are you here?' I couldn't stand the tension that crushed my chest any longer. I needed to know. I always needed to know. Uncertainty was my enemy. My downfall.

'I came back for you,' Tom said, as he stepped towards me. 'Just like I promised I would.'

4

TEN YEARS AGO

'Lizzie!'

I jolted forward on the wooden chair and stared at Rebecca. 'What?' I asked, conscious that everyone at the surrounding tables was now looking at us.

'I was talking to you, but you were...' Her eyes narrowed as she studied me. 'Where were you?'

I felt heat rush to my cheeks. 'Nowhere, I was just thinking.' My gaze instinctively drifted to the coffee shop counter where Tom and Luke were queuing to order our drinks.

'Oh no,' Rebecca groaned.

'What?' I asked again, although the sinking feeling in my stomach told me I already knew.

'Don't tell me you've got a crush on Tom?'

'Don't be ridiculous,' I scoffed, as the café suddenly grew warmer. I was usually more careful. More discreet. But my feelings for Tom had been growing stronger and stronger since we'd started uni in September. No, if I was honest with myself, it had been longer than that. Perhaps it had been a mistake to spend my summer holiday with him. Long lazy days together, sunbathing, swimming and barbecuing on Bournemouth beach.

Not that I would have passed up the opportunity. Those memories were precious treasures that I clung to in the hope that this summer would be the same. If not better.

But it had been just the two of us then.

I pulled myself back to the problem at hand. If Rebecca had picked up on my feelings, were they obvious? Had Tom realised too?

'Well, I know you're not checking Luke out. Not if you value our friendship.'

'Luke?' I pulled a face. 'Seriously?'

Rebecca put her hand on her hip. 'And what's wrong with Luke?'

'N-nothing,' I stuttered quickly. 'He's just not my type, that's all.'

'Hmm,' she grunted, seeming satisfied with my answer. 'But Tom is.'

Rebecca's statement hung in the air between us.

She was right.

And we both knew it.

'I've always suspected you fancied him, ever since I first met you both at the start of the year. But I chalked it up to the two of you just being close, seeing as you've been friends since like infant school or something.'

'Nursery school,' I corrected her, and immediately regretted it.

'Mmm hmm, look who's keeping track.'

I cringed at Rebecca's know-it-all tone.

'How come you two never got together before?'

I shrugged. 'Tom doesn't see me that way. To him I'm just a friend.' I tried to project an air of breeziness to my manner, despite the lead weight wrapped around my heart.

'Are you sure about that?' She arched her eyebrow inquisitively.

'Positive.' I nodded firmly.

'Well, you're not the only one I've caught checking out their so-called friend.'

I leaned forwards to the edge of my seat, until the back legs lifted off the floor and I teetered precariously. 'Are you serious?'

Could Tom really like me that way? Was it possible?

And if it was... Then what? He had a girlfriend now. Surely he wouldn't leave her. Not for me.

But if he wasn't happy... A bubble of excitement rippled through me. If there was a chance, even a small one, then maybe, just maybe...

'Totally.' She smiled smugly. 'Not that you care of course, right?'

I reached out to swat her arm. How could she tease me at a time like this? How could she make fun of my vulnerability? The chair shifted beneath me at my sudden movement. I grabbed the table and managed to push my weight back in the seat, causing the back legs to drop to the floor with a thud.

I shrank down, desperately wishing I could hide from the attention, as Tom and Luke, along with the rest of the crowded coffee shop, turned to stare at me.

'So much for just being friends,' Rebecca whispered amid her laughter.

Her words were like a cold wave of reality crashing over me.

Just friends.

'Yeah, well, no matter what I want, that's all we are. All we can be.'

'You waited too long. You should have made a move before uni.'

'And have him reject me and ruin our friendship? No way.' He was too important to me to risk not having him in my life. We saw each other every day, and when we couldn't be together, we messaged. Losing him would be like losing a part of myself. The part that was exciting and adventurous. The part that kept me going.'

'So your approach was to do nothing about your crush and end up watching him date someone else? How's that working out for you?'

I groaned. 'It sucks.' Now that Rebecca knew, there was no need to maintain the pretence any longer. At least I had someone I could finally confide my misery to.

I'd been alone with my secret for so long. Always wondering why my feelings for him had had to change. It had been so much easier when we were kids. He was my best friend who just happened to be a boy. It was simple and innocent.

Until teenage hormones had kicked in.

Secondary school was a blur of confusion. He occupied more and more of my thoughts. Every decision I made, every outfit I bought, always hinged on one deciding question: Would Tom like it?

But Rebecca was wrong. It wasn't a crush. Not any more. It had outgrown that.

It was love.

'I figured it might.'

'What am I going to do?' I wailed.

I wanted to tell him. I wanted to tell everyone. But I couldn't. If he felt the same way, he would have told me by now. Tom always went after what he wanted. He was so much braver than me.

His silence meant only one thing: he didn't love me back.

'Simple. You just have to show him how irresistible you are, and then he'll ditch Hannah for you.'

I dropped my head to the left as I stared at her. 'Right, like any guy would ever choose me over her.' *Bitterness oozed from my voice. I couldn't even bring myself to say her name.*

Hannah.

I clenched my jaw. She was everything I wasn't. But worst of all, she was what Tom wanted. She'd snapped him up so easily, so quickly. All she'd had to do was smile at him and he was obsessed.

I'd been waiting on the sidelines, hoping one day he'd see me differently. That he'd finally realise what I'd known for so long: that we belonged together.

Until she'd ruined it all.

'They might...'

I raised my eyebrows at her less-than-convincing tone.

'Well, it's not like she's perfect, she's just—'

'Gorgeous, funny, confident, oh yeah, and loaded.' I flopped back in the chair. I didn't stand a chance against Hannah. As long as she was around, Tom would never realise how perfect we would be together.

'Of course it sounds bad when you put it like that.' Rebecca scrunched her nose.

I didn't need Rebecca trying to give me false hope. I might not be Hannah, but I wasn't stupid.

'Here you go,' Tom said as he set a hot chocolate down on the table, before dropping into the vacant chair beside me. 'So, what are you girls talking about?'

'Just catching up on our weekends,' Rebecca said casually, as Luke sat down and draped his arm over her shoulders.

'And what about you, Tom?' I asked quickly. 'What have you been up to this weekend?'

'Hannah and I went to London to meet her dad.'

'Whoa!' Luke almost choked on his coffee. 'It's a bit early for meeting the parents, isn't it? You've only been dating a couple of weeks.'

Tom laughed. 'Normally I would agree with you. But you don't turn down an opportunity to meet a guy like Alan Davis.'

We stared at him blankly.

'Is he, like, important or something?' I asked.

'He owns DEM.' Tom said it in a way that implied I should be impressed.

'Seriously?' Luke's jaw dropped. Clearly he knew what Tom was talking about.

I glanced at Rebecca and she shrugged. Thankfully I wasn't alone in my ignorance.

'Davis Event Management is a hugely successful international event management company,' Tom explained.

'Oh, that's cool,' Rebecca said, lacking enthusiasm.

'It's way more than cool,' Luke informed her. 'Working for a company like DEM is the whole aim.'

'Well, you're looking at their newest employee,' Tom announced proudly.

'No way, he hired you?' Luke stared at him.

'Just one day a week for now. I have no classes on Wednesdays so I can catch an early train to London for the day. Plus I'll pitch in with any events they are short-handed on at the weekends.'

'How did you manage that?'

Tom grinned. 'I guess Davis liked me.'

Luke edged forwards in his seat. 'Do you think Hannah could introduce me to him too?'

There was silence as Tom tipped his head to the left while he contemplated the idea. 'I suppose it wouldn't hurt to ask. Davis did say they were really busy.'

'Yes!' Luke drummed on the table. 'This is going to be awesome.'

'I guess Hannah has her uses after all,' Rebecca said.

'What's that supposed to mean?' Tom demanded.

Rebecca's cheeks flushed. 'Nothing, it's just she's kind of showy and dramatic. She always acts as though she's better than us. But there's no substance to her. Her only purpose in life seems to be looking good and partying hard.'

'So you don't like her because she dresses well and is confident?'

'I didn't say I didn't like her,' Rebecca objected. 'She's just a bit much sometimes.'

'Rebecca has a point. Hannah is a bit excessive,' Luke agreed. 'I mean, I love a drink, but I know when to stop.'

'I thought you wanted a job?'

Luke drew back at the hostility in Tom's voice.

'And what about you, Lizzie? Do you dislike my girlfriend too?'

I swallowed. 'She's—'

'What?' Tom snapped.

'Perfect.' That was the problem. Hannah was perfect. Everything about her. Her looks. Her clothes. And now, even her father. She and Tom belonged together.

The question was, where did that leave me?

5

NOW

For a moment, I forgot to take a breath.

He'd remembered.

He'd remembered me. Remembered his promise.

But...

I drew back. 'Now? After all this time?' My gaze narrowed as I stared at him. 'I haven't seen you since...' My words trailed away. I couldn't finish that sentence. But then, I didn't need to. We both knew when and where we had last seen each other. Some things could never be forgotten. No matter how much we wanted to.

He held his hands out in front of him, his palms facing upward, open and exposed. 'I missed you.'

There was something so simple, so raw and vulnerable about the way he said it that made me feel warm and safe.

He missed me.

I wanted it to be true. I wanted to believe it. To feel it.

But I didn't.

I couldn't.

Not fully.

Too much had happened. Too many years had passed.

If he'd stayed, if we'd ridden it out together, maybe...

I clenched my jaw. I couldn't allow my thoughts to go there.

'I know I should have come back sooner.' He shook his head. 'No, if I'm honest, I know I should never have left. I abandoned you when you needed me. I cut you off. I ran.'

My heart lurched to hear him confess the words I had kept inside me all this time. He *had* abandoned me. He'd left me alone. His career, his life, had soared, while I'd withered away like a flower deprived of water.

'But I had to,' Tom added as he lowered his gaze. 'It was the only way to keep you safe. The only way to protect you. If anyone had realised that we were involved, that I loved you...'

I loved you.

The resentment I'd harboured for ten years dissipated with those three little words. He'd loved me.

We'd never said it to each other. I'd wanted to tell him. I'd wanted him to say it back. But it wouldn't have been right. Not while he was still dating Hannah.

So I'd waited.

And wondered.

But now, finally, I knew for sure. He had loved me.

That was why he'd left me.

Even in my darkest moments of bitterness and hatred, some part of me had still known, deep down, that he was doing it all for me.

'We would have been under suspicion. *You* would have been under suspicion.'

'But you didn't let that happen.' He'd been forced to live a charade in order to protect the secret we shared. The lie that would have destroyed me if it had ever been uncovered. 'You protected me. You all did.'

Tom took a deep breath and let it out slowly. 'So you don't hate me, then?'

I blinked. 'Hate you? How could I hate you? I'm the one that—'

Tom reached out and took my hand in his. 'Don't go there, Lizzie.'

I swallowed. He was right, reliving the past never changed it.

'It took a long time for me to get my head straight...' Tom's voice trailed away.

'Me too,' I agreed. Our eyes met and I felt a connection between us that I'd only ever felt with him. We knew pain and loss. We'd lived it together, even if we'd been apart all these years.

But was that enough?

Tom said he'd come back for me, but what did that even mean? We weren't a couple. We weren't even friends. Not any more. And yet, here he was, standing in my kitchen as though the last ten years had never happened.

A whirlwind of emotions swirled inside me as resentment battled with gratitude and distress battled with adoration. I knew why he'd left. He'd done it for me. But he'd gone so completely. No calls. No messages. Nothing. It was as though I'd simply ceased to exist.

But then, in a way, I had. The life I'd known, the person I'd been, had all faded into nothingness.

Tom, however, seemed no worse for wear for the years we'd spent apart. In fact, it appeared that my absence from his life had made little, if any, impact at all. While I was merely getting through from one day to the next.

And yet, he was here.

He'd come back.

For me.

6

THEN

'You nailed it,' Tom said as he stared at the typed pages in his hands. 'You always had a talent for writing, but this...' He let out a breath as he shook his head. 'It's so powerful.'

'You don't think it's too emotional?'

'No. Not at all. Your story is about loss and grief, it's supposed to be emotional. And you capture it so well. It must have been hard to relive all of those feelings.'

'Relive what feelings? The story is fictional.'

'Yeah, the events themselves are fictionalised, but the emotion is real. I can feel it.' He handed me the story. 'You were thinking about when you lost your gran when you wrote it, weren't you?'

'How did you...?' I stared at him, stunned.

'I know you, Lizzie.'

I felt my cheeks grow warm. Suddenly, his bedroom felt smaller than before. I stepped back to drop the story into my rucksack on his desk, purposefully averting my eyes from his bed that was only a step away from us. 'That's 'cause we've been friends for so long.'

'Of course! We're a team.'

I nodded. 'A great team.'

We smiled at each other.

'We need to capture this moment,' Tom said, grabbing his phone.

'What moment?'

'The day you finished writing your first prize-winning story.'

I giggled. 'You're crazy; we don't know if it will win. I haven't even submitted it yet.'

'You're going to do great. This is just the beginning, Lizzie.'

'You really think so?' I asked hopefully.

'I know so.' Tom gave a short sharp single nod of his head. 'And I need a photo of the writer, so that one day when your books are bestsellers, I'll be able to show it to all my friends and say I knew you before you were famous.'

I reached out and grabbed his arm. 'Well, in that case, you'd better get over here and be in the photo with me,' I said, pulling him towards me. 'Because we're in this together. Remember?'

'I remember,' Tom said as he grinned at me, before turning his attention to the camera on his phone and changing it to selfie mode.

He swung his left arm over my shoulders and leaned towards me as he raised the phone out in front of us. Butterflies soared in my stomach as I smiled at the image of the two of us reflecting back at me from the screen.

This was how we were meant to be. Side by side. Together. Forever.

Tom clicked the button to take the photo and stepped back. Instinctively, I touched my shoulder where his hand had been. It felt like something was missing now.

Tom turned to face me and our eyes met again. 'I believe in you, Lizzie.'

There was something about his expression that made my heart beat faster. Silence engulfed us, but somehow it felt right. It felt charged with all the things we hadn't said to each other. All the things I'd wanted to say but had been too afraid to.

We'd always been close. But there was a line between us. One we had never crossed. One that divided friendship from something more.

But we weren't kids any more.

I stepped towards him slowly, my gaze fixed on his face, searching for any sign that I was making a mistake. I needed to be sure. He needed to want me too.

And then it happened. His body shifted as he leaned forwards to meet me. I felt his breath on my face as he tipped his head to the left and then our lips met. Gentle. Soft.

I closed my eyes, immersed in the moment.

The intensity grew. I wanted more. Needed more. I lifted my hand and cupped the back of his neck, pulling him closer.

But then, suddenly, reality descended upon me like an icy wave. I pulled back and stared at him as my eyes filled with tears. We couldn't do this. He wasn't mine.

'Hannah,' I murmured. Her name was like shards of glass to my tongue. I was being foolish, reminding him of the one reason we couldn't be together. Reminding him of her.

But I had to.

I'd wanted him for so long, but not like this.

Tom blinked as though clearing his focus to study me.

Was he thinking about her now? Comparing my kisses to hers?

In that instant I cursed myself for my timing. I should have kissed him for a little longer. I could have been better. More passionate. More...

Something.

My body sagged, deflated, and I stared at the carpet, unable to bear looking at him a moment longer, while I waited for the words I knew were coming.

'I'll end it with her.'

My head jerked up and I stared at him. My mouth opened and closed, but I couldn't form any words.

He couldn't have said what I thought I'd heard.

It wasn't possible.

He wouldn't choose me.

'I need to break it to her gently. You know how highly strung she can be.'

I nodded, still not convinced that this was really happening.

'She can't know it's because of you. Because of us.'

Us.

My heart soared at that word. It was so small and yet so powerful.

It was everything.

'I work for her dad; if she turns him against me...' *Tom brushed my cheek with his fingertips.* 'My job is at stake here.'

'Take whatever time you need,' *I told him. What did a few more days matter when I'd already waited for him for years?*

'I knew you'd understand, Lizzie,' *he said as he pulled me to him and wrapped his arms around my waist.* 'It's just temporary. Then we can be together. Just us. I promise.'

I nodded slightly as I nuzzled against his neck, breathing in the scent of his coconut shower gel.

We were an 'us'.

7

NOW

He was here now. Perhaps that was enough. Perhaps it was everything. His presence was proof that he cared. That I hadn't been forgotten.

I should have known better than to doubt Tom's motives. There was no hidden agenda. No threat to the quiet little life I had painstakingly built. No sudden desire to come forward and expose my sins.

It was like he said; he'd just missed me.

Maybe as much as I'd missed him...

'You look good,' he said, as his gaze drifted down my body. I automatically tugged at the sleeves of my baggy sweater, pulling them even lower down my wrists. I always wore long sleeves, no matter the season.

'You're even more beautiful than before.'

I shuffled awkwardly, shifting my weight from one foot to the other. They were words I'd always longed to hear, but never had. They were just words that guys said in the movies, not in real life. At least, not to me.

They said them to girls like Hannah.

'Sorry, I didn't mean to make you uncomfortable.'

'You didn't,' I said. But it was a lie. I wasn't used to anyone staring at me the way he was right then. I'd perfected the art of being in the background, like part of the furniture, never quite in focus. And yet, somehow, Tom saw me.

But beautiful? Me? It wasn't true. I was ordinary. Non-descript.

Yet, maybe it didn't matter. The words might not be accurate, but they were still powerful. It was as though they ignited a flame within me. It was tiny and fragile. But it was enough to allow me to feel its warmth.

'So, what are you up to these days?' he asked with a breeziness that made it sound as if we had seen each other ten minutes ago, rather than ten years.

I stared at him, not quite able to believe that was the first question that sprang to his mind. After all these years, after our history, our shared secrets, had we really been reduced to small talk?

'Oh, you know, just keeping busy.' I drummed my fingers against the worktop, conscious of the vagueness of my reply. But at its essence was the truth.

My entire being was about keeping busy. Keeping moving. The trick I had learnt a long time ago was to never allow myself time to think.

To remember.

To regret.

'I always wonder about you when I go into a bookshop. I can't help running my gaze over the shelves, hoping to find your name...'

'You do?' I caught the surprise in my words and knew Tom must have heard it too.

'Of course. I know what a talented writer you are.'

I swallowed. 'I'm a software tester now.' It was a role I would never even have considered when Tom had known me. It was the opposite of everything I'd wanted. Structured. Repetitive. Checking for errors and inconsistencies. There was a right answer. A solution. Its whole purpose was to remove doubt. Remove uncertainty.

'Oh.' I heard the disdain in Tom's voice. 'Didn't you ever make it as an author, then?'

I shook my head.

'What about plays? Do you still write those?'

'To be honest, I don't really write anything these days.' The lie jarred against me. I did write. But I wrote for me now. I never let anyone read my work any more. It wasn't good enough. *I* wasn't good enough.

'That's a shame.' He smiled ruefully. 'Do you remember when you used to have dreams...?'

His words dug into me like a knife and my cheeks flushed with embarrassment. He was right. I'd had big dreams once. But I'd lost them, just like I'd lost everything else.

Including Tom.

Because of Tom. I flinched as the unwanted realisation struck.

My actions had destroyed our fates. I'd pulled at a loose thread, which had unravelled our lives. But it had been Tom who'd placed me in the situation which had triggered it all.

If he hadn't persuaded me to stay in Bournemouth. If he hadn't allowed himself to be ensnared by Hannah. If he'd noticed me sooner. The events that took him away from me wouldn't have happened. My intervention wouldn't have been necessary.

'It's a good job,' I said, with an edge of hostility. 'It pays the mortgage. And I get to work from home four days a week.'

Tom shrugged as if that meant nothing. But then how could he know that to me it was everything? My dreams of research trips, book tours and bestseller interviews had given way to the practicalities of a steady salary, anonymity and the ability to hide in the shadows.

Even just one day a week in the office was stressful enough for me, the thought of facing a crowd of strangers and actually having to talk to them...

'I like my job. My life.'

Tom's eyes met mine and I knew without a doubt that we both knew I was lying.

'And what about you?' I asked, eager to divert the attention.

'Living the dream,' Tom said, straightening his back.

'Still at Davis Event Management?'

There was a flash of surprise in his eyes and my stomach clenched as I realised my error.

'You knew I got a permanent position there?'

I clambered for a response. 'I just assumed you would. I remember it was your goal. You were so driven to achieving it.'

He nodded. 'Yeah, I guess I was.'

I smiled slightly as the knot in my stomach loosened. The lies came so easily to me now. I deflected suspicion with a skill that my younger self would never have believed possible. But like Mum always said, practice makes perfect.

'Actually, I left DEM a couple of months ago, moved on to bigger and better things. You know how it is.'

I nodded. I knew. I'd been one of those things he'd moved on from.

I sank back against the worktop, the granite digging into my back. Reality hadn't been kind to my dreams. But at least Tom had stayed on track.

I already knew it of course. Despite my claim, it hadn't just been an assumption, I knew he'd worked at DEM. I could probably recite his progression there just as well as his own CV. I'd lost count of the number of times I'd google stalked him. My desperate need to keep hold of some tiny connection to him always overrode my intention to let him go.

It was normal. Wasn't it?

It was human nature to be curious. To be interested. To care.

But my investigations had always been discreet. I needed to maintain a safe distance.

At least, that was the plan.

But his arrival had made all my self-discipline pointless and had instantaneously reignited a curiosity in me that I had tried to keep in check.

Was reality as good as the dreams we had once shared? Or had my absence left a void in his life, like his had in mine?

'Are you happy?' I blinked, stunned at the question that had slipped from my lips. Why had I asked that? I didn't want to know. If the answer was yes, then it showed that he'd made the right decision. If it was no...

All that would prove was that the fear that had haunted me all these years was true.

I'd ruined his life.

Along with my own.

'Mostly.'

I couldn't breathe. What did that mean?

'My career is amazing; it's fulfilling, purposeful, important, with a corner office and international travel. I live in a great apartment in London, just like we'd always wanted. I have incredible holidays several times a year. But...'

'But?' I prompted him to continue, even though I knew it was foolish. Whatever hardships his life had endured would undoubtedly come back to one influencing factor: me.

'I guess I never realised how lonely it would be.' He inhaled a long slow breath. 'Then again, I didn't really anticipate doing it all alone.'

My chest tightened. Even after all these years it seemed the burden of guilt I carried could still grow heavier.

I started to open my mouth to say, 'I'm sorry', but I stopped. My apologies wouldn't help him. They were too little, too late. It would take more than that to make up for my mistake.

Much more.

It had been obvious that he couldn't stay with me, not after what I'd done.

8

THEN

'Who's up for a swim?' Tom asked as he leapt up from the sand and started unzipping his jacket.

Rebecca snorted and huddled closer to the wooden breaker we were leaning against on Bournemouth beach. 'Are you kidding? It's March. The sea will be freezing.'

'Aww, don't be such a spoil sport.'

She held her hands up. 'Fine, you carry on. Just don't blame me if you get sick with pneumonia.'

Tom rolled his eyes. 'You'll come swimming with me, won't you, Lizzie?'

'No way! Wait for Luke, maybe he'll be braver than us.'

'Or crazier,' Rebecca teased.

'Oh, come on,' Tom said. He grabbed my hand and tried to pull me up.

I laughed and swatted him with my free hand. But it was the wrong move. He grabbed that hand too and suddenly I was defenceless. He tugged again and this time I didn't have a choice. I squealed as he pulled me to my feet.

'Tom, no!' I laughed as he towed me towards the sea, while I fought to dig my feet into the sand to gain traction. 'I'm fully clothed.'

He arched his eyebrow. 'You could remedy that.'

I gasped. 'We're in public.'

Tom loosened his grip and moved closer to me. 'True,' he whispered. 'Maybe we'd better wait until we're alone...'

Heat crept into my face as I felt his breath on my cheek.

'Maybe we can—' Suddenly Tom's expression changed, and he let my hands fall from his as though I'd scalded him. 'Hannah!' he called as he waved and raced up the beach towards the promenade.

I hunched forward, feeling like I'd been punched.

I stared after him, watching as he flung his arms around Hannah and pulled her into a deep passionate kiss in the middle of the path, oblivious to the obstruction they were causing.

I frowned. Or perhaps they did know. Perhaps that was part of the appeal. The show. The performance. The attention.

Anger seethed inside me. He was mine. We were an 'us'. That was what he'd said. He'd promised.

'Oh, Lizzie.'

I turned at the pitying tone of Rebecca's voice.

'What?' I asked, feigning confusion, but I could already tell Rebecca knew.

'Tell me you are smarter than getting involved with Tom.'

I couldn't speak. I couldn't deny it. And yet to confirm it...

She stood up and joined me as we both watched Tom and Hannah still kissing on the promenade. 'He's dating someone else.'

'It's not like that.'

'It's exactly like that. I thought you were better than that. You're not a cheat, Lizzie.'

Cheat.

The word stung, like a slap to my face.

Rebecca was right. This wasn't me. Sneaking around. Stealing a few moments alone together. Cheating.

How had I come to this?

I wanted Tom, but I wanted all of him. I didn't want to share him. 'It's just temporary,' I reminded myself, repeating Tom's promise to me. 'He's going to leave her,' I added, louder and more certain.

'Does that look like he's breaking up with her?'

'Well, not right now. Not here. He has to do it carefully. His job at Davis Event Mana—'

'Is that what he told you?'

'It's true.' But even as I said it, doubt niggled at me.

Rebecca shook her head. 'Guys don't break up with girls like her, for girls like...'

'Me?' I glanced down at my faded black coat, and knee-high boots that leaked in the rain, and then back at Hannah in her immaculate cream coat and designer jeans.

I didn't have the money to spend on designer labels. But even if I did, it wouldn't be me. No matter how I dressed I would never be in the same league as Hannah.

Rebecca linked her arm through mine. 'Us. Girls like us.'

I smiled ruefully. 'Maybe. Or maybe Tom is different.'

'Maybe. But if you're right, if his career is dependent on his relationship with her, then...' Rebecca shrugged.

I shook my head. 'You don't know him like I do. He'll prove you wrong. He will.'

'I hope so.'

I took a deep breath as I watched Tom and Hannah walking towards us, hand in hand.

'So do I,' I whispered. 'So do I.'

9

NOW

My gaze drifted back to the suitcase that stood in the corner of the kitchen. I wanted to ask how long he was staying in town, but something stopped me.

I frowned slightly as I realised it was fear holding me back. Not that that was unusual. Not for me. But the strange thing was I was both afraid he was planning to stay in Bournemouth for a while, and yet also afraid that he wasn't.

I couldn't even work out which fear was stronger.

I'd spent years hoping he would return.

And now he was here.

Tom was back.

It was exactly what I'd wanted.

But I also knew sometimes it was better to not get what you want.

Tom leaving now, as suddenly as he had come, would be for the best. His presence was a threat to the precarious equilibrium I had salvaged from the wreckage of my downfall.

And yet, I still hoped he would stay.

I rubbed my forehead; the conflicting emotions his return had stirred in me were making my head ache. How could I be excited to see him and yet terrified by his presence? How could I want him to leave and yet stay at the same time?

'How about we go and sit in the living room?'

I blinked and focused my attention on my guest. 'Of course. Sorry, I should have suggested that.' I waved my hand towards the living room, just off the hall to the left.

'I remember the way,' he said with a smile as he carried his coffee mug out of the kitchen.

With a nervous laugh I picked mine up and followed him, cursing myself for being a bad hostess. Tom had come all this way to see me and I'd left him standing in my kitchen instead of inviting him in properly and making him feel welcome.

But then, was he really welcome? In my home? My life?

Every fibre of my being warned me that he shouldn't be. And yet...

'Make yourself comfortable,' I told him, indicating the cream leather sofa.

He lounged back on it while I perched on the edge at the opposite end. 'Rebecca lives in Southampton now,' I told him, conscious of Tom watching my every move.

'I heard.' His voice was steely.

'She's married with two kids. Both girls.'

Tom grunted.

I wasn't sure why I was telling him. He clearly wasn't interested. But then, why wasn't he? I knew from Rebecca that she and Tom hadn't kept in touch after uni; surely it was nice to find out a little about what our old friend was doing now?

Yet his response felt dismissive. Not just of Rebecca. But of our lives before. Rebecca was a part of that. A part of our story. Our connection. The way she was so easily swept aside was a reminder that I could be too.

After all, I already had been once.

'You girls still see each other, then?' I could hear the disapproval in his voice. I'd almost forgotten what that sounded like, it had been so long since I'd heard it. But it still had the power to instantaneously make me withdraw and seek redemption.

'Not that much. She pops in for a coffee every now and then,' I replied quickly, feeling the need to clarify the distance between Rebecca and me. We'd kept in touch, but it had never been the same. Rebecca had remained in my life, but only on the outskirts. The shadows of the past still hung over us, making it impossible to be as we once were.

But then had she pulled away, or had I distanced myself from her?

Truthfully, I knew I'd built a wall around me after the incident. I'd hidden myself away. Was it out of shame for what I'd done? Or embarrassment at the person I'd become? Or perhaps it was just fear.

Not for me. But for everyone around me.

'Ah, I see.'

I glanced at Tom. Did his voice seem more relaxed now? I shook my head. I was overanalysing it. He and Rebecca hadn't seen eye to eye, even at uni, not since she found out about us.

She'd never understood the complexity of the situation. She hadn't known Tom like I had. She hadn't known how important the job at Davis Event Management was to him.

'It's a shame she and Luke broke up.'

I averted my eyes, conscious of my slip. We both knew what had broken them up. The last thing either of us needed was a reminder of that night.

'Do you still keep in touch with Luke?' I asked, desperate to fill the awkward silence. 'You guys were inseparable at uni.'

Tom chuckled. 'Yeah, we were.'

'Did you see him on your way here?'

Tom's body tensed and he glared at me. 'What makes you ask that?'

I drew back, confused by his hostile tone. 'He's in Winchester now, right? I just thought you might have stopped off to see him on your way here.'

'Oh, right.' Tom's muscles relaxed and he smiled. 'I guess I could have done, but to be honest, I just wanted to get to Bournemouth and see you.'

My cheeks flushed. 'You did?'

'Of course; you're my priority.'

My chest swelled with pride, but it wasn't enough to quieten the question that whirled in my head. If I was his priority, why had it taken him ten years to come and find me?

10

THEN

'Do you realise what time it is?' Mum's disgruntled voice carried up the stairs as I padded across the landing and leaned over the banister.

'I just want to make sure she's okay.'

'Tom?' I surged forward at the sound of his familiar voice.

'And why wouldn't she be okay?' I heard the accusation in Mum's tone as I bounded down the stairs. She'd eyed me suspiciously earlier when I'd opted to stay in on a Friday night. Especially when she knew we'd all had plans tonight.

'Lizzie!' Tom turned towards me, ignoring Mum's question.

'What are you doing here?' I asked as I slid past Mum and stood on the doorstep. I pulled my robe more tightly around me, as the cold March air seeped inside.

'What happened to you tonight?' he asked, his blue eyes boring into me. 'You were supposed to meet us at the club.'

I cast a sideways glance at Mum and waited as she withdrew.

'I didn't feel like it,' I replied, as I heard her footsteps on the stairs behind me. I turned away and shuffled to the kitchen. I knew Tom would follow. He'd been in this house enough times, he didn't need a verbal invitation now. He belonged here.

I shook my head. No, he belonged with Hannah. That was the problem.

'I messaged you but you didn't answer,' Tom said as the front door clicked closed behind us. 'I was worried.'

I swung my head round and stared at him. 'You were?'

'Of course I was.'

I grinned broadly.

'You're my best friend, I always worry about you.'

Friend.

My smile dropped into a tight grimace. Was that all I was? A friend? Weren't we more to each other than that now?

'I didn't want to be in the way,' I replied hesitantly. It was true, I hadn't. But mostly, I hadn't wanted to witness him fussing over Hannah, holding her hand, kissing her, when all the time I knew that he should be with me.

He wanted to be with me.

Didn't he?

'You know it's not like that, Lizzie. You could never be in the way.'

'It's Hannah's night. It didn't feel right to be there. Not on her birthday. Not when you and I are...'

'Are what?'

I drew back. What were we?

We weren't dating. Not yet. In fact, aside from that kiss, nothing else had happened between us. Nothing had changed.

It was almost as though our kiss had never happened at all.

Except it had.

Hadn't it?

I filled the kettle with water, simply to give my hands something to do. It was an easy task that required no conscious thought. There was something soothing in that. It gave my brain a moment of respite from the constant see-saw of trying to find meaning in the kiss we had shared.

May have shared.

I shook my head. No, we did. It was definitely real. I could remember it so vividly. That moment had replayed in my head countless times in the last few days. I could feel the passion. The connection. The desire.

Unless...

Was it possible I'd wanted it so much that I had imagined the whole thing? I was always creating characters and stories in my head. It was part of being a dreamer. A writer. But I always knew what was real and what was fiction. There was always a clear distinction between the two.

Or, at least, there always had been before.

Could I still say the same now?

Had this fantasy got away from me?

'What was that about?' Mum called across the landing as I made my way back up the stairs after Tom had left.

'Nothing.' I tried to keep my voice light and dismissive.

She watched me from the doorway to her bedroom. 'Is there something going on between you two?'

'W-what do you mean?' My grip tightened on the banister.

'In all the years you two have been friends, Tom has never turned up on our doorstep in the middle of the night before.'

'It's hardly the middle of the night, Mum.'

'Don't try and change the subject.'

I squirmed.

'I see the way you look at him.'

The accusation hung between us.

'The way I look at him?' I swallowed. What did she see? I thought I hid my feelings well. I was so careful. At least, I'd tried to be. Especially after Rebecca had realised I had a crush on Tom a few weeks earlier.

'You stopped seeing him as just a friend a long time ago. But I thought it was just a crush. He was dating someone else, wasn't he?'

'Hannah.' I forced her name out.

'I guess that explains why you didn't want to go to her birthday party tonight. Does she blame you for the break up?'

I blinked.

The break up.

Mum thought Tom and Hannah had broken up. She thought Tom had chosen me.

My lips parted and then closed again. I couldn't speak. I couldn't lie and confirm her assumption. But to correct her would make me sound so bad.

I'd never liked Hannah, but even she deserved to know. She deserved the truth.

Mum shook her head. 'I can't really blame her, I suppose. Getting dumped always hurts. It must be worse when you're dumped for someone you considered a friend.'

'She's not a friend.' The words slipped out unguarded. It was the truth. I'd never really considered Hannah a friend. She was just someone whose presence I tolerated because I had to. What was the alternative? To spend time with Tom, I had to spend time with her. I couldn't ask Tom to choose between me and his new girlfriend.

I wasn't even faring well now. He'd claimed to have chosen me, and yet, somehow she was still first.

She was still winning.

And I was losing.

Again.

11

NOW

His priority.

The words circled in my brain. Had I ever truly been his priority?

I knew what answer Rebecca would give to that question. She'd lost faith in Tom when he'd hesitated to break up with Hannah.

But I never had.

He'd loved me. I was sure of that.

But had that ever been enough?

'You know I've never stopped thinking about you. I always wondered how you were, what you were doing, who you were with.'

My cheeks flushed with warmth. He thought about me. I wasn't just some mistake from his past that had been buried and forgotten.

He remembered.

He cared.

'I kept wishing things could have been different; that I could have stayed.'

'I wished you could have too.' I turned away and stared out of the window at the fading sunlight. 'Do you remember that night we were all supposed to meet at the club to celebrate Hannah's birthday?'

'You didn't show up.'

I shook my head. 'I couldn't.'

'I was so worried about you.'

'So you turned up on my doorstep at eleven o'clock at night.' Tom winced. 'Your mum was not impressed.'

I chuckled. 'No.' My laughter faded. 'But I was.'

'I've always tried to look out for you.'

'I know.' I nibbled my lip as the past replayed in my head.

'No one can know,' Tom repeated.

'But I have to do something,' I replied, as tears streamed down my face.

Tom shook his head. 'It's too late for that. We can't change what happened. What's the point in ruining our lives too?' He wrapped his arms around me and pulled me to him. I nestled against his chest, feeling his warmth, his strength. 'In ruining your life,' he added in a whisper against my cheek.

I clung to him more tightly, feeling the chill in the sea air.

My life.

He was right. Coming forward wouldn't solve anything. It would just destroy us.

Especially me.

He had been protecting me then too. I'd heard the tremble in his voice as he'd spoken. He was as scared as I was. But did that mean he had been right?

After all this time I still wasn't sure. The same war raged inside me, just as it had back then. Fear compelled me to comply, whilst my conscience battled with the enormity of the secret Tom wanted me to carry.

But I had carried it.

My parents had taught me to take responsibility for my actions. I'd always tried to follow their example. At least, I had, until that moment.

'Are you all right?' Tom asked, concern creasing his brow. 'You've gone quiet.'

'Just remembering how good you've always been to me,' I replied. It was the truth. Tom had always done what he could to protect me. And as much as I wanted to, I couldn't blame Tom for my decision to keep my actions a secret. If I was honest with myself, he had simply told me what I'd wanted to hear. His encouragement had validated my silence.

But silence could be hard to live with.

12

THEN

'I'm going to leave her, just give me a little more time.'

'You keep saying that,' I whined, unable to keep the desperation from my voice.

'You know what's at stake here, Lizzie,' Tom said, reaching for my hands. 'I'm so close to getting everything we talked about. Everything we need.'

'Everything you need, you mean.' I pulled my hands away. He wasn't going to get around me that easily. Not this time.

'I'm doing this for us.'

'You're doing it for a job.'

'For a career. A future. Our future.'

Our future.

I felt a warm rush wash over me at those words. I liked the way they sounded. They were good words. Words worth holding on to.

'This career means money,' Tom continued. 'Exotic holidays, a nice house, and good schools for our kids someday.'

Guilt chafed at me. He cared about me. He just wanted to give me everything he could. 'But I told you, I don't need any of that. I just need you.'

'And that's one of the things I admire about you; you're so sweet and undemanding. But that doesn't mean I should take you for granted. You deserve to be treated well; to be looked after and appreciated.'

He reached for my hands again and this time I didn't pull away.

'Hannah's dad likes me. He's already given me a part-time job at his company and offered me a permanent position once I graduate. Do you know what an incredible opportunity that is? A job at a company like Davis Event Management is a career maker. I could go anywhere from there. But right now it's just a promise; until I have that signed contract, all our dreams could just disappear.'

'You really think he'll keep you on after you break up with Hannah?' I shook my head. Tom was so naive when it came to people. He always saw the best in them. 'A guy as powerful as Davis would find a way to get rid of you if he wanted to, especially if you break his daughter's heart.'

'That's why I have to be so careful, Lizzie. I have to handle it all perfectly. When I end it with Hannah, no one can know it's because of us. Her dad has to think it's come from Hannah; that she screwed up; that she hurt me.'

'How are you going to manage that?'

'I'm still figuring that part out. But everyone knows what Hannah's like; a spoilt, reckless party girl. That's why her dad likes me. He sees me as a steady, stable and hardworking guy. He thinks I'm a good influence on his wild daughter.'

I shook my head at the contrasting image Hannah's dad saw, against the fun loving student I knew Tom to be. But then, that was part of his charm; Tom knew how to be exactly what the people around him needed. It was as though he was a character in the plays I used to write for us as kids. His voice and manner changed depending on his audience. His posture. His confidence. His vocabulary. Everything was adaptable. He blended into his surrounding like a chameleon. He could be everything to everyone. He fitted.

Only I knew the real him.

'I just need a little more time to prove myself invaluable. Her dad needs to see what an asset I am. But more than that, I need to solidify my relationship with him. He needs to be so fond of me that when Hannah and I break up he won't resent me for it. He won't even blame me for it. Instead, he'll feel sorry for me. So sorry, that he'll keep me on. Hell, maybe he'll even promote me.'

'You really think that's going to work?'

'When am I ever wrong?'

I couldn't help but chuckle at that. He was right of course. He was always right. 'I just don't like having to share you with her.'

'I know, and you don't deserve to be put in this position. I hate myself for that. But we have to focus on the end goal and remember that it's only temporary.'

'Promise?'

'When have I ever let you down?'

13

NOW

'Sounds like someone is hungry,' Tom said, as my stomach rumbled loudly.

I glanced at the clock. 'Wow, can you believe we've been talking for over two hours?'

'Time always went fast when I was with you.'

Outwardly I cringed at his corniness, but not even that could stop the tingles of excitement that ran through my body. 'We have a lot to catch up on.'

And a lot that must never be talked about, I added silently.

'Yeah, we do. And we will.'

I smiled. 'I like that prospect.' I realised as I spoke that I genuinely meant it. I could choose to let the past hold me back and walk away now. Or I could enjoy the moment and make the most of having him back in my life, even for just a few brief hours.

Maybe he'd even stay in Bournemouth for a little while. He had a suitcase with him; surely that implied he wasn't planning on heading back to London tonight, right? Perhaps we could meet again tomorrow. We could talk more. Reconnect.

He pulled his phone out of his pocket. 'I'll call us a taxi.'

'Us?'

'To Bournemouth,' Tom said. 'For dinner,' he added when I continued to stare at him blankly.

'You want to have dinner with me?'

'That's the general idea.'

'Out? In a restaurant?' My voice had an edge of panic to it.

'Is that a problem?' Given Tom's puzzled expression, I knew he'd heard it too.

'N-no. It's just...' I struggled for an explanation. One that I could share. One that was reasonable. Normal. 'It's just I haven't seen you for so long...'

'You don't want to share me with anyone else?' Tom teased.

His words cut into me. 'I never did,' I replied flatly and his laughter fell away as he registered my pained expression.

'Sorry, that was...' He shook his head. 'So, how about we order in?'

I wrung my hands together. 'Sure.'

'Pizza?'

I nodded, even though I'd lost my appetite.

'Is Margarita still your favourite?'

I smiled despite myself. 'You remembered.'

'I remember everything about you, Lizzie. How could I ever forget?'

My vision started to blur as my eyes filled with tears. I hadn't been forgotten. At least, not by Tom.

I was so far from the girl I'd once been that I could barely even remember her now. But Tom did. He'd seen the worst of me, and yet even now he could still remember the best too. He still saw her when he looked at me. So maybe, despite everything that had happened, some small part of her still existed in me. Maybe she wasn't gone, but just dormant; buried under years of self-loathing and guilt.

Maybe Tom could help me find her again. Help me *be* her again.

I blinked furiously, determined not to let him see my weakness. My desperation.

'I never asked, do you have a boyfriend?'

'No.' I shook my head. 'Not right now.' I wondered why I'd added that, as though I had options. Instead of the reality, where I was just alone.

But why had he asked? Idle curiosity? Or a more specific interest?

I dug my nails into my palm. I was getting carried away. I had to stop. I had to be realistic. He'd leave soon. He'd be gone. And I'd be left with nothing. Again.

And yet, my heart rate quickened at the remote possibility that maybe, just maybe, no matter where his life had taken him, and who he'd ended up with, he'd never quite got over leaving me.

'And you?' I asked as my nails dug in deeper, while I fought to keep my expression neutral. 'Anyone special in your life?' He'd already said he hadn't intended to do it alone; that implied he was single, didn't it?

But I had to be sure.

I had to know.

He shook his head.

'How come?'

I hadn't intended to ask that aloud. My curiosity had got the better of me. I cursed myself for my stupidity. How would I feel if he asked me that question? How could I ever even begin to answer it? 'Sorry, I didn't mean to pry.' I was giving him an out. It was too late to take it back, but I could, at least, give him a way to avoid answering.

He shrugged. 'No, it's okay. I travel a lot for work. It's hard to maintain a relationship when you're constantly on the move.'

'But whoever you dated must have understood it was your job, your passion.'

'Yeah, they did. Or, at least, they tried to. But to be honest, I kind of prioritised work over them. I can't really blame them for getting fed up.'

'Oh.' My shoulders sagged. Why did it bother me so much? Tom's failed relationships meant he was single. Available.

But then, they also meant he was still a little out of reach. He said I was his priority, but was it true? Would I ever really be? Or was his career his priority now, just as it had always been?

It had never really been Hannah that had kept us apart, but about what being with her could do for his career. She'd had something I had never been able to offer him. Not then. Or now.

'But...' Tom paused. 'I'm not sure that I was ever really with the right person.'

I felt a flicker of hope ignite within me. If they weren't right for him, who was? Me?

'If they were, then I would have made more of an effort. Or, more to the point, it wouldn't even have felt like an effort in the first place. I think losing myself in my work was just an excuse to avoid commitment.'

'I can understand that.' I really could. Hadn't I done the very same thing? I'd focused on my career, on success, to outweigh the void in my life. The thing that was missing. The person who was missing.

Tom.

'Plus,' Tom continued, 'I'm older now. I'm looking for different things in life. A career isn't my only focus. I want a family. A home.' His eyes met mine. 'I want someone to share all that with.'

I swallowed.

It sounded so perfect. He was looking for something serious. Someone to build a life with.

That someone could be me.

Except...

I had less in my favour now than I had ten years ago. My youthful excitement and sense of adventure had been replaced with a preference for a night in with a good book. Even the thought of going out to a restaurant had turned me into a stuttering nervous wreck.

How could I think I could be enough for a guy who liked to travel the world? It wasn't as if he could give all that up. His work meant he would always need to travel, at least, to some extent. He'd always be on the move.

If we did get together, would he expect me to go with him?

And what about if he went alone?

Would he really stay alone?

I couldn't share him.

Not again.

I watched as he tapped away on his phone, ordering our pizza, blissfully unaware of my internal meltdown just centimetres away from him.

He was so close and yet still so far. How could I think I could close that gap?

At best, his return was out of obligation and guilt, nothing more. Even if he didn't realise it yet, he would soon enough.

14

THEN

'Hey,' I said with a sigh as I dropped into the vacant chair beside Rebecca. I really didn't feel like being in a crowded noisy pub tonight, but what was the alternative? Another night at home with my parents, where Mum would spend all evening asking me what was wrong? Plus, I couldn't keep ditching Rebecca. She was my friend. One of the few I actually had. I couldn't risk losing her. Especially not when it was starting to feel like I was losing Tom.

'Wow,' Luke laughed, from across the table. 'Someone's miserable for a Friday night.'

'I'm not miserable,' I objected. 'I'm just...'

'Tired?' Rebecca suggested.

'Right.' I nodded. I was tired. Tired of waiting on the side lines. Tired of lying; of pretending. Tired of wondering when Tom was going to break up with Hannah. And worst of all, I was tired of doubting that he actually would...

Rebecca leaned forwards and squeezed my hand. 'It's going to be okay.'

I smiled at her gratefully. I knew she didn't approve of my relationship with Tom, but she was still supporting me.

Luke glanced back and forth between us. 'Why do I have the feeling I'm missing something here?'

'Girl stuff,' Rebecca and I said in unison, and laughed as Luke grimaced.

He held his hands up. 'I know when to butt out.' He pushed his chair back and stood up. 'Can I get you a drink, Lizzie?'

'White wine, please.'

'You know what you need?' Rebecca asked as Luke walked towards the bar. 'A little time away.'

'Sounds perfect,' I said with a laugh. 'And just where am I supposed to go in the middle of spring term? Or for that matter, how am I supposed to afford it?'

'Easy, Durdle Door and—'

'Durdle Door?' I laughed again. 'Seriously? When you said time away, I thought you actually meant somewhere outside Dorset.'

'Hey, Durdle Door is stunning.'

'It is, but I don't think it counts as time away when your destination is practically on your doorstep. It's not even an hour's drive away from here.'

'It counts if you stay for the weekend.'

'Why would I pay to stay somewhere for the weekend, when I can just drive there and back in the same day?'

'Because it's free.'

I edged forward in my seat, my curiosity piqued. 'Free?'

'My aunt has a static caravan at the holiday park there.'

'Oh, right. I remember you telling me. That's why you applied to AUB, because you loved it so much when you spent summers down here as a kid.'

'Exactly.' Rebecca beamed at me, clearly pleased I'd paid attention. 'Anyway, with all the winter storms we had last month there was some damage at the holiday park. As I'm so close by, my aunt has asked me to go and check that the repairs have all been done.'

She fished in her pocked and dangled a key in front of me. 'Luke and I are driving over in the morning and we thought we'd spend the weekend there. You should come with us.'

'Really?'

'Absolutely. I know it's not the French Riviera. And the weather might not be great.'

I laughed. 'You're really selling it here.'

Rebecca rolled her eyes. 'But it's just what you need to take your mind off you know who.'

'Won't I be in the way, though?'

'In the way of what?' Luke asked as he handed me a glass of white wine.

'Your holiday.'

Luke arched his eyebrows as he turned to Rebecca. 'You mean our romantic weekend away?'

'Oh no.' I shook my head. 'See, that's what I was afraid of. I would be in the way.'

'Not at all. It's really spacious. There's two bedrooms. We'd barely even know you were there,' Rebecca insisted.

'Hi guys,' Hannah called, as she made her way to our table, clinging to Tom's hand as he walked a step behind.

I took a large swig of wine and tried not to glare at her. I hated the way she did that; dragged Tom around like an accessory, rather than her boyfriend. She didn't appreciate him. She never had.

And yet, it was still her hand he was holding. Not mine.

We shuffled our chairs closer together to make room for them to join us.

'You know what?' Luke said, as Tom sat down beside him, leaving Hannah to sit next to me. 'You guys should come too.'

My stomach lurched, and I only just stopped myself from shouting out no. They couldn't come. Not both of them.

Not Hannah.

'Come where?' Tom asked.

'Dur— Ouch!' Luke doubled over, rubbing his shin as he glared at Rebecca. 'What was that for?'

A flash of annoyance passed over Rebecca's features, before she smiled sweetly. 'Sorry, my foot slipped.'

'Hmm,' Luke grunted and twisted on his chair, manoeuvring his legs away from Rebecca.

Tom eyed Rebecca and Luke suspiciously. 'So, where are we going?'

'Luke and I are going to my aunt's holiday home at Durdle Door,' Rebecca said pointedly.

'With Lizzie,' Luke added, earning him another scowl from Rebecca.

'Really?' Tom arched his eyebrow at me, sending shivers down my spine. For a split second I forgot all about Hannah; all I could think about was Tom and I holding hands on windswept walks along the beach and cuddling together in a cosy holiday caravan.

'And we can come too?'

We.

With that one word, Tom brought reality crashing down around me. It wasn't a romantic weekend break with me he wanted.

It was Hannah.

It was always Hannah.

'It's only got two bedrooms, sorry.' Rebecca shrugged in a way that I knew meant she wasn't sorry at all.

She nodded at me. It was a short sharp nod of solidarity and comradeship. She was letting me know she was on my side. Though to be honest, even if Hannah hadn't been my rival for Tom's interest, Rebecca still wouldn't have wanted to spend the weekend with her. As far as Rebecca and I were concerned, there was only one reason Hannah had ever been accepted into our group: Tom.

'There's a decent sized sofa in the living room, though,' Luke offered helpfully. 'I saw the photos,' he explained, when we all stared at him in surprise.

'Well then, that's perfect,' Hannah said, clasping her hands together.

'I don't know,' I said, glancing at Rebecca. 'It sounds kind of crowded.'

'It'll be fun,' Hannah said, wafting her hand in the air dismissively.

No, this couldn't be happening. Hannah was as bad as Tom. Neither of them could take a hint.

'And I'm sure you won't mind sleeping on the sofa, as you're the single one. Will you, Lizzie?'

I tried not to cringe at the emphasis she put on 'single' as four pairs of eyes stared at me expectantly.

I shrugged. 'Whatever.'

What else could I say?

* * *

'I'm not going,' I whispered to Rebecca as we weaved our way to the bathroom later.

She grabbed my arm, bringing me to an abrupt halt in the middle of the walkway. 'No way; you cannot let her run you off. If you really want Tom, you're going to have to fight for him.'

I rolled my eyes. 'You just don't want to get stuck on a couple's weekend with them.' I jerked my head back to the table where Tom and Hannah were sitting. 'You know what will happen, Tom and Luke will be playing games on their iPads and you'll be spending the weekend with Hannah.'

'Ugh.' Rebecca shuddered dramatically. 'This weekend is not turning out as I'd planned.'

'I'm sorry.' I gave her a hug. 'None of this would have happened if you hadn't been trying to cheer me up.'

'Or if Luke knew how to take a hint and keep his mouth shut,' she grumbled.

'A hint?' I laughed. 'Is that what you call that kick you gave him?'

'It was a little harder than I intended.' Rebecca shrugged. 'I panicked. But I swear the guy is so oblivious.'

'So is Hannah.'

'Hmm, I don't know about that. I have a feeling she sees more than people realise.'

'You mean about Tom and me?'

'It wouldn't surprise me.'

Panic bubbled in my stomach. 'Should I warn Tom?'

Rebecca leaned towards me. 'Do you have to? Wouldn't it be a good thing if she did know? You and Tom could finally be honest about how you feel. It would make things simpler.'

'For me, maybe.' I glanced back at Tom. 'But not for him. His job is at stake. His career. If Hannah knows,' I took a deep breath, 'Tom better watch his back.'

'He's not the only one.'

I raised my eyebrows.

'If Hannah does know, the only reason to keep quiet is if she still wants Tom, regardless of his cheating. And as we just saw, Hannah has a way of getting what she wants and—'

Rebecca clamped her mouth shut.

I looked at her nervously. 'And what?'

She shook her head. 'You won't want to hear it.'

'When has that ever stopped you?'

Rebecca shrugged. 'Fair point.' She took a deep breath and I braced myself for what was coming. 'Hannah's not the only one who knows how to get what she wants. So does Tom.'

I pulled a face. 'That's not true.'

'Isn't it? Think about it, Lizzie. What guy in his right mind would want to bring his girlfriend along on a holiday with his...' Rebecca looked at me. I could practically see her mind racing, trying to think of a tactful name to call me. 'Other woman,' she finished hesitantly.

I felt nauseous. The term was insulting. Demeaning.

And yet, it was also accurate.

It was what Tom had made me. What I'd allowed him to make me.

But it wasn't our fault.

It was Hannah's.

She had control over Tom. Not just over his present, but his future too. She'd tied him to her. Trapped him.

Rebecca was right. If I wanted Tom, I was going to have to fight for him. I was going to have to be bolder. Braver. I was going to have to be more like Hannah.

For my relationship.

For our future.

For Tom.

15

NOW

'You've barely eaten anything,' Tom said as I put my plate down and leaned back against the sofa.

'I've had enough.'

'Are you sure?'

I noted the touch of concern in his voice and the corners of my mouth lifted. 'Still looking after me.'

'Always.'

'I've missed that.'

He stared into my eyes. 'I've missed you.'

My heart pounded, but I kept my expression neutral. 'You said that already.' I couldn't let him see the effect he had on me.

'It's worth repeating.'

I smiled as my caution melted away. 'I've missed you too.'

He reached for my hand and a charge of electricity ran through my body. Perhaps I was wrong. Perhaps there was a way to close the gap between us. Perhaps our connection was enough.

'I'm so happy I found you again,' Tom said.

I nodded, even though some part of my brain registered the fact that he hadn't had to search that hard. I hadn't gone anywhere. At least, not physically.

I'd been here the whole time.

Waiting.

For something to change. For things to get better. For life to restart.

Or maybe, what I'd really been waiting for all this time was him.

'What?' Tom asked, studying my face.

'Nothing.'

'It may have been a few years, Lizzie, but I still know you better than that. I can read you. I can tell when you're holding something back.'

I shook my head. 'It doesn't matter.'

'Of course it matters. Everything you think, everything you feel, matters.' He squeezed my hand. 'It matters to me.'

'Okay,' I took a shaky breath. 'I understood why you left. I understood why we couldn't be together. I did. I really did. But,' I shrugged helplessly, 'why didn't you call?'

'Oh, Lizzie.' He shifted on the sofa, twisting his body to face me. 'You have no idea how much I wanted to call you. Or how many times I started to type a text message.'

'But you never sent them.'

'It wouldn't have been fair to you. I couldn't risk anyone realising that you and I were in love; it would have aroused suspicion. There were so many questions already. So many doubts. It wouldn't have taken long for people to start digging.'

'I thought you were mad at me.' I sniffed. 'Maybe even scared of me.'

I wouldn't have blamed him.

After all, I was scared of myself.

Scared of who I'd become; of what I was capable of; what else I might do.

'No, Lizzie. Never.' He pulled me to him and wrapped his arms around me. I buried my head in his shoulder, unable to stop the torrent of tears that I had held back for so long.

'I was so a-alone.' My voice cracked between my sobs. 'I lost everything. Everyone.'

'You didn't lose me,' Tom whispered as he stroked my back soothingly.

'You weren't here.'

Tom flinched at the accusation in my voice.

I'd hurt him.

'If only you'd have let me handle things my way, Lizzie. If you'd been a little more patient we could have been together. We could have had everything we'd dreamed of.'

I pulled away, creating a space between us as his words tore through me.

He was right, of course.

I was the reason that everything had fallen apart. I was my own undoing.

I didn't blame him for running away from me. If I could, I would have run from myself too. In fact, I was stunned that Tom was even here now. If our roles had been reversed, would I have been so forgiving?

It was an impossible question to answer, because I knew Tom would never have done what I did. He would never have been that weak. That impulsive. That reckless.

Unlike me.

But despite my flaws, Tom was back.

And now I had choices; I could do what I always did and dwell on my anxieties and fears. I could talk myself out of this being anything because I was afraid that he would leave again. Or I could focus on the fact that he was here now, and maybe that was enough.

It was a chance to make amends in some small way. A chance to help fill the void in his life that my actions ten years ago had created. And maybe at the same time, fill the void in my own life too.

Despite our successful careers, neither of us had found happiness. We were kindred spirits.

We would take it slowly. Reconnect. Start as friends. And see where things led from there.

There was no rush.

We'd find our way in our own time, our own space.

Tom stifled a yawn. 'Sorry, it's been a long day.'

'Oh, of course,' I said quietly. I lowered my head, feeling a sense of loss as I realised he was about to leave. 'You should get some sleep. We both should.'

'Yeah.' He squeezed my hand. 'You don't mind if I crash here for the night, do you?'

16

THEN

'I can't believe I let you talk me into this,' I grumbled as I walked down the drive to Luke's car, where he and Rebecca were waiting for me.

Rebecca shrugged. 'Like you said, our weekend away wouldn't have been gate-crashed if I hadn't been trying to cheer you up.'

'So that means I owe you?'

'No, it means you can't abandon me.'

Luke laughed as he reached out to take my rucksack. 'I think that means you're coming with us, whether you want to or not.'

Rebecca nodded smugly and clambered back into the passenger seat.

My shoulders slumped. 'So I noticed.' I followed Luke to the back of the car. 'I am sorry, though. I had no idea it was supposed to be a romantic weekend for just the two of you.'

'Yeah, well, it's just gonna be a different kind of weekend now.'

'I can see that,' I said, my eyes widening as Luke opened the boot, revealing a box of wine bottles stashed between their bags. I shook my head, refocusing my thoughts. 'But seriously, thanks for letting me travel with you and Rebecca.'

'No worries.' Luke shrugged as he closed the boot. 'Couldn't let you make the journey to Durdle Door with Tom and Hannah, could we?'

I paused and studied him closely. 'Do you know?'

Luke let out a nervous chuckle. 'I do now. After my screw up last night, Rebecca enlightened me. I'm sorry, Lizzie. If I'd had any clue that—'

I shook my head. 'It's not your fault.'

'I can't believe Tom never told me.'

'It's supposed to be a secret.'

'Yeah, I don't think that's working out so well, somehow.'

'You won't say anything to anyone, though, will you?' I heard the nervousness in my voice. Luke was on the same course as Tom and Hannah, and Rebecca was on mine. It was only through Tom and me that the two groups had merged. So where did Luke's loyalties lie? He was closer to Hannah than he was to me. Would he tell her?

Luke drew a cross over his heart with his finger. 'I've been sworn to secrecy.'

'Thanks.' I felt lighter as I reached for the door handle to the backseat. He might value his friendship with Hannah over mine, but one thing I knew for certain was that he valued his relationship with Rebecca above all else.

'You know, Lizzie, Tom may be my mate, but he's an idiot for putting you in this position.'

'And I'm an idiot for accepting it.' My tone was flat as I tried to read between Luke's words. Or was it my own realisation slipping out? Perhaps I was an idiot for allowing myself to be side lined. To wait without a timescale even in place.

'I didn't say that.'

'No, but that doesn't mean you weren't thinking it.'

'You could end it.'

I tried not to flinch as Luke didn't deny my accusation. His avoidance told me what I had already suspected: he had been thinking it.

I nodded. 'I could.' Yet even as I said it, I knew that I wouldn't. I couldn't. I still wasn't ready to walk away from everything Tom and I had or could have in the future. I had to fight for us. Even if Tom wouldn't.

'But you won't,' Luke said, clearly interpreting my response. He snorted. 'One day Tom has got to tell me his secret to getting all these women swooning over him.'

I glanced at Rebecca sitting in the passenger seat and was thankful she couldn't hear through the closed doors.

'You don't need it,' I said. 'You and Rebecca have something special. Do you really need any more than that? Than her?'

Luke shook his head. 'No.'

Rebecca turned to face him through the window and they smiled at each other.

'I still can't believe she's with me. I'm not about to do anything to jeopardise that.'

* * *

I stood at the top of the uneven steps that led down to the beach. Beyond it, the limestone arch of Durdle Door jutted out into the ocean. In the summer the beach would be crowded with tourists, but today it was practically deserted. There was something so peaceful about the emptiness, despite the bitter wind that whipped around me.

I heard the crunch of someone walking on the stony path behind me, but I didn't turn. I wanted to be alone. I wanted to pretend it was just me and the beach. I didn't want to share this view with some stranger.

'It's weird being here out of season.'

I grinned at the familiar voice. 'Tom!' I swung round and instinctively lifted my arms to hug him, but stopped.

I glanced over his shoulder, my gaze searching.

'Hannah's gone to check out the caravan.' He jerked his head towards the holiday park at the top of the cliff.

'To stake her claim on the second bedroom, you mean?'

Tom winced. 'Don't be like that, Lizzie.'

'Why shouldn't I be? You asked for more time, I didn't know that included a romantic weekend away with her.' Animosity dripped from my voice. I'd never viewed anyone with such hostility before.

'It's not a romantic weekend. It's a group trip, that's all. Nothing will happen with her. You're the one I want.'

I snorted. I was no longer sure that was true.

Then again, had I ever really been sure? Doubt niggled at me, churning my stomach. I missed the way things had been. The way I used to trust him implicitly. The way I could read him and know what he thought. How he felt.

Or, at least, I'd always believed I could.

'Come on,' I said. 'We'd best get back and help them unpack.'

Tom nodded and we walked up to the car park in silence, aside from the crunching beneath our feet. My chest felt heavy as we climbed. It was just the steep path, I told myself. But somehow I couldn't shake the feeling that it was more than that.

The silence between us felt different this time. We'd always been able to spend time together without feeling the need to fill every second with chatter. We could just be together. But this time...

I glanced across at Tom as he walked beside me. This was hardly how I wanted to spend a weekend. Playing fifth wheel to two couples. Especially when one of them included Tom.

'I don't like the look of those grey clouds,' Tom said, studying the sky with disapproval as we approached the cars where the others were retrieving their bags.

'It's atmospheric.' I liked it. It felt like a reflection of my mood.

'You know there's heavy rain forecast. It's going to be a total bore if we get stuck in a cramped caravan all weekend.'

'Hey, it's not a cramped caravan,' Rebecca objected, overhearing Tom's slight on her childhood holiday home. 'It's a luxurious and spacious static caravan and you should consider yourself lucky to have been invited.' She glared at Luke as she spoke. It was going to be a long time before he was forgiven for making that invitation.

'Besides,' Hannah said, as she draped her arms over Tom's shoulders. 'I'm quite sure we can find ways to keep ourselves entertained.'

Tom laughed. 'I'm sure we can,' he said, twisting around to kiss her.

I stared at him, unable to believe what my eyes were seeing. After everything he'd just said to me, here he was, kissing her right in front of me.

Was anything real between us?

Hannah glanced at me as they pulled apart. I frowned. Was it my imagination or was there a glint of smugness in her eyes? The corner of her mouth twitched upwards as she ran her hand across Tom's chest, her gaze still locked with mine.

It felt like she was taunting me. Reminding me that he would never really be mine. He was hers. And she wasn't giving him up.

I shook my head. I was being ridiculous. She was just being Hannah: theatrical and excessive.

'You don't mind bringing my bag in for me, do you, Tom?' she asked, flashing him a dazzling smile. 'I'm a little tired after that drive.'

I bit back my retort. It wasn't even an hour's journey, and it wasn't as though she'd even done the driving. She never did. Tom was always her chauffeur.

'Of course,' Tom said, and his gaze followed her as she flounced off towards the caravan.

'Seriously?' I said, as soon as she was out of earshot.

Tom jerked back to face me.

'Time for us to go,' Rebecca said hurriedly as she nudged Luke towards the caravan.

'You kissed her,' I hissed at him.

'I had to.'

'You didn't have to do anything.' My voice was like venom.

'It won't be for much longer, I promise.'

He reached his hand out for mine, but I pulled away. 'I don't care.' I pouted. But it was a lie. I did care. That was the problem. That was why it hurt.

I cared too much.

'Don't say that. Of course you care. Just like I care about you.'

'You have a funny way of showing it.' He never had a problem showing Hannah how much he cared about her.

'Look, Lizzie.' Tom glanced back towards the caravan, as though checking we couldn't be overheard. 'I have a plan. A way for us to be together. Just you and me.'

'How?'

'That's not important right now. All that matters is it's a way I can get in Davis's good books permanently, even if Hannah and I aren't together.'

'If?'

'When. I mean when,' he correctly hastily.

My gaze narrowed as I glared at him. 'And when are you going to put this plan of yours into action?'

'As soon as I can, I just need to...' Tom frowned as his gaze fell upon the box full of wine bottles beside Luke's car. 'Luke does know we're only here for two days, right?'

'I think Luke's afraid we'll be bored here too.' I chuckled in spite of myself. Tom had a way of doing that. Of distracting me. Of brightening my mood, even when I was mad.

But not even Tom could make me forget what I'd seen.

'I'm serious, Tom,' I said, as my smile withered away. 'I'm not waiting around while you and Hannah are—'

'We're not!' Tom interrupted, clearly guessing where my mind was going.

'You're sharing a room. A bed.'

'I told you, I'll figure it out.'

'Right, because you have a plan,' I scoffed.

'*I do have a plan, Lizzie. I promise, I do.*'

I folded my arms across my chest. 'So, what is this great plan of yours then?'

Tom licked his lips. 'It's best we don't talk about it.'

I rolled my eyes. It was just an empty promise. If he had a plan, why wouldn't he tell me what it was? Why wouldn't he include me?

'*At least, not here,*' *he added quickly, obviously sensing my disbelief.*

I shook my head. 'I'm done waiting. Rebecca was right, you're never going to leave her.'

'*You told Rebecca?*'

I bristled at the accusation in his tone. 'She guessed.'

'*No one was supposed to know, Lizzie. My plan only works if no one knows.*'

'Surely it only matters that Davis doesn't know. And Rebecca won't tell him.'

'*She'll tell Luke.*'

I shrugged.

Tom rubbed his forehead. 'Of course, she's already told him.'

'*It doesn't matter.*'

'*It matters to me.*'

'*Why?*'

'*Because they'll—*'

'*Because what? They'll know you're a cheat? You care more about what they think than about how I feel.*'

'*That's not true.*'

'*Prove it.*' *I folded my arms across my chest and glared at him defiantly.* 'End it.'

'*I will.*'

'*This weekend.*'

'*Lizzie, I can't just—*'

'*End it,*' *I took a shaky breath,* 'or we're done.'

I watched surprise register on Tom's face. He hadn't expected me to issue an ultimatum. But then, neither had I.

It wasn't like me. I was quiet. Accepting.

Weak.

The realisation cut into me. I was weak. Waiting around for Tom to make me a priority. To choose me. Just me.

But no more.

I straightened my back, adding an extra inch to my height. It felt good to stand up for myself. To stand up to Tom. He was so used to winning me over, to persuading me to see things his way. But enough was enough. I deserved better. I demanded better.

'I promise you, Tom, by the end of this weekend you will only have one of us.'

17

NOW

Tom's words whirled around my brain.

You don't mind if I crash here for the night, do you?

'I... Er...' I knew I should say no. I *wanted* to say no. It wasn't a good idea. I couldn't let myself get too attached to Tom. Not again.

But then I'd never been any good at saying no to Tom. And the consequences had been costly.

'I knew I could count on you.'

I blinked. Somehow my hesitation had been interpreted as an agreement.

'You'd never turn me out into the night with nowhere to sleep.'

'Of course not,' I found myself saying, while I wondered what was wrong with staying in a hotel. Wouldn't that have been the normal thing to do?

'But I have to go to the office in the morning,' I told him. 'I work from home most of the week, but on Mondays...' My voice trailed away as I realised I was rambling. Tom didn't need to know all that. He wouldn't even *want* to know.

'That's fine, I can occupy myself while you're out.'

'While I'm out?' I blinked. 'You mean you're planning on staying? Here? While I'm at work?' My mind raced as I tried to process the idea of Tom staying in my home, not just for the night, but tomorrow as well.

Tom chuckled. 'I didn't come all this way just to have one cup of coffee and some pizza, Lizzie.'

'Well, no, but...'

I glanced around the room, wondering what secrets might be lurking just out of sight. Of course, Tom already knew my worst. But there were others. The fall out and repercussions from the first had created more. Secrets were like a chain reaction, one led to another, and another...

'We can have dinner together tomorrow night, after you've finished work, and maybe we can revisit some of our old hangouts over the weekend.'

'The weekend?' My knee bounced up and down restlessly. 'But that's days away, it's only Sunday now.' Just how long was Tom planning on staying? I wanted him to be here in Bournemouth, to see him, to spend time with him. But to have him stay in my house? For a whole week?

Why did he want to stay with me instead of in a hotel? What did that even mean? Something? Nothing? We hadn't spoken in ten years, and yet now he'd practically invited himself to move in. It was too much. Too fast.

I had to be stronger. I had to set boundaries. I had to stand up for myself.

This time.

'I think you'd be more comf—'

'Of course, if you don't want me here, I can always go back home. I'm sure there will be a train this evening.'

'No,' I said quickly. He couldn't leave. I couldn't let that happen.

I'd only just got him back.

'I don't want you to leave,' I said, forcing a smile onto my lips. 'Spending the weekend together sounds great.'

Except, it didn't.

Tom in my home was too much. It was the one place where I felt safe. Where I didn't have to keep up the act that had become my life.

I could sustain it for a few hours. But all day? For a week?

Part of me relished the opportunity to spend time with Tom, to reconnect, to just be us again. The way we had been. I was happy then. I was normal. I was good.

Until I wasn't.

Somewhere along I had got lost.

Could Tom help me find my way back to how I'd been? Or was that person too far gone to be saved?

'It's going to be awesome,' Tom said, grinning at me. 'I promise, we are going to have so much fun, you'll wonder how you lived without me all these years.'

I nodded. I didn't tell him that I already knew the answer to that question. Without Tom, I'd barely lived at all.

But then, was that because of his absence? Or because I'd had to live with myself?

Either way, with Tom back, at least I didn't have to be alone any more. I felt the tension in my shoulders relax slightly. After all, wasn't this what I'd been hoping for? A second chance. For me. For us.

I shook my head. It wasn't realistic.

But somehow that didn't seem to matter. I knew what my life without Tom looked like. It was so far from the future I'd envisaged for myself at eighteen. My world had shrunk. I caught a glimpse of my reflection in the darkened TV screen. I'd shrunk. Running away hadn't solved anything. Maybe it was time to do things differently. Maybe it was time to take a risk.

18

THEN

'It's freezing out here,' I said as I rubbed my hands up and down my arms. 'Whose crazy idea was it to come down to the beach at this time in the morning?' I tried to remember, but everything was a bit hazy. One minute we were in a nice warm caravan and the next we were sitting on the beach in the bitter wind. I reached for the bottle of wine propped up in the sand by Rebecca's feet. Maybe another drink would help warm me up.

'We wanted to watch the sun rise,' Rebecca said, her words slurring slightly as she snuggled closer to Luke.

'We?' he queried. 'You mean you wanted to and somehow you persuaded the rest of us to come with you.'

'It seemed like a good idea at the time,' Rebecca replied, her voice muffled against Luke's coat. 'My parents and I used to get up early to watch the sun rise every time we stayed here.'

'I'm guessing you used to visit in the summer, though,' Tom suggested, as he wrapped his arm around Hannah's shoulders. 'I'm not even sure we'll see it, it looks too cloudy.'

I turned away and fixed my gaze on the grey horizon. What was I doing out here? Watching the sun rise with two couples, while I sat on my own. I pulled my knees up to my chin and took another swig of wine. I should never have come on this trip.

All I really wanted was my nice warm bed, where I could snuggle under the duvet and close my eyes. I yawned, as though the thought of my bed had made me even sleepier.

'It's so cool that you have those little memories with your parents,' Hannah said.

'Yeah well, our "little" holidays might not have been as extravagant as yours, but I liked them.' I heard the indignation in Rebecca's voice.

'I wasn't being patronising,' Hannah said quickly. 'I really meant it; I do think it's cool. We never really did family stuff like that.'

'Oh,' Rebecca said, her tone softening. 'That's too bad.'

'My parents were always working. It's how they met actually, at DEM.'

'Ahh, now that's romantic,' Rebecca said. I felt a twinge of jealousy as Rebecca's hostility towards Hannah evaporated. She was supposed to be my friend. Not hers.

'I guess it must have been, at least, at the beginning.' Hannah shrugged. 'It was Dad's company, his passion. Mum joined when the business started to grow and he needed someone to handle the admin. He hates that side of it. He's a salesman at heart. He wants to be out there networking. Meeting new people. Making deals.' There was something to Hannah's tone; beneath the resentment, there was an edge of pride. She admired that part of him. That large personality. That confidence. From where I sat, it seemed to be a trait they shared. 'He's the face of the business, Mum was the backbone.'

'Was?' I asked, strangely intrigued by her story.

'She left us a couple of years ago. I guess she got bored of being the one left behind while he had his adventures. His fun.'

'I'm sorry.' The compassion in my voice surprised me and I realised that I genuinely meant it. I'd always been close to my parents; I couldn't imagine not having them both there. 'It must have been hard.'

'Dad buried himself further into the business. It was his way of coping. I wanted to help him, to spend time with him. But the only way to do that seemed to be by working with him. I'd always helped Mum with the invoices and stuff, so it wasn't a big deal for me to pick up more of the slack when she left. I thought it might make Dad appreciate me and bring us closer together, you know?'

'Did it work?' I could hear the hope in Rebecca's voice. I wasn't the only one captivated by Hannah's story.

'No, if anything, I feel closer to Mum than him.' She kept her gaze lowered as she dragged her fingers through the sand beside her, lost in her own thoughts.

'She came back?' I asked.

'No. I mean, I still see her in the holidays and we talk on the phone and stuff, but I understand how she must have felt now. I get why she left him. I'm basically just another employee.' For a second that air of self-importance that always surrounded her seemed to slip.

'That's so sad.' Something in my chest constricted. All this time I'd thought Hannah was just some spoilt rich kid, who thought she was better than everyone else. But could I have been wrong about her? Perhaps she was just like the rest of us, muddling through as best as we could, acting as though we knew more than we did. Perhaps her confidence was nothing more than a shield to hide her own insecurities.

Perhaps her shield was just a better act than mine.

It couldn't have been easy, growing up in the shadow of a successful entrepreneur, following in his footsteps in the hope that he might notice her. Did she even want to study event management? Did she want that life? That career?

Hannah scoffed. 'It's life. Besides, unlike the rest of you, I'll inherit a successful business someday.'

And then, just like that, the old Hannah was back. Smug and entitled. That faint simmer of compassion I'd started to feel was instantly extinguished.

She had Tom.

And I didn't

Because of her.

'We should play a game to kill the time,' Hannah announced. 'How about truth or dare? You can go first, Lizzie.'

'Why me?'

'Why not?'

I couldn't think of a reason.

'So, what will it be?' Hannah prompted. 'Truth or dare?'

'Truth...' *I replied hesitantly.*

Hannah sniggered. 'I knew you wouldn't pick dare. You're much too straight for that.'

'Hey!' *Rebecca objected on my behalf.*

'What? You know it's true.'

'Lizzie's a rule follower. There's nothing wrong with that.'

I cringed at Rebecca's attempt at defending me. Compared to Hannah, I sounded like a bore.

'Enough stalling,' *Hannah's voice cut through my thoughts.* 'Truth time...'

I turned to face her, my stomach twisting in knots. There was something about her manner that made me nervous. She was too gleeful. I braced myself for her question.

'Who do you have a crush on?'

I stared at her. How did she know I had a crush on anyone? We weren't close. I'd never shared that with her. And I certainly couldn't tell her who it was. 'I d-don't,' *I stuttered.*

'Come on, Lizzie. You're amongst friends. You can tell us.' *She leaned towards me.* 'Besides, you chose truth, remember?'

I shook my head. 'I don't have a crush on anyone.'

'I've overhead you and Rebecca whispering, I know there's someone. Who is he?'

'Then you need to get your hearing checked,' I said with a forced laugh.

Hannah nudged Tom in the ribs with her elbow. 'Aren't you curious, too?'

'I am now,' Tom replied with a grin. 'Spill, Lizzie. Who's the guy? We need to assess if he's worthy of you.'

'He isn't,' Rebecca said, her tone disapproving.

'Rebecca!' I hissed as I glared at her. How could she do this to me?

'Ah ha!' Hannah exclaimed. 'I knew it.'

'Oh, Lizzie. I'm so sorry. That just slipped out. It's the wine.'

'So, who is he then?' Tom urged.

I gritted my teeth. What was he playing at? Why was he putting me on the spot like this? He should be helping me. Then again, so should Rebecca. 'Just a guy from uni.'

'We need a name,' Hannah demanded.

'You don't know him.'

'It's Hannah's turn now,' Rebecca announced.

'No, we haven't got to the bottom of Lizzie's crush yet.' Hannah jutted her chin out as her eyes bored into me.

'Oh, come on,' Luke groaned. 'This is so boring. Who cares if Lizzie has a crush on some guy we don't know?'

I shot him a grateful look. At least someone was on my side.

'Because I'm curious. Have you told him how you feel? Does he like you too? Why aren't you two together?'

'It's one question only, Hannah.' I was surprised at how steady my voice sounded, while inside I felt like I was falling apart. What had she overheard? How much did she know? I refused to allow myself to look at Tom. Would Hannah be able to read my expression? Or did she already know it was him?

But if she knew, then why waste time playing silly games? Why not just come out and ask?

'Ha, she has you there, Hannah,' Rebecca cheered.

I felt a tiny sense of victory. I'd outmanoeuvred her for once. But I knew it wouldn't last long. My minor triumph was immaterial as long as she still had Tom. I let out a deep sigh. This weekend could have been so perfect if she hadn't been here. She was in the way.

She was always in the way.

'Time to move on,' Luke agreed. 'So, Hannah, truth or dare?'

Hannah snorted. 'Dare, obviously.'

Of course Hannah would choose a dare. She wasn't afraid of anything. She was braver than me. Better than me.

She needed to be cut back down to size. I drummed my fingers against the side of the wine bottle in my hand as I tried to think of an appropriate dare. Something tough. Something daunting.

Something that would teach her a lesson.

19

NOW

I led Tom into the hall and paused. 'The guest room is on the right at the top of the stairs,' I told him, waving my hand unnecessarily in that direction.

The guest room was my parent's old bedroom. I'd redecorated when they sold me the house. I'd intended to move in there myself. It made sense. It was bigger. But, like so many things, the move had never happened.

I'd stayed where I was.

I wasn't even sure why I called it the guest room. My parents were the only people that ever stayed in there.

Or they had been, until today.

Perhaps it was my attempt to convince myself that, at least, something had changed. That there was some form of forward momentum. Even if it was tiny and irrelevant.

Tom nodded. 'Aren't you coming up?'

'In a minute; I'm just going to lock up first.'

He nodded again, collected his case and carried it up the stairs.

I turned to the front door behind me and clicked the lock beneath the latch. Then I returned to the kitchen and put the mugs in the dishwasher before surveying the room, thankful that Tom wasn't present to witness my nightly ritual.

The taps are off. The kettle's off. Hob's off. And the oven's off. My gaze flitted around the room, checking the appliances as I worked through my mental check list.

I pushed the fridge door and then the freezer door. Both were shut.

I scanned the room again, searching for anything I might have missed, before settling on the taps again. I shook my head. 'No, you've already checked everything,' I scolded myself. 'You know it's all turned off.'

I walked to the door, but even as my hand reached for the light switch, I couldn't resist one final glance over my shoulder. Just to be sure...

I rolled my eyes and forced my feet to keep walking.

I climbed the stairs and turned towards the guest room. 'There's space in the wardro...' The words evaporated from my lips as my gaze locked on his suitcase flung open on the bed, its mud-encrusted wheels nestled into the cream duvet cover.

I veered towards it, my hands outstretched, preparing to remove it. But I stopped.

He'd only been back in my life for a few hours. If I started being fussy now I'd scare him straight back out the door. Besides, the duvet cover was dirty now. What difference would it make if I moved the case to the floor, or left it until he'd unpacked? It would have to be washed regardless.

I felt Tom's gaze on me and I turned to face him.

'Is something wrong?'

I shook my head and forced a smile on to my lips. 'No, not at all. I just came to see if I could help with anything.'

The lie grated against me. It wasn't a good way to reconnect. But then it wasn't my first lie. It wasn't even my worst.

I couldn't let him see who I'd become; this version of the girl he'd once known so well. He'd loved me then. It had been complicated and dangerous. But it had been love, nonetheless.

He wouldn't love me now.

He wouldn't even like me.

If the old version hadn't been enough to keep him, he certainly wouldn't stick around for this version.

I needed to be better. Better than now. Better than before.

20

THEN

'Are you crazy?' Rebecca asked. 'That's way too dangerous.'

'Yeah, come on. Climbing to the top of Durdle Door is too much,' Luke agreed. 'Even in good weather and daylight that would be stupid, but the sun's only just starting to come up.'

'Yeah,' Tom said. 'But just imagine how amazing watching the sun rise from up there would be.'

'Fine,' Hannah said, with a shrug. 'If Lizzie goes with me.'

'What?' Tom and I said in unison.

I glanced at towering archway, standing sentry over the bay. 'No way,' I added, shaking my head.

'You're such a coward,' Hannah goaded. 'You're always afraid to go after what you really want.' She tugged Tom's arms tighter around her.

Even in the soft early morning light, there was something about her expression that cut into me. It felt as if she was taunting me. Reminding me that Tom was hers. But how could she know that I wanted him? Was it just a suspicion? Or did she know for sure?

'Guys like adventurous women. Bold. Confident. Not afraid to take a chance,' Hannah continued. 'Women who aren't afraid to prove how much they love them.'

'Women like you, you mean?' I asked, pointedly.

Hannah smirked.

She was right, of course. Guys did like women like that. Like her.

My gaze drifted to Tom. He liked women like Hannah.

Tom would never have dared me to do this. The idea wouldn't even have occurred to him. He knew I wasn't brave enough. Wasn't strong enough.

But Hannah was different.

She was everything I wasn't.

I lifted my chin. But who said I couldn't be more like that? If I wanted it badly enough? If I tried hard enough?

'Fine, I'll go.' My words were so strong, so adamant, it made me more certain that it was the right thing to do.

It was the only thing to do.

I had to prove to Tom, to myself, that I was as good as Hannah.

'I don't think that's a goo—' Tom started.

'Why is it not a good idea for her, but it's a good idea for me?' Hannah asked as she swung round to face him.

'Because you're so much stronger than Lizzie, you can do anything.'

It felt like a void opened up within me; empty and hollow. Tom was the person who was supposed to see the best in me. The person who believed in me the most.

Just like I did with him.

And yet he saw Hannah as superior to me.

His betrayal seeped into my veins. I knew I wasn't perfect. I tried to be, but I always fell a little short. But for Tom to compare me to her, to judge my abilities against hers and declare me inferior wasn't right. It wasn't fair.

He hadn't even given me a chance. He'd written me off too easily.

Resentment bubbled inside me, like a volcano ready to erupt. He was wrong.

'Are we doing this, or what?' I asked, scrambling to my feet. I didn't need to listen to Tom putting me down. Comparing me to her and ruling me out. I was more determined than ever now. If Tom thought Hannah was capable of anything, then I would have to show him that I was too.

'Lizzie, you're drunk,' Rebecca said as I stumbled forwards.

'Yep,' I agreed. 'You don't think I'd actually do this if I was sober, do you?'

Rebecca stood up and staggered towards me. 'That's precisely why you shouldn't be doing it at all.'

I shrugged and turned towards the path that led back to the cliff which jutted out to form the arch. I wouldn't let common sense hold me back. I had to do this. I needed to. Rebecca grabbed my arm, but I shook her off. I wasn't going to let her talk me out of this. There was too much at stake.

Hannah laughed as she stood up and ran ahead of me. 'I bet you won't make it to the top,' she called out.

I gritted my teeth and kept moving forward. I'd show her. I'd make it the top.

Somehow.

'Are you just going to sit there and let them do this?' I heard Rebecca ask.

'It's not like I can stop them,' Tom replied.

'Well, at least, go with them.'

'Fine,' I heard Tom sigh. 'Hey, Hannah, wait for me.'

I stared after him.

Hannah.

It was always Hannah.

It was time that changed. Time I finally showed Tom that I could be as good as her.

In fact, I could be better.

21

NOW

'Goodnight then,' I muttered as I hurried out of the guest room, suddenly eager for some space.

'Oh, er, goodnight.' I heard the surprise in Tom's voice, and maybe even a little disappointment. My hurried retreat wasn't exactly welcoming.

My phone buzzed in my pocket and I paused on the landing. I frowned at the caller ID and hit the green button to answer the video call.

'Is everything okay?' I asked as Mum appeared on the screen.

'I'm all right, but I was worried about you. You missed our call this afternoon.'

'Oh, right. Sorry.' I glanced back over my shoulder towards the guest room. 'I got a bit distracted.'

'I wouldn't have called so late, but you didn't even respond to my messages.'

'Sorry,' I repeated as I stepped into my bedroom and flicked the light switch on, hoping Tom couldn't hear Mum's anguished voice. I was twenty-eight years old and she was checking up on me as though I was still fifteen. 'I haven't looked at my phone all afternoon.'

Mum grunted as I propped the phone up on the dressing table. 'It's unlike you to be busy at the weekend.'

I flinched as I drew the curtains. 'Not that unusual.' I over-lapped the edge of the right curtain over the left, blocking out every ray of light from the lampposts, before straightening the pleats.

Mum shook her head. 'It wasn't a criticism. You're just more of a home bird, that's all.'

'It's not as though I never go out.' I flopped down on my bed, suddenly feeling weary. 'It's just nice to stay home sometimes.'

'Of course it is, dear.'

I tipped my head to the side as I tried to decide if there was a hint of condescension in her voice.

I tried to think of a response, but my mind was blank. I couldn't really object, could I? Not given I hadn't actually left the house all day. I nibbled my lip. Come to think of it, I hadn't left the house all weekend.

'Lizzie!'

My head jerked to the right at the sound of Tom's voice. My gaze instantly fell upon my open bedroom door. Why hadn't I thought to close it? I was so used to living alone, I never usually needed to close my door.

I leapt to my feet as I heard his footsteps crossing the landing. 'I forgot my toothpaste,' he called, his voice growing louder with every step.

I snatched the phone up and angled it away, just as he appeared in the doorway.

'Can I borrow—'

'Who's that?' Mum asked. I could hear the curiosity in her voice.

Tom froze.

I lowered my gaze to the screen in time to see Mum craning her neck as though trying to see around the edges of the camera lens.

'Erm, just a, erm, friend.' I could feel Tom's gaze boring into me.

'In your house at this time of night?'

'Sorry,' Tom mouthed, before retreating.

'He just needed a place to stay for a few days.'

'He?'

'Yes, he.'

Mum leaned closer to the camera, until all I could see were her dark brown eyes filling the screen.

'Oh, Mum, you need to back—'

'*He* as in a boyfriend he?' I could hear the hopeful excitement in her voice. She wanted this for me. A partner. A life. Normality.

'No.' I frowned at the screen. 'I mean, I don't th—'

'What's his name?' Her eager curiosity cut through my indecisiveness.

'Tom.'

I swallowed. I could see the pieces fitting together as her expression changed from curiosity to horror.

'No! Beth, please tell me that it's not Tom Murphy?'

I grimaced.

'You're back with *him*?'

'I'm not *with* him.' *I was never* with *him,* I added silently. At least, not properly. Not fully. He was never completely mine.

'And he's moved in with you? To our house?'

Our house.

It wasn't their house.

Not any more.

It was mine. I'd bought it from them. Admittedly, for less than they could probably have got through an estate agent. But that didn't matter. It didn't make it theirs.

Did it?

I shook my head. Now wasn't the time to focus on that. Some

things were just best left alone. 'Tom hasn't moved in. He's just staying with me for a little while.'

'How long?'

I shrugged. 'I'm not sure.' I hadn't asked and he hadn't said. Our arrangement was impromptu and casual.

'Tell him to stay in a hotel.'

I bristled. It wasn't even a suggestion. It was an instruction. An order. 'We're just taking the opportunity to spend some time together; to reconnect.'

'Reconnect? Are you sure that's wise?'

'Wh-what do you mean?' I knew how risky this was, but I'd never told Mum what had happened. I'd never told anyone.

'That boy filled your head with crazy dreams. You got swept along in the romance of it all. You got swept away by him. And then he cast you aside. He broke your heart, Beth. Do you remember that? He destroyed you. You completely fell apart.'

'That wasn't T—' I stopped myself just in time before I revealed that it wasn't Tom's fault I'd dropped out of uni and hidden away at home.

My parents had always blamed him for it. They didn't know why exactly, but from their perspective, one minute we were dating, and the next he disappeared from my life without a trace. They therefore assumed he was somehow behind me suddenly abandoning my dreams and refusing to leave the house.

'It took us months to get you back on your feet.'

I blinked at Mum's wording. She spoke as if my struggle had been an inconvenience to her. That they'd been the ones to get me through it. As though I hadn't had any involvement in the process.

'And now,' Mum continued, oblivious to my glare, 'you've not just invited him back into your life, but into your home as well.' She shook her head. 'I just hope you know what you're getting yourself into.'

'I'm not getting myself into anything, Mum. We're just old friends catching up.'

Mum pursed her lips. 'Mmm.'

I knew that sound. It was her version of 'we'll see about that'. She didn't believe me. But then, perhaps she was right not to.

Could I honestly say Tom and I were just catching up? Or that I even wanted us to be *just* friends?

Didn't I want more from this? More from him?

A lot more.

'Look, Mum, now isn't a good time to talk about this. It's late and I have work in the morning.'

'Well, all right. I suppose we can talk about it tomorrow.'

'Sure,' I said dismissively. At this point I would have said anything to end the call.

'I'll call—'

'Bye, Mum.' I hung up, vaguely aware that I had cut her off.

I heard Tom clattering around in the bathroom, probably searching for my toothpaste, but I ignored it as the conversation replayed in my head.

I couldn't blame Mum for being wary of Tom, she was just protecting me. She'd seen me at my lowest. Or, at least, she thought she had.

She wasn't to know that she was accusing Tom unfairly.

But that wasn't the only thing she was wrong about...

Technically, I hadn't invited Tom into my life, or my home.

He'd invited himself.

He'd turned up unannounced and asked if he could stay.

I could have said no. I hadn't had to offer him my guest room. That had been my choice.

Hadn't it?

Somehow Tom always seemed to be able to get himself in places. Even those he wasn't supposed to be.

22

THEN

I clambered over another rock. This was such a stupid idea. All I wanted was my bed. Warm and cosy. I paused as Tom scrambled past me without even pausing to check if I needed a hand. I clenched my jaw. Perhaps I could just stay here. I could leave this insane climb to Tom and Hannah. I had more sense than this.

'Maybe you should go back if it's too much for you,' Hannah taunted from further ahead.

Fire burned within me. 'If you can do it, so can I,' I called back as my good sense abandoned me again.

I kept my head down, not daring to allow my gaze to stray as the arch narrowed and the sea became visible to the left and right. Don't look down, I reminded myself for the tenth time.

Or was it more?

I paused as I tried to count, before I realised the pointlessness of what I was doing. 'Just reach the top and get this over with,' I muttered, as I resumed climbing.

'About time.' Hannah towered over me as I scrambled to the top on my hands and knees. 'Didn't think you were going to make it.'

'I'm tougher than I look,' I replied, but even I knew my words would have had more impact if I hadn't sounded so exhausted.

I sank down and sat on a cold hard rock. The sharp edges dug into my legs but I didn't care. I'd done it. I'd reached the top. I glanced back at the narrow, uneven route we had just taken. It looked even more daunting from up here. 'How are we going to get back down?' I wasn't sure I had the energy.

'You could always take the easy route back down,' Hannah said.

I frowned for a second, before I realised what she meant. 'People have got hurt jumping from up here.' I rubbed my head as my words slurred together. I shouldn't have drunk so much. I wasn't used to it. Not even the cold climb had sobered me up.

'There are always risks.' She shrugged. 'That's life.'

'I guess you'd know,' I replied. Hannah was more adventurous than me. I was content to sit on the side lines and observe life, whereas she was out there living it.

Hannah staggered towards me. She could hold her drink better than I could, but she was still drunk. 'You know, don't you?'

'Know what?'

'She doesn't know anything,' Tom said, pulling Hannah away.

'You told her, didn't you?'

'Why would I tell her?'

'Because you're sleeping with her.' Hannah's voice cracked. She sounded so hurt. So betrayed.

We'd done that.

I'd done that.

I curled myself up into a little ball. I wanted to disappear. To avoid witnessing the pain I had caused. But I couldn't.

'We're not—'

'Don't lie to me, Tom.' The venomous streak was back in her voice.

She was wrong, of course. That was a line Tom and I hadn't crossed. But she'd never believe it. Not from me.

I wouldn't if our roles were reversed.

So I kept quiet. This wasn't my battle.

'Okay, okay. Look, I screwed up. I'm sorry.' Tom's voice was soft and apologetic. *I tried not to listen. It was bad enough I was stealing her boyfriend, I didn't need to witness her being dumped too.*

I felt an unfamiliar twinge of compassion for Hannah. I knew the pain of losing Tom to someone else. To imagine my life with him, and have another girl stand in my way. He and I might not have been a couple when he'd met Hannah, but she'd still taken him from me.

I knew loss because of her.

And now, she knew it because of me.

It was sad, and yet, at the same time, there was something disturbingly satisfying about that realisation.

The cold from the rock I was sitting on seeped into my bones and I shivered. Perhaps it was time to leave. The cold and my bitterness were starting to take hold of me. I wasn't that person. Cruel. Vindictive. Smug.

That was Hannah, not me.

I would be gracious in my victory.

'She's pathetic, Tom. She climbed up here with us to try and prove she's as good as me; that she can be brave and daring too. But look at her, Tom. She will never be me.'

Hannah's words cut like a knife despite my intention to be the bigger person. She wasn't going to be gracious and accept defeat. Not to me.

But then, why would she?

She was right. I wasn't her. I was quieter. Weaker.

And as long as that was the case, Tom would always choose Hannah over me.

I was tired and out of breath, but my hatred for Hannah pumped through my veins.

23

NOW

I closed my bedroom door and sagged back against it.

'Do you really think he'll leave me? For you?'

Hannah's taunting laugh echoed in my memory.

I clamped my hands over my ears, desperately trying to block out her voice. But it was no good. I could still see her towering over me as I sat on that rock at the top of Durdle Door.

'You're nothing to him. Just a passing curiosity.'

I leapt to my feet. 'You're wrong.' Anger burned within me as I spat the words at her. Whatever guilt I'd felt for our betrayal instantly dissipated. She didn't deserve Tom. She didn't deserve anything.

'No,' I murmured as I sank to the floor. I had to make it stop. I didn't want to think about it. I didn't want to remember.

I couldn't let the memories take hold of me.

Not again.

'Do you really think he'll leave me? For you?'

The memory repeated. Fragmented and out of place.

'I won't,' Tom yelled behind Hannah.

It was too late. I was spiralling. Stuck in a freefall, reliving the parts of that morning I hadn't been able to block out. They were always disjointed and confusing.

The memories consumed me, making it hard to catch my breath. It wasn't like watching an old movie, it was worse. I relived everything that went along with it. The confusion. The panic. The pain. The guilt.

And the worst part was I knew how it ended.

Hannah's eyes widened with horror as she stared at me. Her arms flailed desperately as she tumbled backwards over the edge of the arch.

It was all my fault.

I'd ruined everything.

One night.

One drink too many.

One bad idea.

One secret that destroyed so much.

No one can know.

I'd spent years trying to escape the past. I'd followed Tom's instructions. I'd built a life on it. I'd started again; cut ties with anyone who'd known me. But there was one flaw with Tom's plan. Someone did know.

Me.

And no matter how hard I tried, I couldn't outrun my own memory.

And now, Tom was back. Along with the memories I'd fought so hard to bury.

I dug my nails into my left arm and pulled them across the skin slowly. My eyes smarted, but I kept going. I needed this. The pain. The release.

But it wasn't enough. I needed more.

I clawed at my arm again. Slowly and precisely. Every millimetre was filled with hatred and desperation.

I groaned quietly as I let my hand fall away.

The pain in my arm was all I could think about. All I could feel. Everything else faded into the background. The lies; the guilt; the self-loathing, which accompanied me in every moment, dulled. My mind felt quiet. Peaceful. Calm.

I curled up on the floor, engulfed in a bubble of calmness that existed around me. For a few brief moments I felt in control.

But I knew it wouldn't last.

It was always temporary.

Relief always gave way to revulsion and shame.

I winced as my arm began to throb. The pain was different now. It didn't feel good any more.

I pressed my right hand to my arm, attempting to dull the agony as I gritted my teeth, refusing to allow myself to cry out. I couldn't let Tom hear. I couldn't let him see me like this. He'd carried a secret for me before and it had destroyed us. I wouldn't burden him with this one too. He'd be afraid for me. Maybe *of* me. There was a darkness within me. One I had to keep hidden from everyone.

Especially Tom.

He'd look at me with disgust and condemnation. He'd want me to get help. To talk.

I snorted. As though talking would help anything.

It hadn't before. It wouldn't now.

This was my battle. Mine to handle alone.

It always had been.

24

THEN

I stood at the front of the seminar room. My hands trembled as I held the crisp white printed pages in front of me. It was my favourite class. It was where I belonged. Where I could be myself.

It was good to be back here. At least, that was what I told myself. I had to get back to normal. Back to conversations that didn't entirely revolve around Hannah.

There was still gossip, of course. Still questions. But thankfully, no one on my course knew her. Except for Rebecca.

I'd only been off for a week. It seemed so much longer. And yet, at the same time, it didn't seem long enough.

How long would it take to put the events of that weekend behind me? How long until I could close my eyes and not see her face?

I shook my head. This wasn't the time for thoughts like that. I had to focus. I had to get back on track.

My classmates slouched in their seats, whispering amongst themselves. I couldn't blame them. Mine was the fifth story of the morning and the clock was rapidly approaching lunchtime.

Usually I wouldn't care. I wasn't here for them. I was here for me. Once I started reading my story they would fall quiet. I could judge the success of my work by their reactions. It was my quest to capture their imagination and hold their attention with my story. It was exciting. Invigorating.

But this time felt different.

I hadn't written all week. The piece I had been working on for today, lay incomplete on my laptop. I could have spoken to the tutor. I could have asked for an extension. Under the circumstances, she would probably have agreed.

But that would have meant talking about the very thing I wanted to forget. She would have asked questions I didn't want to answer. She would have looked at me with sympathy and concern that I didn't deserve.

So I'd stayed quiet. I'd printed out a story I'd already written. One she hadn't heard yet.

A knot formed in my stomach as I recalled Tom's reaction when he had read it almost two months ago. That day had seemed like the turning point for us. I thought it was the beginning of us being together; instead, it had been the beginning of my undoing.

Perhaps it was a bad idea. I should have picked a different story. Any story, except this one.

'Are you ready, Lizzie?' the writing tutor asked.

I nodded mutely. It was an automated response, rather than a willingness to get started.

My eyes sought out Rebecca in the audience before me. She was the one person I knew would be paying attention and rooting for me.

Except...

Her head was bowed forward over her notebook on the desk in front of her. She wasn't looking at me.

She'd been distant since we'd got back from Durdle Door. It was understandable. We were each distracted by our own thoughts. Grieving for what had been lost. I hadn't seen Luke since he'd dropped me off at my house. He blamed me for the nightmare we had found ourselves in.

I did too.

Rebecca and Tom were my only advocates. They didn't agree on much these days, but when it came to protecting me they were united.

It had cost them both.

I waited for the usual rush of adrenaline to course through my veins, to drive my performance and give power to my voice.

But it didn't come.

I cleared my throat and started reading. My voice wobbled more than usual. I wasn't a performer. I was happier sitting behind a desk than standing in front of them, but usually the thrill of reading my work aloud, of seeing the reactions in my classmate's faces, overrode my nerves. I immersed myself in the story, I became the voice of my characters, sharing their world, their hopes, their dreams.

Except this story wasn't about happy endings. It was about loss and pain. Tom had guessed it was inspired by the grief I'd felt from losing my gran. But now the words took on new meaning.

'Loss c-changes you.'

I stuttered over the words.

There was a different truth to them now. I knew a different kind of loss. A different kind of grief.

Loss had changed me. The story no longer felt the same, and neither did I.

My gaze kept returning to Rebecca. She still wasn't looking at me. In fact, it felt as though she was intentionally avoiding me. Avoiding eye contact. Avoiding sharing that moment of encouragement, that silent reassurance that we believed in each other.

'And he...' My gaze dropped back to the pages in my hand and I searched frantically for my place. 'He, er, he...'

I couldn't find it.

I was lost.

The words on the paper started to merge together. I blinked furiously, desperately trying to focus.

The guilt ate away at me, churning my insides. The only distraction from it was the fear that washed over me in waves.

What would happen if the police found something that linked every-thing back to us? To me? A footprint. A witness. Some detail that we hadn't noticed. I frowned as I tried to push those thoughts away. I mustn't think about that.

I swallowed.

Focus, I instructed myself.

I could do this.

This was my safe space. I belonged here. I needed to be here.

Luke thought we should tell the police the truth.

Part of me agreed with him.

Lying was bad. It was wrong. Especially when the lie was this big.

But Tom was right. No one could know.

Not the police. Not Hannah's family. Not even my own.

They wouldn't understand.

Even I didn't understand.

I glanced up again. I squinted through the grey fog that was descending around me. Rebecca was there somewhere, wasn't she?

The sound of my breathing grew louder and faster. I could feel my heart pounding. I wanted to run away. To hide. But I couldn't. My feet wouldn't work.

Nothing worked.

I fought for breath. Short sharp snatches that didn't satisfy my lungs.

The room dipped and swayed, like a ship bobbing at sea.

'Lizzie!'

I blinked at the faint sound of my name being called in the distance.

A strangled wheezing escaped my lungs as I gasped for air.

I felt a hand touch my arm and I jolted. The creative writing tutor's face came into focus. Pale and anxious. She looked so worried.

I took a shaky breath as my gaze drifted over her shoulder to the seminar room. My classmates stared back at me. Hushed whispers and ripples of laughter reached my ears.

Bile rose in my throat. They'd all witnessed my meltdown. They'd seen. My breathing quickened again. My fingers tingled with pins and needles. My palms felt sweaty. I needed air. I needed to not be here.

'I'm...' I wanted to apologise, to ask permission to leave, but my voice wouldn't work, the words wouldn't form. I pivoted on my heel and ran from the room. I didn't even know where I was going.

Anywhere.

As long as I was alone.

25

NOW

The alarm buzzed at 7 a.m., but I was already up, showered and rummaging in my wardrobe, trying to decide what to wear. It was stupid really. Tom had already seen me yesterday. But knowing he was sleeping in my guest room made my morning routine matter more. I crept around my room, desperate not to wake him. I wanted time to prepare for seeing him again. Time to perfect my appearance. Time to rehearse what I would say.

He'd caught me off guard yesterday. I hadn't had time to think, to psych myself up, but today...

I reached for the wardrobe to steady myself. This was really happening. He was actually here. Excitement jarred with anxiety, leaving me in a state of flux. I still wasn't sure this was a good idea, and yet the thought of not seeing him was inconceivable now.

I slid the wardrobe door to the right and studied the clothes inside cautiously, my eyes moving from one end to the other and then back again. It was ridiculous that I felt the need to do so; I'd bought all of the clothes that hung in there yet here I was peering at them as though I didn't know what I'd find.

Realistically though, I knew the problem wasn't that I didn't know what I owned. It was that what I owned wasn't appropriate. Not for today. Not for Tom. Everything was subtle. Comfortable. Safe. I lived in the background; my clothes were part of my camouflage.

But today was different. I didn't want to hide. I wanted Tom to notice me. I needed something which would make me look attractive instead of frumpy.

I continued to stare at the clothes, fingering them thoughtfully as I flicked through the minimal collection. Too formal. Too boring. Too grey. I analysed each outfit, hoping for inspiration. I didn't find any. I only found the end of the wardrobe and the disappointment that hung there.

As I glanced at my watch, I realised I'd run out of time. I was already behind my carefully planned morning schedule.

I drew the wardrobe door closed and glanced at the other door. Slowly I slid it across to the left. It had been years since I'd opened this side. My gaze fell upon the rail of brightly coloured clothes. It had been even longer since I'd actually worn anything that hung in there. They were from another time. Another life.

They belonged to Lizzie.

I pulled out a black skirt and long sleeved red top. I wrinkled my nose as I studied them. Would they even fit?

There was only one way to find out.

I changed quickly and stood in front of the full length mirror. The skirt was a little short and the top a little snug, but the overall effect wasn't bad. I looked different. I looked younger. I looked like...

Me.

I caught sight of red streaks on my left arm. I froze for a moment, before tracing my fingertips across them with my right hand. There was something mesmerising about them. So little. So insignificant. And yet so powerful.

They were my weakness. But somehow, they were also my strength.

I felt calmer today. They had done their job.

For now.

I took a deep breath and I pulled my sleeve down to my wrist. The scars were a reminder that whilst I might look a little more like the old me, the only thing that had changed were my clothes. It was going to take more than dressing the part to find my way back to who I used to be.

But maybe it was, at least, a start.

I sat at my dressing table and studied my reflection as I applied my foundation with extra care. I felt like I was a teenager again, harbouring my secret crush, while trying to make myself more noticeable, more appealing. Back then I'd longed for Tom to see me in a different light; to want me to be more than just his friend. And now... I shuffled on the soft cream stool. What did I want now?

Tom.

I smiled slightly. That part had never changed. I'd always wanted Tom. I probably always would.

But that need was different now. I didn't just want his love. I wanted his forgiveness too.

I have a plan. A way for us to be together. Just you and me.

Tom's promise to me, repeated in my mind. He'd had a plan, and I'd messed it up.

If only I'd waited. If I'd been a little more patient. If I'd kept my jealousy under control just a little longer...

I'd destroyed us. I was the reason he'd left. The reason we couldn't be together. Could he ever forgive me for that?

What if that was too much to ask for? My shoulders sagged as I stared at my reflection. What if Tom's forgiveness, like my own, was unattainable?

And yet, he was here.

Didn't that signify that maybe there was, at least, hope?

He was staying for a week. I had seven days to show him he belonged here. With me.

All I had to do was be exactly what he needed. What he wanted. The perfect girlfriend.

I'd failed last time, before I'd even earned that title. This time would be different. I would be different.

I had to be.

I applied a coat of soft pink lipstick and forced a smile onto my lips. It shouldn't be that hard. After all, my entire life had been an act for the last ten years.

But I knew it wasn't that simple. The self-loathing I felt inside wasn't just for what I had cost Tom and me. We weren't the ones who'd suffered the most. Our relationship had just been collateral damage.

The person whose forgiveness I needed most of all was the one person who would never be able to give it.

Hannah.

26

THEN

'So tell me a little about what's going on.'

I shuffled uncomfortably under the therapist's gaze. She smiled at me encouragingly, but her question felt intrusive. She wanted me to open up and talk about my feelings. My problems. My secrets.

I shrank back into the chair, wishing it would swallow me up and I could disappear. This was the last place I wanted to be.

'In her referral, your GP mentioned you've been having some issues attending your classes...'

It was the GP's fault I was here. I'd gone to see her for help and instead she'd sent me here. I'd wanted her to give me a tablet or even some disgusting-tasting medicine that would instantly cure me. I wanted it to be treatable. Fixable. I wanted it to be something normal. Something real. I didn't want to be crazy. I wanted it to go away as quickly as it had come on.

'Lizzie?' the therapist prompted.

'It's stupid.'

'You can tell me anything. It's just us here.'

'I want to run away.'

'Run away from what?'

'*Everything.*' I shrugged. '*Everyone.*'

'*Everyone?*'

'*Sometimes there are too many people.*' I paused as I struggled to find the words to explain. '*It's like they're surrounding me. Watching me.*'

'*And how does that make you feel?*'

'*Scared.*' I sniffed. '*I'm afraid I'm going to do something stupid. Afraid that they'll all see; that they'll all know.*'

'*Know what?*'

'*That I don't belong. That I don't deserve to be here.*'

'*A lot of students feel overwhelmed in their first year at university. It's a big change.*'

I shook my head. '*It's not that much of a change. I still live at home. And I have friends here. Sort of.*'

'*Sort of?*'

'*Things are strained between us at the moment.*'

'*Why?*'

I nibbled my bottom lip. '*Rebecca and Luke broke up and Tom...*'

'*Tom...?*'

'*He's not really around right now.*'

'*Tell me about him.*'

'*He's my best friend. We've known each other since nursery school and we've been friends ever since.*'

'*You two sound close.*'

'*We are.*' I swallowed. We were, I added silently. I'd ruined that. But this wasn't about us. This was about getting me back to normal. Getting me right. Then maybe he'd come back... '*It never used to bother me to sit in a huge theatre, or to be crammed in on a full bus,*' I said, shifting the conversation away from Tom, before she could ask any more questions. I couldn't talk about him. I couldn't tell her why he'd left. Why I was alone. If I did, everything would unravel.

'*When did you start to feel uncomfortable in those situations?*' The momentary crease of her brow told me she'd noticed my change in direction, but she didn't question it.

'A few weeks ago.'

'Had you felt particularly stressed or anxious about anything before then?'

I shook my head. 'No, everything was fine. I was fine.' My voice wobbled slightly. I had been fine, until...

'Had anything happened to change that?'

I clasped my hands together, desperate to stop her from seeing the tremor that had started at her question. It was too close. She was too close.

'Lizzie?'

My gaze met hers. I could tell from her expression that she knew I was holding back. 'I...' I licked my lips. All I had to do was tell her the truth and this would all be over. She would tell me what to do next. She would help me.

'Tom and I, we started dating.'

My shoulders slumped. I'd bailed. Again.

'Okay.'

'But, we shouldn't have done. He had a girlfriend.'

'Ah, I see. And the panic attacks started after you two started seeing each other?'

I nodded. 'Yeah, but...' She assumed it was about a boy, that I was some lovestruck teenager who couldn't handle the guilt of dating Tom behind Hannah's back.

But that wasn't the worst thing I'd done.

'Have you talked to Tom about the panic attacks?'

'No.'

'Do you want to?'

'He would normally be the first person I'd go to. I can talk to him about anything. Or, at least, I could.'

'So what's different this time?'

'We're, erm, not really hanging out together much right now.'

'Is that your choice or his?'

'He has a lot of stuff going on.'

'So your best friend isn't really available to you right now? How does that make you feel?'

'Lost.' The confession slipped out. I hadn't even realised it, but as I said it I knew it was true. Tom was the one I would turn to, the one I could always count on, and yet right now, when I needed him most, he was the one person I couldn't confide in. Without him I was lost and alone.

'And what happened to his girlfriend?'

I couldn't catch my breath. 'W-what?'

'You said he had a girlfriend, not has. So are they no longer together?'

'Er, no.' I swallowed. 'She, erm, she died.'

I braced myself for the inevitable reaction that would follow that news. The sympathy. The questions.

'I'm sorry.'

Even though I'd being expecting it, her compassion was like a vice crushing my chest.

I didn't deserve her pity. Her concern.

'Do you want to talk about it?'

I shook my head as Tom's instruction to keep quiet replayed in my head. But inside the words I could never say screamed, desperate to escape; to be heard.

Because somewhere deep down, beneath the emotions I was supposed to feel, there was something else: relief. A tiny part of me was glad she was gone.

Glad that I'd killed her.

27

NOW

I paced back and forth in my kitchen, too nervous to stand still even for a moment. I ran my fingers through my hair, straightening it again. My breath caught as I heard the bathroom door click upstairs. My hand slid from my hair to my side. And I stood frozen in place as I listened to the soft thud of footsteps crossing the landing above me.

What was I doing? I couldn't just stand here waiting for him.

The realisation that waiting for him was exactly what I had been doing for my whole life sucked the air from my lungs.

Would it be the worst thing for you two to spend a little time apart?

Mum's question stirred in my memory.

She'd always believed I was too dependent on Tom, even when we were kids. What if she was right? Maybe I should have chosen another uni, one further away from home. Maybe I should have had the adventures I'd always dreamed of and not let Tom change my plans. I'd stayed for him, but he could have come with me.

If he'd wanted to.

But then that was the problem. I'd always wanted him more than he'd wanted me. I cared the most. Sacrificed the most.

Whereas Tom...

What had Tom done?

He'd brought Hannah into our lives.

A floorboard creaked on the stairs and I pivoted on my heel, reached up and swung the cupboard door open by my head. I might still be waiting for him, but, at least, I couldn't let him know that was what I was doing.

'Morning,' Tom said as he entered the kitchen.

'Oh, hey.' I turned and smiled at him. 'Did you sleep well?'

'Yes, thanks.' He smiled too and my stomach did a little flip. I'd missed that smile.

I paused, waiting for him to comment on how I looked.

'I'd love a cup of tea if you're making one,' Tom added, nodding towards the open cupboard behind me. I turned back to the shelf neatly lined with mugs.

A wave of disappointment crashed down over me. 'Right, tea. Yes.' I grabbed two mugs from the cupboard and turned to flick the kettle on. I pulled the milk from the fridge and opened the top, ready to pour it into the empty mugs.

'Not like that, Lizzie,' Tom said. I could hear the frustration in his tone as he ushered me aside. 'Here, let me do it.'

I stepped back, the open bottle of milk still in my hands. I squirmed uncomfortably as the waist band of my skirt pressed against my stomach. I felt out of place in my kitchen and in my clothes.

'Where do you keep your teapot?' he asked as he fished a couple of teabags from the tea caddy.

I shook my head. 'I don't have one.'

He clicked his tongue and dropped a tea bag into each mug with disdain. 'Well, I guess this will have to do, then.'

'Sorry.' The apology slipped out automatically. I was screwing up already. I needed to be more careful if I wanted to keep him.

Why did I always screw everything up? He'd never stick around if I couldn't get my act together enough to even make a cup of tea right.

Tom took the milk from my hands. 'Why don't you go and sit down and I'll finish this.'

I nodded and sat at the kitchen table obediently. My stomach churned; I'd screwed up again. This was not the impression I wanted to make.

Tom's opinion was the most powerful thing. His approval could build me up, but his disapproval tore me down. It had always been that way, even when we were kids. It made me try harder to please him. To be the way he wanted me to be.

Yet as I sat subdued and remorseful, I felt a flicker of resentment simmer inside me. His disapproval was always reserved for me. He never criticised anyone else that way.

He'd never criticised Hannah.

28

THEN

'You've done what?' Mum stared at me, her jaw gaped open and eyes wide, soapy hands dripping water on to the tiled kitchen floor, from the washing up she had just abandoned.

'I've dropped out of AUB.'

Mum shook her head. 'You can't just drop out.'

'I can't go back. Every time I go to class I can't breathe.'

'What are you talking about? You love your classes.'

'Not any more.'

'Oh, you're just a bit overwhelmed. University is different to college. But you'll get used to it. You'll adapt.'

I shook my head. 'It's not that simple.'

Mum waved her hand. 'It'll just be a phase. You need to push past it.'

'I can't.'

'Of course you can. It's all in your head.' Mum dried her hands on the tea towel. 'You're so sensitive. You're always getting so caught up in your fictional world that I think sometimes you forget how to live in the real one.'

'That's not true,' I whispered. I knew the difference. And yet, for some reason, my objection lacked conviction.

'You just have to get back in there and it will get easier. We always taught you to be strong and face your fears. You can't run away any time things get a bit difficult.'

'You don't understand.'

'This is your dream, Lizzie. This is what you wanted. What you worked for.'

'I know.'

Mum tipped her head to the left. 'Your dad and I have always supported you. We never wanted to discourage you from writing. We knew how much you loved it, and how passionate you were. But that doesn't mean we didn't have reservations.'

Reservations?

I felt like the kitchen floor was shifting beneath me. What reservations? They'd always been encouraging. They believed in me.

Didn't they?

'We were afraid you were too emotional, too fragile, for a career where your thoughts and feelings are so exposed. We know how much of yourself you put into your stories. We were always afraid of how you'd handle rejection.'

'You never believed I'd get my work published.' The realisation reverberated through me.

'I didn't say that. We've always had faith that you were good enough. We just weren't sure if you were strong enough. Writing is so subjective. Success isn't guaranteed and it's certainly not instantaneous.'

'I know that.' Of course I knew that. Everyone did. I wasn't some naive kid who still believed in the romanticised version of being an author. I knew it involved hard work, dedication and limited degrees of success.

But it didn't matter.

No, that wasn't true. It did matter. It had always mattered. But it wasn't enough to dissuade me.

Writing wasn't something I chose to do because I wanted success and fame. It was something I had to do. I needed to do.

Writing was part of me, just like breathing. It was instinctive. Essential.

It was me.

'*I know you've had a rough month. Losing your friend like that...*' She rubbed my arm. '*If you need someone to talk to...*'

'*I already,*' I swallowed, '*I've already seen a therapist.*'

'*Oh, you have? You didn't say.*' There was a flash of hurt in her expression.

I hadn't gone to her for help. I'd wanted to. I'd thought about it. But if she'd asked too many questions I knew that my secrets would all come tumbling out.

What would she do then?

Tom, Rebecca and Luke had protected me, but was it out of friendship, or fear? I knew Luke's answer to that, but the others...? I couldn't place my parents in the same predicament. Doing what was right, or protecting their daughter.

They would choose me.

I think.

But I knew that choice had consequences. They would look at me differently. They would question what else I might do. Who else I might hurt.

And beneath it all, the guilt of carrying that secret would weigh heavily on them. I knew well enough that you couldn't rationalise guilt away. It didn't dissipate just because you wanted it to.

'*Did the uni arrange that?*'

'*Er, well...*'

Mum shook her head. '*Never mind, that's not important. The only thing that matters is, is it helping?*'

I scrunched my nose. '*It's not really my thing, you know, talking to a stranger, telling them all my private thoughts and feelings.*'

'No.' *Mum smiled slightly.* 'You've never really been much of a talker. You always preferred to work through your feelings through your writing. You had us so worried when you were younger with the way you treated those fictional characters as though they were real friends.'

'Not even writing is helping this time.'

'Oh, honey. I'm so sorry. I hadn't even realised you and, er, Hannah, was it? I hadn't realised you were so close. I thought she was only part of your group because she was dating Tom. I didn't realise you'd all stayed friends after the break up.'

Guilt chafed at me. I'd never told her the truth about Tom and me. I'd never told her he and Hannah hadn't broken up. How could I?

'How is Tom doing? It must be hard on him, losing someone he'd cared about, even though they weren't together any more.'

I shrugged. 'I guess.'

'We haven't seen him round here recently. Actually, come to think of it, we haven't seen him since before you all went to Durdle Door that weekend.'

'He's had a lot going on.'

'But you're his girlfriend. He should be making time for you, especially when you're struggling.'

'He doesn't...' I sniffed back a sob.

'He does know you're struggling, doesn't he?'

I shook my head. 'We haven't really talked for a while.'

'Oh, Lizzie!' Mum flung her arms around me and squeezed me tightly. 'I always knew that boy was no good for you.'

I pushed her away. 'It's not his fault,' I snapped.

'Why do you always defend him?'

'He's been busy. He's helping Hannah's dad out as much as he can.'

'Really?' I could see from her bemused expression that she found this strange.

'He works for her dad, remember? They get on really well.'

'I hadn't realised that.' She nodded slowly. 'It's really good of him to be *there for her father when he's going through such heartache.'*

'He's a good guy, Mum. I know you've never been able to see it.'

'Oh honey, I'm sure he has his admirable qualities, and this is certainly one of them, but...' She inhaled sharply. 'There's just something about him that always felt a little off. And him being there for Hannah's family is good of him, but that doesn't make it okay to neglect the person he supposedly loves.'

'He's not neglecting me, he's—' I clamped my mouth closed. I couldn't confess that Tom's absence was to protect me. He had to play the part of the mournful boyfriend to keep suspicion away from our relationship.

Our love.

My jealousy.

'He's what, dear?'

I shrugged helplessly. 'He's so much more than you could ever imagine.'

'You really do love him, don't you?'

Tears trickled down my cheeks as I couldn't keep my emotions in check any longer. 'So much.'

Mum pulled me towards her again, and this time I allowed myself to be comforted in her arms. 'I'm just so grateful that you weren't up on those rocks that night.'

'Oh Mum.' I choked back a sob.

'To think that someone so young could just die so tragically like that, it's terrifying. And her poor family, they'll never know for sure what she was doing up there. If it was an accident, or if she—'

'Mum, don't.' I shook my head. I couldn't think about how Hannah had died. I couldn't think about how her family would forever wonder what had happened.

'Just promise me...' Mum lifted my chin and stared into my eyes. 'Promise me that you would never do something like that.'

'We don't know if it was suicide.'

'But it could have been. She and Tom hadn't long been broken up. I

know how hard love is at your age. How it can feel like the only thing that matters. And break ups,' she shook her head, 'they can crush you.'

A heaviness descended on me. That lie by omission still hung between us. She thought Hannah was heartbroken. Dumped.

But it had never even come to that.

Had it?

'It wasn't Tom's fault.'

'I wasn't implying that it was. I just want you to be careful. If he—'

'If he dumps me, you mean?'

'That's not what I said.'

I pulled away again. 'But you were thinking it, weren't you?'

'I am just concerned. Your friend died in such tragic circumstances. You're having panic attacks in class. And your boyfriend is nowhere in sight. It would be a lot to deal with at any age, but especially when you're so young.'

'I'm eighteen,' I said indignantly.

'When you get to my age, you'll realise just how young eighteen really is.'

I folded my arms across my chest. I hated the way she dismissed my feelings because of my age. I was old enough to know I loved Tom. Old enough to know he loved me.

And old enough to know that I should never have been up on the top of Durdle Door that night.

My arms dropped to my sides, the fight in me slipping away into nothingness.

I may have been old enough to know better. But Mum was right, I was still too young to prevent myself from making bad decisions. Or for being brave enough to deal with the consequences.

'I can't go back,' I whispered.

'But what would you do instead?'

I shook my head. 'I don't know. I don't care. Just not that. Not there.'

29

NOW

'There's a spare key on the hook if you want to go out. And there's food in the fridge if you want to make yourself some lunch. Or there's a corner shop just down the road,' I said as I stood in the kitchen with my coat on. Tom dropped a couple of slices of bread into the toaster, showering crumbs across the worktop.

I reached for the dishcloth to wipe them up. 'I've put my—' I was too slow. Before I could get there, Tom reached out and brushed the crumbs away with the side of his hand.

I watched them fall to the floor like flakes of snow. The cloth in my hand was useless now. I stared at the crumbs, wishing they would melt away. They didn't. I bit back the reprimand that almost escaped. I couldn't tell him off. It wasn't his fault. He didn't know how things worked here. He didn't know the rules. They didn't exist when he knew me before. They weren't necessary then. I'd created them to help me regain control. To cope. To survive.

Tom turned towards me and I realised he was waiting for me to continue my sentence.

'I've put my phone number on a Post-it note on the fridge,' I told him as I put the dishcloth down and picked up the broom instead.

'You can message me if you need anything,' I rambled on as I swept around his feet.

'Relax. I'll be fine. I might have been away for a few years, but I still know my way around the place pretty well.'

'Right.' I chuckled nervously. 'Of course you do.' I glanced around the kitchen again. 'Just make sure you turn the toaster off when you're done—'

'Lizzie!'

I raised my hands in surrender. 'Okay, okay. I'm going.' Reluctantly, I walked to the hallway and slipped my shoes on.

Tom followed me and leaned against the pristine white door frame.

I inhaled sharply. *Don't complain*, I instructed myself. *Don't criticise.*

I let my breath out slowly, attempting to instil a sense of calm.

It didn't work.

My home felt wrong. Invaded. Tarnished. He was messing things up already. How could I leave him here unattended? Unsupervised?

'You're wearing those?'

I followed Tom's gaze to my sensible flat black slip on shoes. 'They're comfortable to walk to work in,' I said quietly as I took a step back, wishing I could hide my feet.

After all the care I'd taken in selecting an outfit, Tom hadn't even noticed my clothes. But something as unimportant as a pair of shoes to walk in, he'd decided to pay attention to. I glanced at the shoe rack, hoping to find an alternative, but the only options were a scuffed pair of ankle boots, or trainers that had once been white. I restrained the groan of frustration that threatened to slip from my lips.

'Hmm,' Tom murmured. 'But you change them when you get to work, right?'

'O-of course,' I stuttered over the lie. I had no other shoes.

The disapproval faded from his features. 'Well, I guess that's not *so* bad, then.'

I breathed a sigh of relief as his gaze met mine. I'd pacified him. For now, at least. But perhaps I'd better go shoe shopping before he spotted the state of my trainers...

'Have a good day at work.'

My heart sank at the reminder that I didn't have a choice. I had to go to work.

'Thanks,' I replied, mustering a watery smile.

'What time did you say you get home?'

Had I said? I shook my head, shaking off that irrelevant thought. I must have done. My thoughts were preoccupied this morning; it was hardly surprising that I couldn't remember what I'd said already. 'About 6 p.m.'

The corner of Tom's mouth twitched slightly, and I felt a tug on my heart as I realised he was trying to smile and mask his disappointment. It was a long time to desert him for. I tipped my head to the side. 'You're sure you'll be okay?'

Tom rolled his eyes. 'I think I'll survive.'

I drew back at the gruffness of his tone. I'd probably embarrassed him, by noticing his vulnerability. I mustn't do that again.

I picked up my key from the hook by the door and slipped it into my pocket. I paused as I cast a final glance around me. It felt strange going out and leaving Tom in my home. I was torn between a sense of guilt at abandoning him and unease at leaving him unattended.

It was my home.

My private space.

I took another breath. I was being overprotective. It was Tom. Of course he was welcome here.

My morning routine had been disrupted, and along with it, my sense of equilibrium. I needed balance. Routine. Consistency. I depended upon it. But all the checks I would usually carry out before I left the house, like unplugging the toaster, checking the hob, the taps, the lights, were all pointless. Tom was still using these things.

Would he remember to turn them off if he went out?

'Aren't you going to be late?'

Tom's question jolted me out of my musings and I reached for the door handle.

'See you tonight, Lizzie.'

I glanced back at him. An unexpected impulse to give him a hug goodbye caught me off guard. I tried to ignore the sudden pounding of my heart. My impulse didn't mean anything. It was just because he was there, seeing me off to work, like a boyfriend would...

I turned away quickly, before Tom realised what I was thinking. He'd always been good at doing that. But suddenly my momentum dissipated and I froze.

My grip tightened on the handle. It was just a door. My door. All I had to do was turn my wrist and pull. It was so simple. So easy. And yet, so hard.

'Lizzie?'

There was a hint of concern in Tom's voice. To him I must look crazy. Maybe I was. It shouldn't be this difficult to leave my own home.

This door had been my nemesis for years. It was my protector, keeping the world out. But it also kept me in.

I glanced at Tom and plastered a smile on my face. 'Have a good day,' I told him as I summoned all my courage to pull the door open.

I stepped outside and closed it behind me quickly, before I could change my mind. But the soft clunk as it shut made my chest tighten.

I wrapped my fingers around the key in my pocket and fought the urge to allow myself to unlock the door and retreat back inside. To do so meant failure.

My feet were welded to the spot. I refused to allow them to turn back. Yet they didn't move forwards either.

But they had to. I couldn't stand here all day. I was being silly. I was just going to the office. Just like every Monday. Today was no different. No harder. No scarier.

Except it was.

Everything felt off today. More than usual.

30

THEN

Sunlight filtered into my bedroom through the small gap in the curtains. I glanced at the clock: 10 a.m.

I sighed and pulled the duvet over my head. If I was quiet, Mum and Dad would think I was still asleep. They would leave me here. Alone.

I closed my eyes. Alone was good. Alone was safe.

If I went downstairs, Mum would quiz me about what I was going to do. Not just with my day, but with my life. Each heartbeat vibrated through my body at the thought of it. I needed to apply to a new uni. Pick a new course. I needed to decide what I wanted my future to be.

But how could I?

I didn't even want to get out of bed, let alone leave the house.

The thought of it made me sink deeper under the duvet.

Everything felt too big and complicated. I couldn't make a decision that affected the rest of my life when I couldn't even manage to get up for breakfast.

Faint tapping on my bedroom door interrupted my thoughts. I lay still and I held my breath as the door opened with a slow shhh sound as it brushed across the carpet.

'Lizzie,' Mum whispered. 'Lizzie.' Her whisper grew louder as the floorboards creaked, indicating her approach. 'You need to get up, honey.'

I fought the urge to shake my head. I didn't need to get up. I wanted to stay here, hidden, for the foreseeable future.

Maybe even forever.

I knew as I thought it that it was bad to think such things. Wrong. Weak. And yet, that still didn't dull its appeal.

'You have an appointment with the therapist in an hour.'

I groaned automatically as something inside me withered. Mum had insisted I book another appointment. Compliance had seemed the easiest option.

At the time.

'I don't want to go.' I was aware that I sounded like an insolent child. But I was powerless to stop the whine in my voice.

'We talked about this.' I felt the mattress dip and I could envisage Mum sitting by my feet, just as she had done whenever I'd been sick as a child and she'd come to check on me and keep me company. There was something reassuring in the familiarity. The closeness.

'Your dad and I are worried about you. It's been weeks since you dropped out of uni and all you do is hide up here in your bed all day. It's not healthy.'

The air beneath the duvet felt hot and thin. Suddenly Mum's presence didn't feel comforting. It felt claustrophobic. They knew I was hiding. They'd been discussing me. Analysing me.

'Come on.' She tugged at the duvet, breaking my cocoon. 'You have to get up now, or you'll be late.'

I shrugged and tried to retrieve the duvet from Mum's grasp, but she held firm. What did it matter if I was late? What did anything really matter any more?

'Now, Lizzie.' I flinched. Mum hadn't used that tone with me in years. It was still effective.

I dragged my legs over the edge of the bed and sat up grudgingly. I hoped that would be sufficient to satisfy her so she would leave.

It wasn't.

'Go and take a shower,' she instructed, without showing any indication of budging from her position.

I didn't have a choice. I had to obey. Arguing with Mum had always been futile. One glance at her set jaw and unwavering expression told me that even though I was older now, my chances of success still hadn't improved.

* * *

My heart pounded and my legs felt weak, as though they would give way at any moment. All I had to do was open the front door, step outside and walk down the driveway to the car. It wasn't a big deal. It wasn't difficult.

Except it was.

'What are you standing there for?' Mum asked, giving me a nudge forward. 'Come on, let's go.'

I side stepped out of the way, allowing her to pass. She cast a sideways glance at me before reaching for the latch and pulling the door open.

I stared out at the world beyond the threshold. Somehow it seemed as though all the oxygen was slipping away through the open door. My breathing became laboured. Quick shallow gasps that didn't satisfy my lungs.

I heard Mum sigh. The patience she was trying to hold onto was starting to slip. I had to get it together. I couldn't fall apart in front of her. Not again.

I fought to regain control. But it wasn't working.

Nothing worked.

The hallway dipped and swayed. Everything started to blur. Tears streamed down my face. I wasn't even sure why I was crying. It was just a door. Just a driveway. I wanted to run away. To hide. But I couldn't.

My feet were welded to the spot. I couldn't move. Dark patches appeared at the edges of my vision. I was going to pass out. I could feel it.

'Don't start that nonsense.' There was an edge of frustration to her tone. 'We haven't got time for it.'

I nodded, obediently, as a loud sob escaped. She was right. It was nonsense. I was being stupid. It was just the driveway. The same driveway I had walked down nearly every day for my whole life.

And yet somehow it was no longer the same. I was no longer the same.

Mum couldn't understand. She'd tried. She was still trying. But the daughter she'd known had simply disappeared. All she was left with was this shell of my former self. Sad. Tearful. Panicked.

She couldn't understand why. She couldn't figure out how to fix it. How to fix me.

With every day that passed I became more reclusive and she became more frantic. My failure somehow became her failure. It was a mother's job to keep her kids safe and well, that's what she said. But she couldn't make me well. Plasters and paracetamol wouldn't work this time. Eighteen years of experience as a mother hadn't prepared her for this.

Mum thrust smelling salts under my nose. I flinched as my eyes smarted. But I inhaled deeply. I took the little brown glass bottle from her and clung to it, wafting it back and forth below my nose as the darkness gradually faded into grey.

'Just don't think about it,' Mum said as she hooked her arm through mine and pulled me forward, escorting me outside, while my body trembled and each breath rasped in my chest.

It had become her favourite phrase. I wasn't even sure what it was I wasn't supposed to think about.

I don't think she knew either.

* * *

I sat in the waiting room, my body rocking back and forth in my chair. I read the posters on the notice board. I hadn't even been here ten minutes, but I'd already memorised them.

I read them again anyway.

Perhaps I should feel triumphant that I was here.

But I didn't.

The mere fact it had been such an effort felt like a failure in itself. I'd gritted my teeth and pushed through. Mum wouldn't let me do anything else.

I eyed the door. Through there was freedom. But I knew I wouldn't make it. I glanced to my right, where Mum sat beside me, flicking through a magazine. She didn't trust me enough to leave me here alone.

She was probably wise.

I felt someone watching me and I turned to my left without breaking my rhythmic rocking. A woman was staring straight at me. My eyes met hers and I turned away quickly, feeling as though I'd done something wrong. I shrank lower in the seat and wrung my hands together. I must look crazy to her.

Then again, perhaps I was crazy.

I was here after all.

Heels clicked along the corridor and I automatically turned towards the sound. Cold dread descended over me as I recognised the therapist I'd seen a few weeks ago. Part of me hoped she'd call someone else's name. I wasn't ready. I didn't want to see her. I didn't want to move.

And yet at the same time I wanted to get it over with so I could go home, back to my duvet where I could hide from everything and everyone.

She paused at the doorway, her gaze locked on to me. 'Do you want to come through, Lizzie?' she asked with an encouraging smile.

I continued to rock back and forth a couple more times as I summoned my strength to stand, before nodding and following her to the consulting room.

What else could I do?

I didn't feel like I was in control of anything any more. Least of all my presence here.

'Last time we spoke you were struggling at university,' the therapist said once we'd sat down. Her gaze seemed to linger on my sweater just a fraction of a second too long. It probably struck her as wrong for the season. A little too thick and warm for the sunny late-April weather. Or perhaps she recognised it from our last session.

I could have worn something else.

I should have done.

And yet, for some reason, I rarely did these days. There was something comforting about the familiarity and consistency. I'd got through our first session. Maybe if I kept everything the same, I could get through this one too.

The same silver dropper earrings. The same cream sweater. Same blue jeans. Same ankle boots with the worn down heels. There was so much I couldn't control, that it made the things I could matter even more. Regardless of how minuscule and seemingly irrelevant they may seem to anyone else.

I'd never been superstitious. I'd rolled my eyes whenever Mum searched for a second magpie or threw spilt salt over her shoulder. And yet now I was worse than she'd ever been. She'd never believed her outfit could dictate the course of her day.

'So how are things now?' the therapist asked, when I ignored her subtle attempt to probe.

'I dropped out.' Three words were all it took to voice my failure.

'But I remember you telling me how much you loved your course.'

'I did. Before.'

'Before what?'

I twisted my hands together in my lap.

'You mentioned you were experiencing panic attacks.'

'T-they got worse.' I stared at the floor between us. It felt wrong to admit it. As though saying it aloud made it true. If I didn't talk about them, I could pretend they didn't happen. Or, at least, that they weren't that bad. That I wasn't that bad.

But I was.

'They happen all the time now. I-I can't even leave the house without falling apart.' I looked up at her, finally meeting her gaze. 'What's wrong with me?'

'What you've described is called agoraphobia.'

I'd heard the term before, of course. But it was something I only knew of from movies. It wasn't something that affected real people. It wasn't something that affected me.

'But it's not just being outside, it's everything.'

'Agoraphobia isn't necessarily a fear of open spaces. It doesn't always restrict people to their houses.'

'It doesn't?'

'It's more about feeling trapped or unable to get help. That can be in the open, or it can be in a crowd, standing in line, in an enclosed space, or when using public transport.'

I swallowed. I felt seen. Exposed.

I wanted to shake my head and tell her no. It couldn't be. I wasn't that bad. I wasn't that crazy.

But I was.

'You mean...' I struggled to form the words. 'That it's a thing? A real thing?' I stared at her, bewildered. 'People experience that? Other people? Not just me?'

She nodded. 'It's a real thing. It's not just you.'

Perhaps it should have made me feel better. Despite how I felt, I wasn't alone. Other people had the same feelings, the same panic. Enough people to have already given it a name.

But it didn't matter.

It didn't make anything better. If anything, it made me feel worse.

It wasn't the kind of illness that could be picked up in a blood test or an x-ray. *That kind of illness would have been real. Physical. Acceptable. Bad. Scary. But acceptable.*

This was different.

This wasn't real.

It was all in my head.

Like the characters in the stories I wrote, it was fictional. Imaginary. I chose to daydream. To create. And now I chose to allow myself to feel sad. To panic.

It didn't exist. Not really.

Hannah had lost her life and I was wasting mine.

It felt wrong.

I felt wrong.

31

NOW

'Are you okay, Beth?'

I glanced up to see Kate staring at me as she wheeled her recycling bin to the edge of her driveway.

I nodded silently on my doorstep, unable to find the words to tell her I was fine when it was so far from the truth.

'So what's the story with that cute guy last night?' she asked, abandoning the bin and walking across my lawn, curiosity clearly outweighing her domestic chores.

'St-story?' I stuttered, as panic seeped into my veins.

No one can know.

The memory cut into me like steel.

'There's no story,' I added, but my voice sounded hollow and unconvincing, even to me.

'Well, now I'm more convinced there is.' Kate laughed. 'You know you're a terrible liar?'

I laughed awkwardly. She had no idea what an accomplished liar I actually was. No one did.

'I thought I could sense a spark between you two last night, and now I'm sure of it.' She smiled smugly. 'So, how long did you date for?'

'Just a couple of months.' It felt strange admitting it out loud. It had been a secret for so long. Few people knew.

It'd had to be that way.

'At school?' Kate asked.

'No.' I shook my head. 'We didn't get together until uni.'

'Ah, so I guess he moved away after uni, then?'

I nodded.

'That's so sad.'

She was right: it was sad. But his departure wasn't the reason we'd split up. He'd already disappeared from my life long before he moved away.

Not that I was about to tell her that.

'Do you think you'll see him again?' There was a hopeful tone to her voice.

A frown flitted across my brow as I pondered whether her excitement was for me, or for the possibility that she might get to see him again too.

'He's still here,' I told her, determined to keep my tone neutral this time.

Kate's eyes widened as her gaze flicked towards my house, as though she expected to find him lingering in a window. 'He's staying with you?'

'Just for a few days,' I added. But was it? What would happen after the weekend? We hadn't agreed a duration. Come to think of it, we hadn't exactly agreed upon him staying in the first place. Had we?

My head felt heavy and sluggish. There was a familiarity to it; that sense of confusion. Uncertainty.

Stress was a trigger. That was what the therapist had said. It overwhelmed the senses. Slowed the thinking.

It made sense. My body and mind were on high alert today. My routine had been disrupted. Of course my brain felt overwhelmed and slow to respond.

Kate edged closer. 'Tell me everything,' she instructed.

'There's nothing to tell.'

Kate scowled at me. 'Nope, not buying it. Your university boyfriend shows up to surprise you *and* spent the night with you. There is definitely something to tell.'

'It wasn't like that. He stayed in the guest room.'

'Really?' I heard the surprise in Kate's voice, but was there a hint of something else too?

'Things between Tom and I are complicated,' I said.

'Well, clearly Tom has fond memories of your time together, otherwise he wouldn't have reached out to you. Maybe he wants a second chance.'

A second chance.

Kate's words repeated on a loop.

I stared at her. Wasn't that exactly what I'd wanted too? I'd thought I had to reinvent myself to find it. But maybe it had never mattered who I was. Perhaps all that mattered was who I was with.

Maybe what I needed all along was a second chance with Tom.

'You never know,' Kate continued. 'This could be your chance to rewrite history.'

Could it?

The idea circled in my brain. It was so appealing. So idyllic. The chance to correct the mistakes I'd made. To restore what had been damaged and lost.

But it wasn't that simple. I couldn't go back.

And yet...

'I wish that was possible,' I said wistfully.

'Anyway, at least tell me he kissed you?'

I shook my head.

'Hugged you?'

'We're just friends.'

'Friends hug.'

I rolled my eyes at her. 'It's comp—'

'Complicated. Yeah, yeah, I know.'

I nodded, satisfied.

'But Beth, when a guy you haven't seen in years suddenly tracks you down and spends the night, there's nothing complicated about his motives.' She winked at me, before pivoting on her heel and waltzing back to the wheelie bin, clearly feeling smug that she knew what was happening here better than I did.

Or, at least, she thought she did.

The problem was, there was a lot more to our story than Kate knew. Than anyone knew for that matter.

It was the way it'd had to be.

For him.

For me.

For Hannah.

32

THEN

'You're going to be late!' Mum yelled up the stairs.

I gripped the sink and glanced at the locked bathroom door. How had I let myself get talked into this? A different uni. A different course. But the outcome was still the same.

'You'll miss the bus.'

I swallowed, forcing the nausea back down. I had to leave.

'Lizzie!'

'Don't call me that,' I snapped as I flung myself into action. 'I'm Beth now.' I had to be Beth. Different. New.

I ran down the stairs. Every step was an effort. I wanted to retreat. To hide. To lock the door and never set foot outside again.

But I couldn't.

I pulled my ankle boots on and grabbed my bag. 'Bye,' I called as I rushed out the front door. I heard it slam behind me. The sound filled me with terror. My fingers instinctively felt for the key in my pocket. I clung to it like a lifeline. I refused to allow myself to look back. I knew the temptation would be too strong if I did. I would grasp the key, ram it into the lock, fling open the door, and return to the safety inside.

I focused on putting one foot in front of the other. I couldn't be late. I couldn't miss the bus. My fast walking became a jog, and soon I was running. It struck me as ironic, that I was running for a bus I didn't want to catch, to go to a place I didn't want to be.

But what was the alternative?

If I went home, Mum would know I had failed. She'd have that look on her face, the one that showed her disappointment. She wouldn't let me stay home, she'd make me catch the next bus. The process would repeat. I wouldn't be free.

And if not home, then where?

I had nowhere else.

Reaching the bus stop, I checked my watch. I'd run so fast that I was early now.

I took a shaky breath.

The whole day loomed out ahead of me. The bus ride. Classes.

On the surface, each was so simple, and yet I knew better. Nothing was simple any more. My mind and body had turned against me. I was in a constant battle with myself.

And somehow I always seemed to be losing.

I shook my head. One thing at a time.

All I had to do was keep going.

Nothing else really mattered any more. Life wasn't about doing what I wanted, there was no bigger picture, no grand plan. At least not to me.

It was just about going through the motions. Staying on the bus, in the lecture theatre. Staying in university.

This time.

I focused on the characters in my head. Telling myself stories was the only way I knew to keep my feet in place. I might have given up on my dreams of being published, but I'd never stop writing. I couldn't. I needed it now more than I ever had before. It was a distraction. An escape when I couldn't leave.

It was the only thing keeping me going.

I swayed back and forth, staring down the road on constant alert, *waiting for the bus that I loathed. I pictured Tom's face. I could see him standing outside the uni, waiting for me. All I had to do was get on the bus and it would take me to him.*

He'd grasp my hands in his and apologise for having left me. It had crushed him to do it, but he'd had to. There were people who'd wanted to destroy us. Bad people. But it was all in the past now. We were safe. The threat that had loomed over us, had gone.

'Run away with me,' he'd whisper.

I'd nod without hesitation. I'd go anywhere with him.

We'd be together again.

Everything would be all right then.

I'd be all right.

The bus pulled up in front of me, I sighed at the intrusion. I wanted to stay in my fantasy. Where I was unafraid. Where I was normal. Where I was loved.

Reluctantly I clambered on board and sank into a vacant seat. My breathing quickened and I twisted my hands together in my lap. No, I couldn't let the panic take hold.

Think about Tom, *I told myself.* He's waiting for me.

My thoughts wandered as I stared at houses out of the window. Tom and I would have our own house one day. I assessed them, pondering which style was more us. It needed to be perfect. Spacious enough for the family we would have, but not overstated.

I just needed to stay on the bus and get to uni. He'd be there waiting. And then, our lives could begin.

Eventually the uni came into view. I hurried out of my seat and staggered down the aisle, clinging to the handrails as the bus swung me back and forth. I craned my neck, my gaze scanning the pavement around the bus stop.

Disappointment washed over me like a cold salty wave as the bus came to a halt. He wasn't there.

I stepped off the bus and paused. Some part of me was still hoping

Tom was on his way, that he was simply running late. Just like normal. He'd still come.

But even as I waited I knew he wouldn't. It was just a daydream. A fantasy. And yet, it had still felt so real.

I took a deep breath. I couldn't postpone the inevitable any longer. I had to get to my first lecture. Today wasn't the day that I was going to escape this life. Today wasn't the day for Tom and me to be reunited.

But maybe tomorrow.

33

NOW

I glanced at my watch and cursed. Between Tom's disruption to my routine and Kate's curiosity, I was late. I ran down the driveway.

Late.

The word ricocheted against me. I was never late. Not for anything. I couldn't be. It wasn't permitted.

Lateness was another form of failure.

And I couldn't fail.

Not again.

I couldn't miss the bus. I couldn't be late for work. I had to go. I had to.

The alternative was...

Memories crashed around me, snatching the breath from my lungs. Even skipping one day was a disaster. Running away made the fear stronger. It made my world shrink a little more. If I chickened out today, next week would be worse. It never got easier, but I knew I couldn't let it get worse.

Worse led to giving up.

Staying home.

Never going out.

Never leaving.

I quickened my pace. I wasn't going back to that.

The only thing I had in my favour was my determination. It would have been easier to quit. To allow myself to curl up and wither away into nothingness. But there was something in me, something stubborn, that persisted. It wouldn't let me give up.

It wasn't the belief that I could get better. I wasn't naive. Better was out of my reach. I'd accepted that now. Deep down I knew that I didn't even deserve to get better. I'd avoided punishment for my mistake, at least officially. But my own incarceration was equally effective. There was no time off for good behaviour here. I was my own life sentence.

The bus was already at the bus stop as I approached. I surged forward with a final spurt of energy and jumped on board. I swiped my card and dropped into the nearest available seat, panting for breath.

My body cursed me for the unaccustomed exercise. It made it worse. It made it harder. My determination started to dwindle. How could I stay focused when my senses were in overdrive now? My heart raced. It was too fast. I pressed my hand to my chest. This fast couldn't be good, could it?

I shook my head. No. I wasn't going there. I couldn't let myself go there. I was fine. I was safe.

Wasn't I?

I clasped my hands together in my lap, my mind automatically checking my body, my senses, my surroundings, searching for a sign of something out of place, out of kilter.

I fumbled in my bag for the bottle of water I always carried.

I couldn't find it.

I searched again. And again.

It wasn't there.

I groaned inwardly as I remembered seeing it on the kitchen worktop, waiting to be refilled.

I'd never gone out without it before.

But then, I'd never woken up with Tom in my house before.

I focused on my breathing. It didn't matter. I could manage without the water. I had to.

It was only a short journey. I could do this. After all, I did it every week. I sucked in a deep breath and let it out slowly.

Somehow it never seemed to get any easier.

'Face your fears.' That's what everyone said. But they were wrong. Facing your fears didn't eliminate them. At least not for me. My fears remained to be faced again the next day, and the day after that. It was continual. Endless.

But at least I was doing it.

The fear was my constant companion. It was always a battle between me and it. But I still fought. I hadn't given up. I couldn't. Not again.

The therapist I used to see would tell me I was strong. But I knew it wasn't strength that kept me going. It was a greater fear.

I knew what giving in meant. I knew what that life was like. Trapped in the house. Trapped in my own head. I'd been there before. I wasn't going back.

But success was always short lived. The process repeated again the next time. Knowing I'd won once was no guarantee for a repeat performance.

I tried to replicate it. If I did exactly the same things, in exactly the same order, maybe, just maybe the result would be the same too. I knew it was a long shot. But it was all I had. My dwindling hope of relative normality was hinged upon creating certainty.

Think about something else, I instructed myself. Distraction was the key to staying in places I didn't want to be. I used to fixate on

Tom; on the idea that he would return; that he would be waiting for me when I reached my destination.

He never was.

I told myself that it didn't matter. That there was always tomorrow. He'd be there then. I just had to be patient. To keep believing.

Eventually the disappointment had become too much. I'd stopped watching for him. Stopped giving a double glance at every guy that had the same build and the same hair colouring.

I made up new stories with new characters. They were my distraction. My salvation. My addiction, perhaps.

It was an ongoing game with imaginary friends. Their adventures. Their stories. Their lives. It was like watching a TV series, but without needing the TV. They were with me all the time. Lurking in the background, ready to spring forward when I needed them most. Sometimes they were fuzzy, like a bad signal was interrupting their strength, as reality occupied too much of my thoughts. But if I concentrated hard enough, reality could slip away. Not completely. Never completely. But I could immerse myself in the story. Focus on creating the perfect plot. The perfect line. The perfect escape.

I would reach my destination, or survive the duration of a meeting, without bolting for the door.

They made me calmer. They made me stronger.

Solving the plot was like a puzzle that required full attention. It was harder to panic if my brain was occupied elsewhere.

The anxiety didn't go away. My senses were still on alert. But the alarm was more distant and muffled. The threat was more manageable. More controllable. More survivable.

Sometimes I would scribble their stories into my notebook or tap them frantically into an app on my phone. But some days it was better to just stare into space, to watch them; direct them; focus on them.

They lived the life I couldn't. Because the truth was, no matter what name I called them, or how I imagined them to look, at their essence they were always based on Tom and me.

I knew they weren't real. They were just characters from a story. The book I was writing in small pieces each day. They were my sanity. And possibly my craziness.

But they'd achieved more than the therapist ever had.

The rituals I followed were what got me out of the house. They enabled me to get on the bus. But the stories were what kept me in my seat.

It wasn't a perfect solution. Perhaps it wasn't really a solution at all. Just a plaster on a deep wound that really needed surgery. It pulled the edges closer together, but couldn't heal the rift.

Maybe I'd stopped seeing the therapist too soon. I'd written her off as being unable to help me. But maybe I hadn't given her enough of a chance. I hadn't really even told her the full story for her to know how to help me.

I couldn't.

I couldn't tell anyone.

My fictional world was all I had.

But then, perhaps it didn't have to be that way. Not any longer.

The impossible had happened. Tom was back. In my life. In my home.

Kate was wrong. I couldn't rewrite history. But maybe I could change my future. I could be the kind of girl Tom had always wanted. The kind of girl Hannah had been. I was a better actress than I had been ten years ago. If being Hannah was what it took to win Tom back, then so be it. It wouldn't be real. But maybe that didn't matter. Not as long as Tom was mine.

I would start with new shoes. New clothes. A new me. My excitement grew as I felt the future I'd longed for stretching out ahead of me. This time it was within reach. All I had to do was not be me.

Hannah wouldn't be afraid to go shopping. She wouldn't need to avoid crowds. To avoid people. So I wouldn't be afraid either.

I knew even as I thought it, that it wasn't realistic. The fear wouldn't dissipate just because I wanted it to. It never had before.

But I'd go anyway.

I'd *live* anyway.

34

THEN

'I like your shirt,' the therapist said as we sat across from each other in our usual seats.

'Thanks,' I replied with a gracious smile. It had been Mum's choice. Blue; her favourite colour. But it had long sleeves. I liked long sleeves.

'Are you comfortable wearing it?'

I nodded like I was supposed to. I was getting good at doing what I was supposed to now. What was expected. What was acceptable.

That was why I'd let Mum persuade me to wear something new. I surrendered a little bit of the control I found in keeping things the same, to appease everyone else.

'It's a good sign,' she said. I watched her as she spoke. Was she happy for me, or was it a touch of pride that after months of seeing me twice a week, I was finally 'better'?

At least on the outside.

'You seem calmer and happier,' she observed.

I fought the urge to fidget and kept my careful pose, straight backed in the chair. I wouldn't allow myself to rock. Normal people didn't rock back and forth.

I was normal now.

I had to be. Maybe then Tom would come back.

He liked things to be uncomplicated and simple. He liked women who were calm and capable.

He liked normal.

'How's the new uni?'

I shrugged. 'It's uni.'

'That doesn't really answer the question.'

'I get the bus each day. I go to every class. I stay in my seat for the whole lecture. I do my coursework on time. I pass my tests.'

'But how does it feel to do all that?'

Hell.

It was as simple as that. Every moment of every day was hell.

But I endured it.

I survived.

It was all a means to an end. Every day I made it through brought me one day closer to being back with Tom.

I couldn't give up. I couldn't lose sight of the goal. The purpose.

I was just biding my time. Making it through the emptiness, the darkness, until Tom was back.

Everything would be all right then. I would be all right.

I forced my lips into a smile. 'Good.'

There was a tiny crease in her forehead as she studied me. Despite my performance, doubt still lingered. Maybe my act wasn't convincing enough. Or maybe my recovery had been too sudden. Too unbelievable.

'I mean, it's still hard,' *I added.* 'But it feels good that I'm doing it. That I'm winning.'

She nodded. 'I'm so happy for you.'

I smiled again.

She'd fallen for the lie.

Everyone did.

It turned out I could hide a lot with a smile. It didn't even matter if it was real or fake. But then it had been so long since it had been real, perhaps everyone had forgotten what that looked like.

I had.

'I think we could stop our sessions now, if you feel ready for that?'

Panic fluttered in my chest. It was the result I'd wanted. And yet, now she was offering me the escape I'd worked for, I wasn't sure I wanted to take it.

I wasn't ready.

What if I couldn't keep up the act?

What if without her I relapsed?

She thought the biggest issue was to get me to leave the house. To make it through the day without being paralysed by panic attacks that made me retreat further into myself.

She was wrong.

There were bigger risks than my reclusiveness. The torture I subjected myself to was nothing compared to what I could do to other people.

There was a side to me that I didn't recognise. Things I would never have believed I was capable of. And yet, Hannah's death was proof that I was.

What if someone crossed me again? What if I envied them for the life they had that was so much better than the way my own had turned out?

Would I take it from them too?

Was anyone safe?

'You can always go back to the GP for another referral if you need to come back again.'

There was a safety net. A way back.

I nodded, feeling slightly pacified.

'You're going to be great, Lizzie.'

I flinched slightly.

'Sorry, I mean Beth. I know you prefer that name now.'

'I'm leaving the past behind me and making a new start,' I said adamantly. 'It deserves a new name.'

'It does,' she agreed. 'You've made a remarkable recovery, Beth.'

I grinned. She would expect me to look proud.

She was right. It was a remarkable recovery. It was just a shame that none of it was real.

She stood up and I copied her.

Perhaps I should tell her. Admit the truth. Tell her I still needed her.

But I didn't.

Coming here twice a week was just another place to dread going. Another journey to psych myself up for. Another bus ride to grit my teeth through.

Leaving was for the best. It was one less battle to face. One less person to lie to.

Despite what she thought, she hadn't helped me.

It wasn't her fault.

How could she help when I couldn't answer her questions truthfully? I couldn't tell her the real reason I was here. I couldn't tell her who I really was. What I'd done.

She was treating the character that I had become. A cut down, edited version of myself.

Who would have known that all those years I'd spent writing, making up stories and characters would become my life? Not in the way I'd thought. Not as a career. A passion. But an existence.

Beth was a new start. She was more confident. Stronger. Determined. Beth could do what Lizzie couldn't.

She could survive.

35

NOW

'Beth?'

I tapped my pen against my lip as my brain ran in circles, chasing the answer that still eluded me. Despite Kate's optimism at Tom's return, I couldn't overlook one question: why now?

'Beth?'

'Huh?' My head jolted up as I realised someone was calling my name.

Jen was standing beside my desk, staring at me expectantly.

'Are you coming?' Jen asked.

'Coming?' I frowned. 'What time is it?' I glanced at my watch. 'Oh no!' My stomach lurched. 'The monthly team meeting.' I grabbed my notebook and phone as I leapt to my feet, sending my chair scooting backwards behind me.

'You must really be in the zone today,' Jen said, leaning forward to peek at my screen.

I forced out a feeble laugh. 'Yeah, I guess so.' I switched off my computer screen before Jen saw how little work I'd actually accomplished this morning.

'You're usually the first one in the conference room,' Jen said, straightening up, a slight crease etched into her brow.

'I like to be early.'

Jen chuckled. 'So I've noticed.'

I froze. She'd noticed. Had everyone? What else had they noticed?

Did they realise that it wasn't really about preferring to be early, but a fear of being late? Was my seat selection in the conference room predictable? Did they notice I always sat by the door? Did they see me watching it? Checking it was still there? Still accessible?

Did they know why?

Panic swelled inside my chest, as my hands started to tremble.

I wasn't early today. My seat would be gone. I'd have to sit somewhere else.

What if I had to sit at the back? I'd be away from the door. Blocked in. Trapped.

'I just, er, I need...' My words tumbled out as my brain frantically scrambled for an appropriate escape.

'Ah, bathroom stop.' Jen nodded. 'Don't blame you; these meetings go on forever.'

'Right.' I nodded a little too enthusiastically, seizing upon the excuse she had given me.

'I'll see you there. I'll save you a seat if I can.'

Jen turned and started walking down the open-plan office towards the conference room. I paused a moment longer before heading in the opposite direction. I held my head high and walked purposefully towards the back staircase. I kept my gaze locked on the doors ahead, praying no one stopped me.

Look like you belong, I instructed myself silently. It was one of the tricks I had learnt over the years. If I looked like I knew exactly what I was doing and where I was going, people were less likely to question me. Even if, like right now, I was going in completely the wrong direction.

My hand trembled as I reached for the door. I pushed it open and triggered the sensor, plunging the stairwell into light. I headed down the first few steps until I heard the door close behind me.

I stopped and glanced back over my shoulder. I'd made it out.

Now I just had to hope no one came this way. It was unlikely. No one else had reason to.

Only me.

And even I shouldn't be here.

The whole department was scheduled to attend the meeting in the conference room at the other end of the building. Forty members of staff crammed in to one room. There weren't even that many seats in there.

I glanced at my watch.

10.58 a.m.

Now that I was alone, the flaw in my plan began to sink in. I'd effectively trapped myself in the stairwell. Some of the staff in my department were based on the ground floor. If I walked through their office now, chances were, someone would spot me. I would get swept along in the mass exodus to the conference room.

I took a shaky breath. It was safer to stay where I was.

Safer.

I snorted.

I was acting as though I was facing something perilous, when to everyone else it was just mundane, and at worst, inconvenient. I was being ridiculous, hiding in a stairwell just to avoid a meeting. But then it wasn't really the meeting I was avoiding. It was the people. An entire department of them, corralled together in one small space.

Admittedly, it wasn't that small. But it felt it to me. Anywhere felt small when I was surrounded by people; when they congregated in walkways, obstructing the exit; when they cut me off from escaping without causing a disturbance to get past them.

I hated that; feeling as though I was in the way; an inconvenience; an embarrassment. They'd ask what was wrong, where I was going. Everyone would look, stare.

Just like before.

36

THEN

I lingered at the back of the unfamiliar lecture theatre, jostled by bags as the other students pushed past me. I was in the way. I should take a seat. Any seat.

'Hey, Beth.'

Beth. That was me now. My gaze shifted as I searched for the voice that was calling me.

'Over here.' A girl I'd met during orientation week was waving at me. 'Come sit with us.'

I forced my lips to curve upwards. I was fitting in. Making new friends. This was good. Except... My gaze trailed across the long narrow row of seats between us. Why did they have to be sitting so far along the row?

'Come on,' she urged.

My shoulders hunched as I shuffled along the row to join them. I could already hear someone behind me, following me, blocking me in. I was committed now. I couldn't turn back. I couldn't leave.

I could sense them gaining on me until they were impatiently walking at my heels, silently urging me to hurry.

I reached my destination and slowly lowered myself into the vacant seat. I perched my messenger bag on my lap, as my hand continued to grip the strap still draped over my shoulder.

'Beth, these are my friends: Julia and Zoe.'

I nodded at them, my brain too preoccupied to find words.

My heart pounded, my chest tightened, my palms sweated, my head spun, and my stomach churned as bile rose in my throat. Only one thought filled my head: Escape.

It wasn't rational. It wasn't necessary. It wasn't as though I was actually in any danger. And yet the overwhelming fear remained.

I fought against it. It wasn't supposed to happen again. Not here. Not now.

I was better now.

I was normal.

Tom wouldn't come back if I wasn't.

I had to keep focused on that. He was my purpose. My strength. I could do anything for him.

I would do anything.

And yet, in reality, my optimistic determination wasn't enough.

It was just another lie.

Around me, other students scrambled in their bags for pens and notebooks, but I couldn't move. I couldn't do anything. All my energy was focused on the momentous task of simply staying in my seat.

I was vaguely aware of a hush descending on the room, signalling the lecturer's arrival. A PowerPoint slideshow appeared on the screen at the front as he launched into a well-practised session.

I needed to focus, to take notes, to understand. I couldn't drop out a second time. I gritted my teeth as I released the bag strap and rummaged for my notebook. I could do this. I had to do this. I couldn't run away. Not again.

Hannah wouldn't run away.

I gripped my pen and started to copy notes from the screen, but their *meaning was lost to me. I glared at the wobbly childlike writing as my pen trembled against the page.*

I tried not to panic, but it was too late. The lecturer's voice faded away as a familiar roaring sounded in my ears. I tried to focus on my breathing; long slow deep breaths. It was the only hope I had of keeping the darkness at bay. I felt pressure building in my head as the roaring intensified.

It wasn't working.

I knew what would happen next.

I shook my head as I felt my lips part to mutter an inaudible no. I couldn't faint. Not here.

I grabbed my belongings and clutched them to me as I leapt up and pushed past my neighbour without even waiting for him to move out of the way. I surged on, ignoring the grunts and curses that punctuated through the roar. I clambered over feet and bags, desperate to reach freedom, as blackness claimed the edges of my vision.

I had to get out.

I had to escape.

I reached the end of the row as the floor beneath me dipped and swayed. I staggered drunkenly back up the stairs towards the door.

'Was it something I said?' the lecturer asked. His tone showed he wasn't amused, but a ripple of laughter surrounded me. I kept my head down, my gaze fixed on the floor.

Keep going.

The instruction reverberated through me, spurring me on as my vision grew hazy. I fumbled for the handle and tugged the door open.

I stumbled into the deserted corridor and drew a shaky breath as I collapsed against the wall opposite. The door banged shut, making me flinch. But I didn't care. I was out.

I closed my eyes and sank to the floor, still clutching my notebook and bag. I sat there frozen, not daring to move, until the dizziness slowly began to ebb away.

Cautiously, I opened my eyes. I stared at the solid blue door to the lecture theatre. I knew I should go back inside. But I also knew I wouldn't. Not today.

I should have waited outside until the last minute and then sneaked in to a vacant seat by the aisle. It might have helped.

A little.

Next time I would try that.

I knew there would be a next time, even as my body trembled at the thought of it. I wouldn't give up. I couldn't. Too much was at stake.

37

NOW

A throbbing sensation caused me to glance down at my left hand. My knuckles had turned white as I gripped the stair rail tightly. I took a deep breath and uncurled my fingers slowly.

The lights clicked as they switched off. I was tempted to remain still; hidden in the darkness. But I knew it was too risky.

The darkness was never safe.

Besides, anyone using these stairs would trigger the lights, and they would see me. They would question why I was in a dark empty stairwell. It would be too obvious that I'd been hiding.

I shifted position, triggering the lights again. I felt exposed in the brightness. Vulnerable.

I stayed alert, ready to spring into action and start walking the second I heard a door opening. It needed to appear as though I was on my way somewhere. I needed to look like I had a purpose; to look like I belonged.

I was good at that; at looking the part; appearing to fit in.

Appearances could be deceptive.

I shook my head, trying to shake off the heaviness that always descended upon me when I thought about the past. When my colleagues talked about their university days, they made them sound like an adventure filled with excitement, new friends and new experiences. For me it had been something I endured. I survived because I couldn't afford not to.

The alternative was so much worse.

I checked my watch again.

11.01 a.m.

It was too soon to go back yet. There would always be someone who was running late for the meeting, driven by the need to send one last critical email or a phone call they had to make.

I might as well make use of the time and respond to some emails. At least it would occupy my mind and alleviate some of my guilt for skipping the meeting. After all, I was still working...

I turned my phone on, flicked to my work emails and tried to focus, but it was no use, my attention was still fixed on Tom.

He'd been back in my life less than twenty-four hours and I was already screwing things up again. I was back to running away and hiding, just like before. If he hadn't turned up on my doorstep last night I would have stuck to my routines today. I'd have gone to the meeting. I'd have been present. At least in body. My mind would admittedly have been focused on counting the minutes until I could leave. But I'd have been there. That counted for something. It had to.

Why had Tom had to come back now? I'd spent years wanting him to return. Needing him to. But he'd waited too long. Our time had passed. I'd moved on. Everything was fine as it was. The last thing I needed was the past messing things up.

I squirmed as the lie grated against me. Things weren't fine. Not even close. They hadn't been for years. One moment; one mistake had destroyed everything, me included.

Tom was a reminder of that. Of what I'd done. Of who I'd become.

I should tell him to leave and then the past could return to where it had been; buried at the back of my mind. But whilst I might not think about it, at least, not as obsessively as I once had, it didn't mean I'd left it behind.

I carried it with me every day. It influenced the life I led. Or more accurately, the one I didn't.

I glanced at my phone. I could message him now. Tell him to leave before I got home. I wouldn't even have to face him again.

I lowered the phone to my side.

Maybe if Kate hadn't planted the idea of how good it could be to reconnect. If she hadn't started me thinking about the good times Tom and I had shared. If I hadn't remembered the person I used to be before my mistake changed things. Maybe then I could have told him to go.

Maybe.

If I hadn't messed things up, Tom and I would have been together. We'd have been happy.

And Hannah would still be alive.

I couldn't change what had happened to Hannah. But I could change what happened with Tom and me now.

Maybe ten years was penance enough.

38

'What happened to you?' Jen asked as she approached her desk.

'I got waylaid.' I rolled my eyes, as though my absence had been an inconvenience rather than the intentional escape it had been. 'Didn't like to disrupt everything by sneaking in late.'

Jen shrugged, as though it wouldn't have been a big deal. 'Well, you didn't really miss much.' She lowered her voice. 'To be honest it was a total waste of time. You'll have had a far more productive morning here.'

I tried not to fidget. I wasn't sure dwelling on the past counted as productive.

'I'll fill you in over lunch, if you like?' Jen continued as she sat down.

'That would be great, thanks,' I replied, trying to keep the panic from my voice at the thought of facing the crowded staff restaurant with Jen instead of eating my homemade sandwich at my desk, like I always did.

Jen tipped her head to the right. 'Are you okay, Beth?'

'I'm fine.' The lie slipped easily from my lips. I'd had years of practice. No one questioned it. No one cared enough to see beneath the surface, to—

'Are you sure?'

I blinked. 'I...' I couldn't think of a response. The question was so unexpected, so personal, so concerned.

'W-why do you ask?'

Jen hesitated for a moment. 'To be honest, I'm not sure. You just seem different today.'

I felt as though I was sinking. The shield of invisibility that had protected me for so many years was slipping. People didn't notice that I wasn't okay. They didn't realise that I got through the day by gritting my teeth and white-knuckling it. It was how this worked. How *I* worked.

Present but never really part of things. Liked but not loved. Seen but not known.

Until now.

'You know I'm here if there's ever anything you want to talk about.'

I stared at her. 'I'm fine.'

The corner of her mouth twitched upwards. 'You said that already.'

'Right.' I rolled my eyes. 'Of course I did. But I mean it. I *am* fine.' Even as I said it, I wondered which one of us I was trying to convince.

'Okay. Well, the offer's there if you change your mind. There's no expiry date.' She turned to her computer and started typing.

'Jen?'

She turned back to face me.

I nibbled my lip. 'Thanks.'

Jen smiled and for a brief moment I was reminded of Rebecca. That concern. That interest. That friendship.

I'd had friends since, of course, like Kate. But it wasn't the same.

The friendships were superficial. They, like everyone else, didn't really know me. They only knew the act. The person I'd become to survive.

It was safer that way.

For me.

And maybe even for them.

39

'Lunch?' Jen asked at 1 p.m.

'Erm, actually, I kind of need to make a phone call.'

'Sure, no worries. I can wait.'

'No, you should go on without me.'

'Are you trying to get out of having lunch with me?'

'No! Of course not.' The truth of Jen's accusation jarred against me, filling me with guilt.

'I promise to give you the abridged version.'

I blinked.

'Of this morning's meeting. That's what you're trying to avoid, right?'

'Right, I mean, no. Not at all.' I felt flustered.

'Relax, I'm only teasing you. Go and make your call.'

I nodded obediently as I picked up my phone and walked to the stairwell, feeling confused. Were we still meeting for lunch?

I rubbed my forehead. My ability to keep it together really was slipping today. I took a shaky breath. It was further proof that I needed to make this call.

I opened the contacts list and scrolled to the Rs.

My finger hovered over Rebecca's name.

Since my conversation with Jen earlier, I hadn't been able to stop thinking about Rebecca. She was the one person who would understand what Tom's return meant to me.

And understand the threat it posed.

I tapped her name and clicked the call button. I paced back and forth at the top of the stairs as the phone rang.

'Hi,' I heard the questioning tone to her greeting. We hadn't spoken in a while. No doubt she was wondering why I would be reaching out now.

'Hi Rebecca, how are you?'

'I'm good.' There was a guardedness to her words. 'What about you?'

'I, er...' I ran my fingers through my hair and tucked it behind my ear playing for time.

'Lizzie?' That name jarred against me. It was like stepping back in time; first Tom now Rebecca.

'I just needed to talk to you.'

'About?'

'Tom.'

Silence fell between us. 'Why would we ever need to talk about him?' she asked finally.

'Because he's back.'

'In Bournemouth?'

'In my house.'

'You let him into your home?'

Her bewilderment echoed my own. Why had I let him in? Why had I let him stay?

'Please tell me you don't still have feelings for him?'

I swallowed. Both of us had our answer now.

'But I didn't think you'd kept in touch with him. At least that's what you told me before.' There was an edge to her voice.

'I didn't. I hadn't heard from him since...' I paused and took a shaky breath. 'Since that trip to Durdle Door.'

'I still can't get over him never calling you after that.'

'He couldn't. It wouldn't have been right.' My response was automatic. Instinctive. Yet, even as I said the words, doubt started to creep in.

He couldn't call, could he?

'Oh, Lizzie.'

My legs felt weak and unable to hold me, and I sank down to perch on the top step as something inside me withered at her pitying tone.

'He always knew how to play you.'

'He's not playing me. He just—' I clamped my mouth closed.

'He what?'

'He missed me.'

'Then why did it take him ten years to come back for you?'

'He was busy.'

Rebecca snorted. 'Busy? Lizzie, do you hear yourself? Busy is maybe an excuse for forgetting to return a phone call for a couple of days, but not for disappearing for ten years with no contact.'

'He was keeping the secret. Protecting me.'

'We all kept the secret, Lizzie. But I still talk to you.'

'Occasionally.' I bit my lip. The word had slipped out with an accusatory tone I hadn't intended it to carry. At least, not aloud.

I heard Rebecca's sharp intake of breath.

Silence hung between us. I should apologise and tell her I hadn't meant. I should tell her I was wrong.

Except, I wasn't.

'Fair point,' she conceded. 'But our lives went in different directions. It's hard to find the time to keep up with everyone.'

'I get it.' I truly did. It was me who'd dropped out of uni. Her life had just carried on without me. It was probably easier for her that way. I was a reminder of that night.

But I didn't need a physical reminder. Talking to Rebecca wasn't a trigger for my guilty conscience. It was my companion every single day. Being able to talk to Rebecca just made me a little less alone with it.

As Mum always said, misery loves company.

But it wasn't fair. Not to Rebecca. She shouldn't have to share my burden. She'd already done enough.

'I shouldn't have called,' I said quietly.

'Why did you?'

'I...' I frowned. 'I'm not sure.' I'd known her opinion of Tom. I must have known she wouldn't be enthusiastic about his return. Or, at least, I should have done. And yet, I'd still called. Still wanted to tell her. Confide in her. 'Perhaps because you're the only person I could really talk to about this.' My shoulders sagged. 'But you're right, I shouldn't have done.'

* * *

'Pull it together, Lizzie,' Rebecca whispered beside me as I eyed the door.

I gripped my hands together as they rested on the desk in front of me and tried to steady my breathing. 'I'm trying.'

'Try. Harder.'

I jerked my head round and stared at her, stunned by the harshness of her tone.

Her eyes met mine. 'You're drawing attention to yourself. We can't afford that. You can't afford that.'

I lowered my gaze. 'I know. I'm sorry.'

'Maybe you should take a few days off.'

'What?' I asked too loudly.

'Shhh,' Rebecca whispered as the lecturer looked in our direction.

'Being here isn't doing you any good. You've barely attended any classes. Even when you do come, you leave early, or sit there lost in your own world. You're so far behind, Lizzie. How are you going to catch up?'

'I can. I will.' My heart pounded in my chest. I had to catch up. This was what I wanted. I needed to be here.

Rebecca leaned closer to me. 'Take some time. Get away from here for a while. You're never going to be able to put all this behind you while you're still stuck here.'

'But this was my dream.'

Rebecca's eyes met mine. 'This isn't a dream any more. It's a nightmare. The only way to end it is to get out.'

* * *

'I never said that,' Rebecca objected.

'Not exactly, but you don't want to know, not about Tom. Not really about me, either.' I reached up, grabbed the stair rail and pulled myself to my feet. 'I'm sorry, I should let you get on with your day.' I started to lower the phone to hang up.

'No, Lizzie, wait!' The desperation in Rebecca's voice made me stop and I lifted the phone to my ear again. 'I'm the one who should be sorry. Tom wasn't the only one who screwed up ten years ago. I did too.'

I shook my head. 'I don't understand.'

'I was worried that Tom wasn't good enough for you, but I tried not to interfere and you got hurt. I won't do that again. I can't. Let's meet.'

'Really?' My eyes narrowed. 'You just want to tell me why he's no good for me in person.'

'No, well, I'll try not to. We can talk it through together.'

'You'll keep an open mind about Tom?'

'I promise, as long as you do the same.'

I sighed. Why couldn't she accept that Tom coming back into my life was a good thing? That I was happy?

Doubt niggled at me. I was happy, wasn't I?

'Just be cautious, that's all I'm saying. Don't let yourself get swept up in his promises again.'

Again.

I heard the emphasis she placed on that word. She sounded like Mum. Cynical and overprotective. Neither of them understood. Neither of them realised how important Tom was. How everything hinged upon him.

Or then again, maybe they did. Maybe that was the reason they were so concerned. Maybe my life shouldn't be dependent upon anyone else's. Not even Tom's.

Maybe I should only be reliant upon myself.

'Okay, fine,' I agreed before she could lodge any further doubts in my head.

'Great, how about lunch on Saturday?'

'I can't. Tom has plans for us to spend the weekend together.'

'Oh, well, I could meet you for coffee on Friday afternoon, but I guess you'll be working?'

'I could get the time off.' I had a full year's quota of annual leave to use. It wasn't as though I went anywhere to make use of any of it.

Usually.

'Great. So where should we meet?'

My breathing quickened as though I was running, instead of simply standing still. 'I, er...'

Usually, I would have invited her to my house. It was easier that way. The problem was Tom was there now, and I knew they wouldn't want to see each other. But if she couldn't come to the house, that meant we had to go out.

I had to go out.

'I could meet you by the pier.' The beach was the only other place I ever felt safe. Open and spacious. Even on a busy day, there was still enough space to be alone. But most importantly, it was easy to leave. 'There are little kiosks where we can buy coffee or ice cream.'

'I remember,' Rebecca said fondly. 'We had some good times on that beach.'

My stomach tightened. Maybe the beach wasn't a good place to meet. Rebecca was right, it was full of memories. And even the good memories always led back to one thing. The night I lost everything.

40

'I saw you coming,' Tom said, greeting me at the door as chatter from the TV spilled from the living room.

'Oh, er, thanks.' I smiled at him, while inside my emotions whirled around like a spinning top.

Had he been waiting for me? Watching for my arrival? My pulse quickened. Had he missed me that much?

He always knew how to play you.

Rebecca's accusation sprang into my head, causing my smile to waver.

Was she right? Was that what Tom was doing? Had he before?

'Did you have a good day?' he asked.

I could hear the genuine interest in his voice. He cared. About me.

Rebecca was wrong. Tom had never played me. He never would. He wasn't perfect. He made mistakes. But so did everyone.

So did I.

'It's better now,' I told him, as my smile lifted back into place.

I knew I should be cautious. Tom and I were a dangerous

combination. I also knew that I shouldn't get my hopes up. He was just visiting. At some point he would leave.

And yet, there was something heart-warming about coming home to someone waiting for me.

Not just someone.

Tom.

Kate was right. This was what I wanted. He was what I wanted.

There had never been anyone who had quite measured up to Tom. Even though we'd never been a proper couple, he was the standard by which I compared other guys to.

Not that there had been many. Dating was too much like hard work. It involved leaving the house. Going out. Meeting new people. Making connections. Sharing details about myself. My vulnerabilities.

My secrets.

There was too much I couldn't explain. Too much to hide.

Even from Tom.

We stood in the doorway staring at each other. I couldn't get in unless he stepped back, but he didn't move.

He looked as if he was about to say something. But he stopped.

'So, I'll just, er...' I slipped my bag off my shoulder and edged forwards slightly. I couldn't get into my own home.

'Oh, right. Sorry,' Tom said, stepping back, allowing me to pass.

'How was your day?' I asked as I slipped my shoes off, but I paused as a familiar scent filled my nostrils. I sniffed. 'Is that...?'

'Mum's casserole.'

'You cooked?' My eyes widened as I stared at him.

Tom laughed. 'Don't sound so surprised. It does happen. Occasionally.'

'Sorry, I'm just not used to coming home from work to find a home-cooked meal waiting for me.'

Tom shrugged. 'I just wanted to do something to say thank you for letting me stay. I really appreciate it, you know?'

I smiled. 'You're welcome.' I felt lighter somehow. The doubts that warned me to be cautious ebbed away a little more. It had been the right decision to let him stay. He was good to me.

My life was so different with him back in it. It was better. I was better.

'Come on through to the living room,' Tom said, pulling me back from my thoughts. 'I'll pour you a glass of wine before we eat.'

'Oh, I don't have any wine—'

Tom laughed. 'In addition to cooking, I also go shopping too, you know?'

'Right, of course.' I laughed awkwardly. 'Let me just go and freshen up first.'

I padded up the stairs to my bedroom in my bare feet, and opened the wardrobe. I pulled out a pair of jeans and a navy top and closed the door. I started to turn back towards the door but my bedside cabinet caught my eye.

The drawer was slightly open.

That was strange. I was very particular about how I left things. There was an order to everything. I never left drawers or cupboards open.

I couldn't.

Things needed to be exact. Perfect. Or they unbalanced the whole day.

I walked towards the cabinet and opened the drawer fully. Instinctively I reached in and straightened the little pile of note-books and old diaries that lay in there. It was unlike me to leave them out of alignment.

I shook my head as I closed the drawer. Tom's presence must have thrown me off this morning more than I'd thought.

I walked towards the bathroom with my change of clothes.

Funny thing was, I didn't even remember going in that drawer this morning…

I opened the bathroom door and froze.

The toilet seat was up and damp towels were strewn over the floor, along with a pile of discarded clothes. I inhaled sharply as I placed my clothes on the side of the bath. I scooped up the laundry and took it to the kitchen.

'You could have left that,' Tom called from the sofa as I walked past the open door to the living room, my arms loaded with his clothes and towels. 'I would have dealt with it later.'

'It's fine,' I said breezily. 'I've got it.' I separated the heap into the two laundry baskets I kept by the washing machine.

'At least leave it until after dinner,' he said, appearing in the kitchen doorway. He held a glass out towards me. 'Look, your wine is ready for you.'

'I'm done,' I said as I dropped the final towel into the basket.

I caught Tom rolling his eyes as I took the glass from him, but he turned away silently and walked back into the living room.

A familiar sense of unease settled around me as I followed him, like a heaviness weighing down on me. Tom's presence disrupted my routine. It was my home and yet I felt out of place. Floundering. Lost. In just a day he was more at home here than I was. How had that happened? Had he taken over? Or had I been overly accommodating? Was I so determined to make him comfortable here, so he would want to stay, want to keep me, that I had displaced myself in the process?

Or perhaps his ease at being here had just highlighted my own sense of guardedness. Perhaps I had never really been relaxed here, because I was never really relaxed anywhere.

41

'To us,' Tom said as we clinked our wine glasses.

I shuffled back on the sofa and reluctantly pressed the glass to my lips. I should just have told him that I didn't drink. The absence of wine in the house wasn't an oversight, it was an intentional decision.

But if I told him that it would raise a question.

He'd understand, of course. Or maybe he'd even guess the reason himself. Either way, the one thing we agreed never to talk about would be brought back to the forefront of our minds.

It was the reason he'd left me before. Reminding him might make him leave again.

I couldn't take that risk.

I took a tiny sip and forced a smile on my lips.

'Oh, Lizzie,' Tom said as he reached for my hand. 'You have no idea how much I've missed you.'

'I've only been gone a few hours.'

'I'm not talking about today. I'm talking about all these years being forced to stay away from you.'

Forced.

He made it sound as though there was a wall between us. A physical one. Tall and impassable.

'Uni wasn't the same after you left. I'd walk past the bench where you used to like to sit and write, and it just felt wrong. You weren't there.'

'You knew I'd left, then?' There was an edge to my words. I'd often wondered if he'd noticed my absence. One day I was there, the next I was gone. Other than Rebecca, no one had commented. No one had cared.

Not even Tom.

It wasn't as though I'd gone far. I was still in Bournemouth. Still in the same house where I'd always been. He could have come to see me. He could have called. Texted. Anything.

Something.

'Of course I did. It was lonely without you there.'

'I'm sure there were plenty of other people to talk to.'

'Don't be like that.'

'Like what?'

'Don't put yourself down. I didn't want other people. I wanted you. You were special to me. You *are* special.'

Special.

I felt the word vibrate in my chest. I was special. Even after everything I'd done, after everything I'd become, Tom still thought I was special.

'I...' I didn't know what to say. I didn't feel special. I had once; when he'd told me he wanted me. That he would leave Hannah for me.

But he never had.

I hadn't given him enough of a chance.

The timer on the oven beeped and Tom leapt to his feet. 'Dinner's ready.'

I followed him to the kitchen. 'Can I help?' I asked as he picked up the oven glove and opened the oven door.

'No, you can sit down, thanks. I have it all under control.'

I complied, feeling strangely displaced. It was odd watching him manoeuvre around my kitchen. He seemed so at home there. As though he belonged.

Tom set the dish down on a heatproof mat in the centre of the table, which he had already laid, and sat down beside me. 'Here you go,' he said as he heaped a ladle of casserole onto my plate.

'When did you learn to cook? I remember your mum complaining that you were never interested in learning when we were kids.'

'It's a necessity when you start living alone. I moved to London straight after uni and had to start fending for myself. I couldn't rely on Alan to feed me every night.'

'Alan?'

'Hannah's father.'

'You're close to him?'

'He was distraught after losing Hannah like that. I think having me around helped. I was a link to her. A reminder.'

'It must have been so hard for you.' Somehow I managed to speak, but my voice sounded distant and hollow.

'It was,' Tom replied as he stared at me, but it was as though I was transparent. He wasn't really seeing me at all.

But then again, maybe he never really had.

'She was too young. Too...' His voice cracked.

* * *

Cold rain seeped through my clothes as my body shook.

'Lizzie.' I was vaguely aware of Tom's voice. He sounded so far away.

I didn't respond. I couldn't.

I stared at the space where Hannah had been standing. I glanced down at my trembling hands that were still outstretched in front of me.

What had I done?

My vision blurred as a throbbing pain reverberated through my head. Everything felt fuzzy, as though I was a little removed from reality.

I leaned forwards and strained my eyes as I scanned the water below. I frowned. What was it I was looking for?

I flinched as Tom touched my arm. 'We need to go, Lizzie.'

'No.' My word was barely audible.

We couldn't leave.

Could we?

'We can't stay here.' He tugged at my arm, forcing my reluctant muscles into movement.

The stones shifted beneath my feet and I lurched forward. Tom's grip tightened and I winced as his fingers dug into me.

'We have to hurry.'

I tried to shake my head, but the movement made me heave. I didn't have any choice but to follow him. I wasn't strong enough to stand my ground. But more than that, there was something about Tom that made my body comply despite my exhaustion. There was an urgency to him. A fear.

I felt it too. Somewhere deep inside me, I knew something was wrong. Like waking up after a nightmare, feeling unsettled.

But this was worse.

The only thing I knew for sure was, I was already awake.

* * *

'I'm sorry.'

Tom blinked, as though my apology had drawn him back from his own world. 'Really?'

A vice tightened against my chest. 'Of course.' I fought to breathe. 'What happened to her was just so awful.'

Tom nodded. 'But it wasn't as if you liked her, though. Did you?'

'Well, no—'

'I think you'd have liked her, if you'd got to know her better. Everyone that knew her liked her.'

'I'm sure I would—'

'She didn't deserve what happened to her.'

'No.'

It was all I could say. All there was to say.

No one deserved that.

Not even the girl I'd killed.

42

We ate our meal in silence. I couldn't think of a way to start another topic without seeming dismissive of Hannah's memory.

She was the one mistake I could never earn redemption for.

But to Tom...

I pushed a carrot around my plate. Tom was what I'd wanted for so long. But what about me? Did he still see me the same way he once had? After what I'd done, was that even possible?

* * *

'Can you see her?' Tom yelled as we reached the beach.

Luke staggered as he waded back to shore, gasping for breath. 'I t-tried to find her, but the current is so strong.' His teeth chattered as he shivered. 'We need to get help.'

'No,' Tom said sharply. 'We can't call anyone. We can't be here.'

'W-we can't just l-leave.' I winced as Rebecca's sobs grated in my pounding head. 'We h-have to do s-something.'

I put my hand to my head. Despite the throbbing, I knew Rebecca was right. Something was wrong. I frowned, trying to focus my thoughts. But everything felt jumbled and fragmented. What did we need to do?

Cold water dripped onto my face and I tilted my head up towards the sky. Why were we standing outside in the rain?

'Luke, you need to get Rebecca back to the caravan. Now!' I flinched at the sharpness of Tom's instruction.

'What are you talking about?' Luke objected. 'Hannah is out there.'

'Hannah?' I murmured. There was something about Hannah. Something important.

'We can't be here,' Tom repeated.

'We didn't do anything wrong.' Luke was defiant.

'Didn't we?' Tom asked as he looked straight at me.

My knees started to crumple beneath me, but I didn't care. It was okay. I could just sit here for a little while. I could rest my eyes. I could sleep. And then, when I woke up, everything would be better. All of this would just have been a bad dream.

* * *

My impatience had cost us before. My doubt. My suspicion. I needed to be more patient this time. I needed to show him I trusted him.

I paused. I did trust him, didn't I?

My thoughts drifted back to the open drawer. What if it hadn't been me who'd left it open?

But what reason would he have to snoop through my belongings?

I shook my head. No, I was being ridiculous. He was Tom. The Tom I had grown up with. The guy I'd loved my whole life. I knew him better than that.

I'd been distracted this morning; that was the only explanation.

And yet, doubt still niggled. I'd never forgotten to close the drawer before. I'd never been able to walk away from something that wasn't in its proper place. I couldn't. I'd tried. But even the slightest thing out of alignment played on my thoughts, as though it had the power to alter the course of my day.

'So, what did you do all day?' I asked as I collected the plates and carried them to the sink, unable to look him in the eye as I questioned his movements.

'What are you doing?' Tom asked.

'I'm cleaning up,' I said, stating the obvious as I turned the hot tap on and squirted Fairy liquid into the washing up bowl. 'Did you find everything you n—'

'I'll do that,' Tom insisted, approaching behind me.

'You cooked—'

Tom placed his hands on my shoulders and pivoted me around to face him.

'I told you, this is my thank you.'

Instead of moving away, his touch lingered for a moment before running slowly down my arms to my hands. His fingers intertwined with mine. I smiled as tingles ran across my skin.

My mind went blank. Neither of us spoke.

This was uncharted dangerous territory and yet despite all the reasons I should keep my distance, somehow it felt right.

We were connected.

We always had been.

And now, finally, we were holding hands. Like a couple would.

This is where we should always have been. Hannah had intervened. Her presence had been an obstacle, preventing Tom from being able to act on his feelings for me.

But her absence had been worse. It had torn our worlds apart.

Until now.

'You mean so much to me. You always have,' Tom whispered softly in my ear.

'You mean a lot to me too.' *You mean everything to me*, I added silently.

'I'm so glad we're back together.'

Together.

Were we back together?

Was that what this was? Could it be that simple? That easy? That fast? Could the years that had stretched between us disappear just like that?

Tom released my left hand as he turned and led me out of the kitchen, through the hall towards the stairs.

'Tom?' I whispered nervously.

'I want you, Lizzie. I've always wanted you.'

I followed silently as he led the way upstairs and into my bedroom.

He pressed his lips to mine. Softly at first, but his urgency grew as his body moved closer.

This was what I'd wanted, I reminded myself, despite my body's assertion otherwise. It was what I'd dreamed of for the last ten years. This moment. Tom.

I'd longed for the life that we could have had together...

But at the same time I knew there was a reason it hadn't worked out for us before.

It had been easy to blame Hannah. To see her as a rival. But even with her gone, Tom still hadn't been mine. She'd divided us in death even more successfully than she had when she was alive.

I'd given her that power.

But, nonetheless, the hope of a life with Tom had kept me going when it would have been so much easier to give up. But I had it now. I was no longer alone. I was part of something.

I never imagined it could be with Tom. Yet somehow that made it feel more right. We were connected. Our lives were intertwined. They always had been. He needed me as much as I needed him.

I pushed the door closed behind me, cocooning us inside.

Us.

We were an us now.

43

I stared at the ceiling as Tom slept beside me. We'd never spent the night together before. Never slept side by side. Never really done any of the things that normal couples did.

It was what I'd wanted for so long. It was finally ours. Finally *mine*.

I should feel excited. Happy. Complete.

Instead, I felt strange and wrong.

It didn't make sense. There was no one to come between us this time. No one lingering in the shadows. We were free to be together. At last.

And yet, that sense of unease still remained.

Just be cautious.

Rebecca's plea echoed in my mind.

Don't let yourself get swept up in his promises again.

Is that what I'd done?

He hadn't really promised me anything. Not explicitly. But the implication was there, wasn't it? We were back together, that's what he'd said. That implied a future, didn't it?

My breathing felt laboured, as though somehow Tom's presence in my room was stealing all the oxygen. My room seemed to shrink with the two of us in it. I needed space to think. To breathe.

Every movement he made aggravated me further. I needed him to be still. I needed him to disappear. To not be there. Not so close. Not in my space.

There was a disturbing familiarity to it. That claustrophobia. That panic.

I'd thought Tom was the solution. That he was the missing piece that had destined my relationships with anyone else to fail. I thought with him it would be different. I would be different.

I would be whole. Well. Normal.

But not even our intimacy had quietened the fears that bubbled inside me. It hadn't eliminated the distance between us. If anything, it had made it more obvious.

Hannah had stolen too many years from us. Her memory still dominated my thoughts, reminding me that I would never be her. Did Tom think about her too? Did he compare me to her?

Our first time should have been special, instead it was ten years late and yet somehow it still felt too soon. I'd followed Tom's lead. It was what he'd wanted, but maybe I should have told him I wanted to wait. Wanted to reconnect first. To get to know each other. Spend time together. Rebuild what had eroded between us over the years spent apart.

I glanced across at Tom in the darkness. No, I was just being overly cautious. Tom knew best. He knew what was right for us. For me. He was my Tom. He wouldn't steer me wrong.

Maybe that unsettled feeling in the pit of my stomach was just my own insecurities. The fear that Tom would be gone again soon. That lingering doubt, telling me that he would never really be mine. That I would never quite be good enough to keep him.

Or perhaps no amount of time and taking things slowly would be enough to eradicate the guilt of knowing that everything we had together led back to the one unforgivable mistake I had made. My happiness had come with a price that Hannah had paid.

But was it fair to keep tearing myself apart for it? Hannah wasn't blameless. She'd taken what should have been mine. She'd taunted me. Belittled me. She'd made me the person I'd become. Without her I would never have done what I had.

I was good.

Once.

The question was, where did it end? It was part of me now. That darkness. That evil. I'd fought for Tom before. I knew what lengths I would go to.

I was more invested now. More connected to him.

I had more to lose.

More to protect.

I rolled over to the edge of the bed away from him. But it wasn't enough. Tremors vibrated through my body. I expected him to wake up at any moment and ask what was wrong.

But he didn't.

His snoring grew louder.

I slipped my feet out of bed and onto the soft carpet. There was a chill in the air despite the mild spring weather. But then, perhaps it had nothing to do with the season. I tiptoed out of the room in my bare feet. I stood on the landing wondering where to go. It was my home. I could sleep anywhere. But nowhere seemed right. The guest room was occupied by Tom's stuff. It felt wrong to go in there.

I wanted my own room. My own bed.

Alone.

That thought jarred against me. It didn't make sense. I wanted Tom. I needed him. So why didn't I feel right now he was finally with me? How could I want him, and want to be alone at the same time?

My heart thudded as I wiped my sweaty hands against my

nightdress.

His presence in my home, my life, should have been like the missing piece of a jigsaw being slotted into place. He should fit. We should fit.

So why didn't we? I crept downstairs and flicked the kitchen light on, blinking as my eyes slowly adjusted to the brightness. There was a starkness to the light. An eeriness in the emptiness. The silence.

That was never good. I needed noise. I needed distraction. I needed to drown out my own thoughts.

I filled the kettle and switched it on. I didn't really want a cup of tea, but it was something to do. Something to occupy my hands. My thoughts.

The kettle seemed to boil more slowly than usual. I popped a tea bag in a mug and fetched the milk from the fridge while I waited. Tom would hate the way I was making it, I realised.

I sank down to the floor and sat on the cold tiles. How would I explain my absence if Tom woke up and I wasn't there? I couldn't tell him his presence made me feel claustrophobic. That wasn't right. It wasn't fair. It wasn't even as if he'd done anything wrong. Just been there. Present. Close.

The kettle clicked off as it reached the boil, but I ignored it. I leaned forward, rested my head on my knees and stared at the floor between my feet.

There was something familiar about the sensation. Something on the edges of my memory, like a dream I couldn't quite grasp.

I focused on it. I wouldn't let it slip away. I had to know. I had to remember.

* * *

I felt strange. The bouncing was making me nauseous.

Why was I bouncing?

I forced my eyes open. A weak jittery movement. I could see my arms hanging lifelessly beside my head as heavy rain pounded against me. I tried to lift my body and realised the ground was above me.

No. That couldn't be right.

It was me who was upside down.

I was being carried.

By who? Where were they taking me?

I tried to lift my body up. If my head wasn't upside down maybe I could think more clearly. My vision blurred and I closed my eyes again. There was something calming about the darkness. Inviting. Quiet.

I stirred as I felt something soft and dry beneath me. I nestled into it, grateful for the stillness.

Tom's voice intruded on the calmness; it was sharp and authoritative. 'Rebecca, go and shower. Luke, clear some of these bottles—'

'Tom, she's bleeding!' I heard the panic in Rebecca's voice. Someone was hurt. Bleeding. I was vaguely aware of the chaotic activity surrounding me, but I was so tired I couldn't keep my eyes open any longer. The chatter and clanging faded into the darkness.

'Lizzie, you can't sleep now.'

I tried to open my eyes, but my eyelids felt heavy and the effort made my head hurt even more.

'You have to stay awake...' Tom's voice faded away as I let my eyes close again.

* * *

'Lizzie!'

'No,' I murmured. My body was stiff and uncomfortable. I groaned as I summoned the strength to straighten my legs, but my feet pressed against something solid and unfamiliar.

An uneasiness descended upon me. Something wasn't right.

It didn't feel like my bed. In fact, it felt more like I was sleeping on a sofa. But even my foggy brain knew that didn't make sense. Why would I be sleeping in the living room?

I squinted as I struggled to summon the strength to push myself up. My head spun from the movement and I pressed my fingertips to my forehead.

I dragged my legs down, and my feet touched something cool and hard. I leaned forwards, attempting to see the floor as I curled my toes, trying to reconcile the unaccustomed sensation with my memories. The living room had soft fluffy carpet, not a laminate floor.

This wasn't my house.

The revelation reverberated through me. Thoughts swirled in my head, but my brain was too heavy and sluggish to catch hold of them. If I wasn't at home, where was I?

I turned my head slowly, assessing my surroundings. There was something familiar about them...

I licked my lips as I tried to bring some moisture back to my dry mouth. I grimaced at the bad taste on my tongue. It was sour and nauseating.

What was that?

It reminded me of the stench of stale beer.

I started to shake my head but winced at the movement. It couldn't be beer. I didn't drink that. I'd never liked it. I wasn't a big drinker, but when I did drink I preferred wine.

Wine.

How much had I drunk last night?

From the pounding in my head it would seem the answer was too much. But that was unlike me. Why would I drink so much?

Tom.

Everything I did was usually about Tom.

A hazy memory started to surface in the dark recesses of my mind. The holiday park. We'd all gone to spend the weekend at the holiday park in Durdle Door. I glanced down at my makeshift bed on the sofa as clarity seeped into my drowsy head. I'd been relegated to the sofa as there were only two bedrooms. I remembered now.

'Here, drink this,' Tom instructed as he marched towards me and thrust a mug of coffee at me, oblivious to the scowl I was giving him.

I slowly lifted the mug to my lips, the muscles in my arm complaining at the small movement.

'Come on!' he urged impatiently.

There was something about his tone that made me comply, despite my body's reluctance. Tom was always so calm and yet right now he sounded... I squinted at him, as I tried to identify this new mood.

'Once you've drunk that you need to go and shower.'

I drew back. He was being bossy and hostile. I didn't need him to tell me when to take a shower. I'd shower when I felt like it.

I glanced down and my eyes widened as I took in the state of my grazed knuckles and mud-encrusted jeans. Bright red streaks ran across my right hand. I froze. Was that blood?

My gaze drifted back to Tom, and as our eyes met, I instantly knew what his tone was.

Not bossiness.

Not hostility.

It was fear.

'W-what happened?'

'Don't you remember?'

Remember?

I summoned the memories from last night. They were patchy and disjointed. The drinking. The laughter. What was I forgetting? There had to be something.

Something important.

I tried to shake my head, but the movement made me queasy.

'Who's next for the shower?' Rebecca called as she rushed in, her wet hair clinging to her face.

She froze as she saw me. Maybe it was my muddy clothes, or hungover hunch, or maybe it was the panic that I felt bubbling inside me.

'What's wrong with her?' Rebecca asked Tom.

'She doesn't remember.'

'Huh,' Luke grunted as he stooped to pick up an empty wine bottle. 'That's convenient.'

Rebecca shook her head. 'Luke, she's not faking. Look at her. How hard did she hit her head?'

'My head?' I raised my right hand to my forehead where the throbbing was accentuated. My fingertips traced the edges of a plaster that I had no recollection of being applied.

What had happened to me? My eyes darted back and forth from one to the other as they all stared at me.

No, not all. There was someone missing.

Hannah wasn't there.

Hannah was always there.

Always present.

Always in the way.

Until now.

'You're telling me we could all go to prison 'cause of her, and she doesn't even remember?'

'Prison?' I leapt to my feet, but the movement was too rapid and I stumbled forwards.

Tom grabbed my arm and held on to me as I regained my balance. 'No one's going to prison.'

I let out the breath that I'd been holding. Luke was just trying to scare me. He was so stupid.

'Not if we stick to the plan,' Tom added and my stomach plummeted.

It wasn't a joke.

Something had happened

Something bad.

And whatever it was, it looked like it was all my fault.

44

I forced myself back up onto my feet. I needed movement. I needed to distance myself from the memory I wished I had left locked away. Dormant and undisturbed.

One step at a time, I reminded myself. That was the key. Never think about the past. Never think too far ahead. Focus on the present. This moment.

Make the tea. That was all I had to do right now. Just make the tea.

I poured the water into the mug and stirred, before fishing the tea bag out and adding the milk. It was wrong. But I didn't care. It was my way. My tea.

I set my mug on the kitchen table and started to pull a chair out, but stopped. There was one thing I could do to help distract me. I marched to the living room with a renewed sense of purpose and picked up my laptop. I brought it back to the kitchen, placed it on the table and sat down before opening the novel I'd been working on.

Writing was the only solace I had. I could lose myself in creating adventures for my characters. They lived the life I never would.

Bold and exciting. Whatever problems faced them, there were always solutions. For them there was always a way to find redemption. The quintessential happy ending.

My fingers paused above the keyboard, as I searched for the perfect line, the perfect description. But even my characters couldn't distract me tonight. I couldn't focus on fiction when reality was so overwhelming and all-encompassing. My thoughts swirled in continual circles. With one central focus: Tom.

He was a reminder of who I'd been before. Happy. Calm. Free. But he was also a reminder of who I could be. The darkness. The jealousy. The anger. I knew them now. I lived with them. Always fearful of when they might retake control. Of what else I might do.

Was Tom's return an opportunity to recapture what I'd lost? To find my old self? But, if so, which version?

I'd found a balance to the life I lived now. It was a precarious tightrope. But I was used to it. I knew how to deal with it. How to get through the day. How to survive.

But it wasn't enough.

It was empty. Lonely.

I tried not to think about it. I had to focus on the present moment. One step at a time. It was the only way I could get through it. If I lifted my head and looked further ahead at the road that lay in front of me, all I could see was more of the same. A vast expanse of nothingness.

It was dangerous to think like that. To consider the future. To remember the past. I lived somewhere in between, in the place where existence was possible. Not life. Not living. Just survival.

To aim higher involved risk. And I knew that risks had consequences.

Hannah was proof of that.

I cursed myself for allowing my thoughts to drift to memories of her. It was best not to think of her. Or, at least, try not to.

If only Tom hadn't brought her into our lives. Into my life.

'I thought you said you didn't write any more.'

I almost sent the laptop flying as I swung around at the sound of Tom's voice behind me. 'I don't,' I stammered. 'Not really.'

He drew closer, squinting at the document displayed. 'Sure looks like a story to me.'

I pulled the screen down, shielding my words from his view. 'It's just notes, nothing major.'

'Why are you being so secretive?'

'I'm not b—'

'I think it's great that you're writing. I was so disappointed when you told me you'd given up. You always had such a great talent.'

I lowered my gaze to the floor. 'I don't know about th—'

'It's so pointless now, though. All that time and effort you put in over the years, just gone to waste.'

His words hung between us.

A waste.

He was right, of course. I'd wasted my effort. My time. My life.

'What do you write about?' Tom asked. 'Do you still base them on your experiences?'

'Yeah, kind of. I mean, I fictionalise them, but the inspiration comes from an experience, an event, an emotion, or maybe even just something I've heard or seen.'

'It makes sense. You always used writing as a kind of catharsis, didn't you? Like when your gran passed away, or those girls used to tease you at secondary school. You used those emotions, that pain, and channelled it into your writing.'

'Right.' I'd spent so long on my own in the last few years that I'd forgotten how it felt to have someone know me. Know what I liked. How I functioned.

'So what inspires you these days?'

'Just stuff, you know...' I was being evasive. But what choice did I have? I couldn't tell him the biggest source of inspiration was the grief and guilt I carried over Hannah. My writing was part of my continual search for a way to come to terms with the past. To find a way to leave it behind me and move on.

Or perhaps, it was a way to ensure that I never allowed myself to forget. Because if I was honest with myself, I knew deep down that I didn't deserve to move on.

I never would.

'Can I read them?'

'Oh...' I instinctively leaned closer to my laptop. 'I don't really write them for anyone else to read.'

'You used to let me.'

'Things change. People change.' I stared at the floor and studied a little trail of crumbs that nestled beside the cupboard. I stood and picked the broom up from the corner of the room.

Tom sighed. 'Yes, I can see that.'

'What does that mean?' My shoulders slumped as I started to sweep the kitchen floor.

'You used to take chances.'

'You're right. But I'm not that girl any more. I haven't been for a long time.' I gathered the crumbs into a neat little pile in the middle of the floor.

'Maybe it's not too late to find her again.'

I glanced out at the hall floor. I may as well sweep out there while I had the broom in my hands. 'Sometimes you can't go back.'

'You don't really believe that, do you?'

'I'm not sure.' I tried to feign indifference, but the truth was I desperately hoped that I could. I needed it to be true. To be possible.

I waited for Tom to tell me it was achievable. That he'd help me. That I wasn't too far gone to be saved.

'You know it's not even three-thirty in the morning?'

'Mmm hmm.' It was the only sound I could muster, without betraying my disappointment.

'Don't you think it's a little early to be cleaning the house?'

'It won't take long,' I said, ploughing my energy into the task at hand. I shoved the shoe rack out of the way. I had to keep going. Keep cleaning. Keep the momentum.

If I stopped now my thoughts would take over. I would spiral. I couldn't allow that to happen. Not in front of him.

He already realised I was different. Maybe too different to fit with him and his life; the one we had both once dreamed of.

'Have you started submitting to publishers yet?'

'N-no, I told you, it's nothing.' I didn't look at him. I couldn't. 'I just write for me. For fun.'

Tom scoffed. 'Then where's the point?'

I stared at him blankly.

'You're just wasting more time if you're not actually going to do anything with it.'

I watched as he turned and marched out of the kitchen and up the stairs. He didn't turn back.

It felt as if he'd given up on me. As though I wasn't worthy of continuing to talk to. But then, what else was there to say? He was right.

45

I sat at my desk in the corner of the living room. It was the space I had dedicated to work. It helped to have a routine. A specific spot. When I was here I was in work mode. Focused. Disciplined.

Usually.

I jumped at a sudden roaring cheer. My head jerked to the right and I scowled at the football match that filled the TV screen the other side of the room.

'Er, Tom...?'

He leaned back on the sofa, propping his feet up on the coffee table.

I inhaled sharply. He had only been here a couple of days. He was still getting used to how things worked here, I reminded myself.

He was taking a break from work. Relaxing. It was natural that he'd want to be lazy and just chill out in front of the TV. Although, I still wasn't sure why he had chosen to do that in my house. All day. Every day.

It was tempting to ask him. To question his timeframe. His plans. His purpose. But I didn't. I pivoted on my swivel chair and stood up. He'd understand, I told myself as I walked towards the sofa. Of course, he'd understand. 'Tom?'

He glanced up at me. 'Taking a break already?' He chuckled. 'I knew this working from home thing was a cushy number. You're never at your desk for very long.'

'No, actually, I was trying to work, but...' I pointed to the TV. 'Like I told you yesterday, I'm used to working in silence.'

'Can't you just tune it out? Once you focus on your work you'll forget I'm even here.'

The crowd cheered again and Tom punched the air. 'Yes!'

I drew back as his yell resounded through the living room.

'There's a TV in my bedroom, maybe you could watch it in there?'

'But I want to be close to you.' Tom pouted.

His expression tugged at my heart. He wanted to be with me.

'Unless you're sick of having me around already?' He stared at me, as though searching my face for any sign of hesitation.

'No, not at all,' I said quickly. I wanted him here.

Didn't I?

My head felt jumbled.

A second chance.

Kate's words echoed in my brain.

I'd lived alone for so long I'd forgotten what it was to have company. I just needed to adapt. To be flexible. Accommodating.

'Well, how about using your headphones then?' I suggested.

Tom grunted, apparently less than enthusiastic about my compromise, but he picked up his headphones and complied without comment.

* * *

I rubbed my forehead, but it did nothing to alleviate the throbbing headache. I pushed my chair back. Perhaps food would help. It had only just turned noon, a little earlier than I usually ate, but at least it was an excuse to step away from my laptop for a little while.

As I stood up I glanced at Tom. The football match had ended, and been replaced by a film. Fortunately, that meant his cheers and groans had also ceased. Aside from craning his neck to the side to see around me as I crossed the living room in front of the TV, Tom didn't move.

I let out a sigh as I walked into the kitchen, opened the fridge and pulled out a tub of margarine. It was weird having Tom here while I was working. I was used to the quiet, the emptiness. But now I was aware of him wandering about, watching TV or making phone calls, while I tried to focus.

I liked my own structure and order in my home. Everything had its place here, including me. But Tom... He didn't really fit. He flitted about, without his own space, jarring against the routine that existed.

He stacked the dishwasher wrong. Used too much hot water. It was all trivial, but somehow it still mattered. It was my home and yet I felt as though I'd lost control. Things weren't where I left them. Or they'd appear where they didn't belong.

I rolled my eyes. I was making too much of it. They were just typical adjustments that were all part of living together.

But then, I hadn't expected us to be living together. It felt too soon. But what was the alternative? To ask him to leave felt wrong too. I wanted him here. With me. I wanted this life. This future. I just needed to catch up.

I had to let go of my own routines. My own needs. I had to think about us now. Not just me.

I liked my freedom to be lazy, to be obsessive and tidy. To watch TV until midnight or eat junk food all day. To stay in my pyjamas because I was too depressed to summon the energy to get dressed. But I couldn't do any of these things with Tom here. I had to smile, to be bubbly and cheerful. I had to be okay. Normal.

I couldn't be me.

* * *

I snuggled against Tom's chest, his left arm draped around me, whilst he scrolled through the films on Netflix, searching for something to watch.

'I-I have to go to the office tomorrow afternoon.' I silently cursed my stutter. I needed to sound casual or he'd realise I was lying.

Why was I lying?

The question sprang into my head. I hadn't even considered telling him the truth. I'd automatically planned to lie.

Was lying so ingrained in me now that it had become instinctive? Or was it that I knew he would disapprove?

I'd heard the hostility in his voice when I'd talked about Rebecca the other day. How would he feel if he knew I was actually meeting her? I'd already told him I hadn't seen her in years. He would think it was odd that I was meeting her now. He'd realise that I wanted to talk about him. About us.

He'd realise that I had doubts.

The revelation sent icy cold shivers through my body.

I had doubts.

I shouldn't. I couldn't. I wanted this too much to doubt it. But at the same time I knew the dangers of us being together. I knew the lengths I would go to in order to keep him. He brought out a side of me that I had never even known existed.

'Okay.'

Tom's casual acceptance made the guilt worse. He trusted me implicitly.

Even though he, of all people, should have known better.

'I have a meeting,' I added, feeling the need to justify myself; to make it less of a lie. I did have a meeting. Sort of.

'Great,' Tom said.

'Great?' That wasn't the response I'd expected. I'd anticipated curiosity, questions, even disappointment. Instead, he sounded almost enthusiastic.

'I think you spend too much time in the house,' Tom said. 'It's good for you to get out a bit more.'

My hands felt clammy. He'd realised already. He'd noticed I didn't go out much.

'Yeah, absolutely.' I nodded with fake eagerness. I had to do better.

I felt his chest rise and fall as he took a deep breath and let it out slowly. He almost seemed relieved.

I wanted to ask why, but something stopped me. Was he simply glad that I hadn't been offended by his observation? Or was he happy that he would have some time alone?

Did he need a break from me already?

46

I rocked back and forth in my seat as the bus travelled the familiar route into Bournemouth town centre. Why was I putting myself through this? I never caught the bus other than to go to work. Why had I accepted Rebecca's invitation? Why hadn't I, at least, suggested we meet closer to home, somewhere I could have walked to?

Tom.

Guilt engulfed me. He was the reason. If we'd met near to the house there was a risk that he might see us, that he might discover my lie.

My phone pinged, disrupting my thoughts. I rummaged in my bag, silently praying that it wasn't Rebecca cancelling our plans. I couldn't make this journey for nothing. What would I do all day? Where would I go?

My eyes widened as the phone sprang to life and a message from Tom appeared on the screen. I lurched forward in my seat, almost sending my handbag tumbling to the floor.

Why was he messaging me? I'd only just left; surely there couldn't be an emergency already, could there?

I hope I didn't get under your feet too much the last few days. I haven't chased you out of your own home, have I?

I froze and read it again.

Had he realised how much he'd disrupted my routine? Had I made him feel unwelcome? Or in the way?

Not at all. It's lovely to have you staying with me.

I frowned at the message I'd written. My words weren't entirely true. He had got under my feet, and it wasn't exactly lovely, more like disconcerting, to have him staying.

But it had been a long time since I had told the truth to anyone.

Liar.

My hand trembled and I almost dropped the phone.

But then a laughing emoji pinged onto the screen and I smiled. He'd been teasing me.

We'd found our rhythm, just like we had when we were kids.

It feels good to have you back in my life.

I stared at the words on the screen. What did he mean? In what way? My mind raced. I wanted to ask, but I couldn't. I couldn't be desperate and clingy. I needed to handle this better this time. I needed to get it right.

I had to stop letting my thoughts race ahead of me. I had to stay in the here and now. Focus on what I knew. He'd messaged me. He hadn't had to. He'd wanted to. It was a sign that he wanted to be here. Wanted to be with me.

Right now that was enough.

Another message came through.

We have so much wasted time to make up for.

My stomach lurched. My intention to stay focused on the present evaporated instantly. What if there was too much to ever make up for? Would I get it right this time?

I tugged at the collar of my shirt and turned away from the screen, unable to face his words. Familiar scenery passed by the bus window and my spine straightened sharply as I realised where we were.

Sorry. Gotta go. The bus is almost at my stop.

I pressed the bell to signal to the driver to stop, slipped my phone into my bag and shuffled down the bus, clinging to the rails as the driver braked.

I stepped onto the pavement in Bournemouth Square and waited as the bus pulled away. I stared after it, still stunned. The trip had never gone that fast before. I glanced at my hands as I held them out in front of me. I wasn't even shaking.

I smiled as I turned and walked towards the beach with an unfamiliar lightness to my step.

47

'Hey!' Rebecca called, waving at me as I approached the crowded pier. She gave me an awkward hug. 'I'd forgotten how crazy this place gets in the summer.'

I glanced uncomfortably at the surrounding crowd. 'Yeah, me too.'

Confusion flashed across her brow. 'Oh, right. I guess you locals go to the quieter parts.' She shrugged.

I nodded, as though that was the reason. As though I actually went anywhere.

'Anyway, it's great to see you, you look...' Rebecca paused as she assessed me. 'Hot. Why on earth are you wearing a long sleeved shirt in this weather?'

'I burn easily.'

'You've heard of this thing called sunscreen, right?'

I rolled my eyes. 'I see you haven't changed.'

'Why change perfection?' Rebecca shrugged before breaking into a broad grin.

'And you're as modest as ever,' I added and we both laughed.

It felt good to laugh again. I'd missed that. I'd missed her.

'How about we get ice creams and have a walk along the prom, just like we used to?' she suggested.

I glanced down the prom where the crowd started to thin out and smiled. 'Sounds perfect.'

We headed towards the closest ice cream kiosk. 'So how are things going with Tom?'

'Good,' I said as we joined the queue.

'Really?'

'Yes, really. You don't need to sound quite so dubious.'

Another lie. They came as easily as breathing now. Did I even know what the truth was any more?

'Sorry.' Rebecca wrinkled her nose. 'It's just I worry about you. I don't understand why he's back.'

'Is it so impossible to believe that he really did just miss me?'

'Yes.'

'Gee, thanks.' I turned away and stared at the waves as they crashed on to the shore.

'He abandoned you.'

'He was in a difficult situation.'

'Why are you still defending him?'

'Because, it's true.'

I knew he wasn't perfect. I wished he'd handled things differently. Better. But I didn't like Rebecca tearing him down. I needed to believe that Tom was a decent guy; that his feelings for me had been genuine. Were genuine. Perhaps because it meant so much to me to have him in my life, I needed it to have meant something to him too. Or perhaps because he'd made me feel important; worthy; loved. I needed those feelings to have been real. Because if they'd been a lie, then where did that leave me?

'What happened to you giving him a chance?'

'Right. I did promise I would, didn't I?' She sighed. 'This is going to be harder than I thought.'

'Old habits die hard, I guess,' I said and we both laughed again, but my laugh felt feeble and forced.

'What flavour would you like?' Rebecca asked as we stepped up to the counter. 'Let me guess, mint choc chip?'

'Always.' I smiled, secretly pleased that she'd remembered.

She paid the guy behind the counter and handed me my ice cream. 'I am worried about you, though, Lizzie.'

I gritted my teeth as we started walking along the promenade. 'Because Tom's back?'

'No. At least, not just because he's back. To be honest, I've been worried about you for a long time. You changed after you dropped out of uni. You're so different to how you used to be. You're so pale and—'

'And what?'

'I don't know exactly; kind of like the life has gone out of your eyes. You were always so vibrant, so energetic and now you just seem so,' I could see her searching for the right word, 'small.'

I tried not to flinch. It was how I felt. How I tried to be. Small and insignificant. Unnoticed. Distant. It was safer that way. Not just for me. But for everyone. 'Of course I'm different.' I tried to brush her comments away. 'Things change. People change.'

'True. But you changed after Hannah—'

'I don't want to talk about her.' I cast a nervous glance around us.

'Maybe you should.' She caught hold of my elbow and steered me off the crowded promenade on to the beach. 'Maybe we both should.'

My head jerked back and I stared at her. 'You still think about...?' I couldn't finish my sentence. I couldn't bring myself to say it.

'Of course I do.'

'But you're happy. Your life is so amazing. A great husband. Lovely kids.'

'That doesn't mean I can just forget the past. It's a part of me. A part of all of us.'

'But you didn't do anything wrong.'

'I was there.' Rebecca took a deep breath. 'And I was part of the lie. The cover up.'

Bile rose in my throat. 'You regret protecting me.' It wasn't a question. I could tell from her tone that the lie had haunted her. She wished she'd told the truth. She wished she'd turned me in.

'I don't regret trying to protect my friend. But...'

'What?'

'I feel guilty about the lie. I feel guilty that Hannah's family never got answers. They never got closure.'

'So you do regret it.' My legs felt weak and I sank down onto the sand, holding the ice cream that I no longer had any desire for.

'No.' She shook her head firmly, as she sat down beside me. 'But I'm starting to wonder if keeping that secret really did protect you.'

'Of course it did. The truth would have destroyed my life. It would have destroyed me.'

'And what did the lie to do you?'

'I... I...' I couldn't speak. The words wouldn't come. How could I explain it? How could I tell her how that lie had affected me? It had given me freedom. It had kept me out of prison. But at the same time the lie had trapped me in a prison of my own making.

'I knew you were struggling. I saw you freak out in class just after it happened. I started to come after you, but I froze.'

'I get it. It was weird. No one knew what to say to me afterwards.'

'No, that wasn't it. Or, at least, not all of it. The truth is I didn't know how to be there for you when I was barely holding it together myself.'

I stared at her. She'd been struggling that much? How had I not seen that? What kind of friend did that make me? 'I knew you'd taken the break up with Luke hard, but I didn't realise things were so bad.'

'It wasn't just Luke. It was everything. If we hadn't gone to the caravan that weekend. If Luke hadn't brought all that wine. If we hadn't got so drunk. Or started that game.'

'It wasn't your fault. You couldn't have known what would happen. No one could.'

We nodded at each other silently. We didn't need words. For the first time I knew that I wasn't alone in reliving that night and wondering what I could have done differently. Better.

Knowing Rebecca felt the same way didn't change anything. It didn't undo the mistakes that any of us had made. But somehow it made it a little less lonely. Maybe I was a little less broken than I'd thought. Maybe some of how I felt was normal.

'So, tell me everything,' Rebecca said.

'E-everything? I w-wouldn't even know where to begin.'

'I know you changed courses. Changed uni. Changed career.'

I nodded. We'd kept in touch enough over the years to know the key facts of each other's lives. But we didn't know the details.

I hadn't asked. And neither had Rebecca. I'd chalked it up to neither of us caring that much. But maybe it wasn't out of disinterest, but out of fear. I didn't want to know the bad parts of her life, the ways that I had screwed things up for her. But equally, I didn't want to know too much about the good either. It made the gap between us bigger. She was succeeding. She was living. While I was barely surviving.

'Was it my fault?'

'Your fault?' I stared at her blankly. 'How could it be your fault?'

'I encouraged you to take a break. I only meant for a week or two, just to clear your head. I knew you were struggling. I thought it would help.'

'You were right. I couldn't keep going to class like that.'

'But you never came back.'

'I couldn't. Too much had changed. I'd changed. I felt so...' I searched for the right word.

'Lost,' Rebecca finished for me.

Our eyes met and I knew that she was speaking from experience. She'd felt it too.

'I feel so guilty,' she said.

'I keep telling you, you didn't do anything.'

She took a deep breath. 'I let you down. I should have messaged more. Called more. I should have come round to see you. I tried a couple of times but your mum said you didn't want visitors, so I left. I just gave up.'

'I pushed you away. I pushed everyone away.'

I'd isolated myself. I'd shut myself away at home, unable to leave. It was the only way I could cope. If I could even call it coping.

The one person I'd wanted to see was the one person who'd never called at all.

Tom.

Perhaps it was fitting. After all, I'd already given up on myself. His disregard simply reinforced that I wasn't worth it. I wasn't missed. I wasn't needed. I wasn't loved.

'I thought you were better off without me,' I said softly. 'You were safer without me.'

* * *

I stood at the top of the cliff as blue lights flashed around me.

'Lizzie?' I heard Tom's voice beside me, but I didn't turn round. I couldn't.

My gaze was locked on the beach below where a blanket was draped across the sand. 'T-this can't be h-happening,' I stuttered quietly as my body shook.

'Don't look,' Rebecca said on my other side, as she wrapped her arm around my shoulders. 'You don't want to see this.'

I shook my head. I needed to see. I needed to understand.

'Tell me what happened.' I said to Tom.

'I already told you.'

He was right. He had. But I must have misheard him. What he'd said didn't make sense. It wasn't possible. 'Tell me again.'

He glanced around, checking that the four of us were alone. 'Hannah was taunting you. Laughing at you.'

I nodded slightly. I remembered that. I remembered the sound of her laugh and the scornful tone of her voice mocking me.

'She knew you had a crush on me.'

'But it's not just a crush. We're together. I'm your girlfriend.'

'You got mad,' Tom continued as though he hadn't heard my correction. 'I've never seen you so mad. You were yelling at her. Screaming. You grabbed her.'

I shook my head. 'I don't remember that.' It didn't sound like me. I didn't yell. I didn't attack people.

But then it wasn't just anyone. It was Hannah.

I hated her. Loathed her.

I'd fantasised about something happening to her. Anything that would get her out of our lives. Out of Tom's life.

I'd wanted her gone.

And I didn't care how.

'She tried to defend herself. She fought back. She grabbed a rock and swung it at you.'

My fingers instinctively traced the cut on my forehead. I remembered the jarring pain of the impact. The dizziness. The darkness. The sensation of falling.

'You stumbled and she tried to manoeuvre around you, but then,' Tom paused, 'you lunged at her.'

I squinted, trying to recall that moment. But there were gaps in my memory. It was like trying to see the horizon through fog. I could catch glimpses of images, outlines of shapes, but the moment I focused on them the fog grew denser, obscuring my view.

'The next thing I knew, Hannah was falling,' Tom continued. 'There was nothing I could do. It all happened so fast.'

I remembered that too. Her wide eyes. Her scream. Her arms flailing as she tried to grab hold of me. I could still recall the feeling, that instinct inside me that told me to help her.

But I didn't.

I just watched, frozen, unable to move, as she tumbled backwards over the edge.

'You have to tell the police,' Luke said, glaring at me, before turning back to Tom. 'I know you care about Lizzie, but we can't protect her. We shouldn't. She doesn't deserve it.'

'You're wrong,' Rebecca hissed. 'Lizzie would never do that. She couldn't.'

'Let the police decide,' Luke said.

'If you tell the police, who do you think they'll believe? The girl who can't remember anything, or Tom's accusations?'

'I'm not making accusations, I'm just telling you what happened,' Tom said indignantly.

Luke shrugged as he stared at Rebecca, ignoring Tom completely. 'That's not our problem.'

'She's our friend.'

'So was Hannah.'

48

'You still think you pushed her intentionally?' Rebecca asked. 'You really believe you could have done that?' She shook her head. 'You wouldn't. You couldn't.'

I took a shaky breath. 'I hated her so much.' It crushed me to think that I was capable. But it was futile to deny the truth.

'That doesn't mean you would attack her. It doesn't mean you would push her. I never believed that you did.' She leaned to her left so her eyes met mine. 'And I still don't believe it.'

Tears welled up inside me and I fought to catch my breath. There was something so powerful in hearing those words. The conviction. The belief. The trust.

But she was misguided. Naive.

'Tom told us what happened. He wouldn't lie. Not to me. He'd done everything he could to protect me. He even turned against Luke to save me.'

* * *

'You know the police are going to want to talk to us,' Luke said as we stood on the cliff top, watching the coast guard on the beach below. 'We have to tell them we were all out here this morning. They could find evidence. We could have been seen.'

Tom shook his head. 'We ran away, Luke. We left Hannah out there. We didn't call for help. We didn't report it.'

'You wouldn't let us.'

'You went along with it. You all did.'

Luke nodded. 'You're right, we did. But we shouldn't have done. And once we explain that we were in shock, that we were scared—'

'Do you really think that would make everything okay? Do you think Lizzie is the only one with something to lose?'

'What are you talking about?'

'How much had Hannah drunk?' Tom fired the question at him.

'I don't know.'

'Who brought all the wine?'

'That's irrelevant. She didn't have to drink it. That was her choice.'

'Can you prove it?'

'What?' Luke looked dazed. 'No. I mean, how can I?'

'And why did you let her climb in that state?'

'It wasn't my idea.'

'But you didn't stop her.'

'Well, no.'

'Did you try?'

'You were with her. Not me.'

'But I was drunk too. You didn't try and stop me. You didn't try and stop any of us.'

'You're trying to pin this on me,' Luke snapped, his eyes wide.

'I'm trying to show you that none of us can afford for the truth to come out. We all have too much to lose.'

'You and Lizzie were the ones up there with her. If anyone's going to be under suspicion it's you two.'

'And what do you think will happen if the police start investigating me? What will happen to you?'

'What are you saying?'

'I'm simply reminding you that you have something to lose here too.'

* * *

'He lied to Hannah about you.'

'That's different. He was protecting his career. Why would he lie about this?'

'Tom has always lied to protect himself. You can't trust him, Lizzie.'

'What are you saying? That he pushed Hannah?'

'It's a possibility.'

I snorted. The idea was ridiculous. Tom wasn't like that. Tom wouldn't hurt anyone.

And yet, somewhere deep inside me, a tiny slither of doubt niggled. After all, there was a time when I would have said the same about me.

I shook my head, feeling disloyal. 'If that was true why would he come back? If I was nothing more than the person he pinned his crime on, he wouldn't care about me. He wouldn't come back for me.' Tom had covered for me. He'd lied to the police to protect me. He wouldn't have done that if he was just using me.

'I don't know. I haven't figured that part out yet. But I do know you. Or, at least, I did back then. And I know that his version of events never made sense.'

'Perhaps you only thought you knew me. Perhaps there was a side to me that no one knew. That no one saw. Until it was too late.'

'So you really believe it? You think that you did it? That you could?'

'Who knows what anyone is capable of in the right circumstances? Or rather, the wrong ones. I was jealous, I know that. I remember having this rage bubbling inside me every time I saw her with him. The way she flirted, the way she put her hands on him, kissed him. It was always such a show with her.'

'For your benefit. I still think she knew about you two. She was marking her territory. Reminding you he was hers.'

'I should have ignored it. Ignored her. I should have been more patient and trusted Tom more. He had a plan. He just needed a little more time.'

Rebecca scoffed. 'And what was this great plan of his?'

'I don't know actually.' It was a question that had often circled in my brain. The plan that had been the solution to everything had always remained a mystery. I shook my head. 'I screwed everything up before he had time to implement it. And then afterwards it was irrelevant. Not that I could have asked him; he disappeared off to London to support Hannah's dad and by the time he came back I'd already dropped out of uni.'

But why hadn't he told me beforehand? He'd known I was anxious. Impatient. He could have shared his plan with me. He could have given me peace of mind.

Unless... I swallowed as a heaviness descended upon me. What if he'd never had a plan?

What if he'd lied?

And if he'd lied to me about that, then what else might he have lied about?

I felt cold despite the warmth of the sun. There had always been a part of me that had jarred against Tom's recollection of events. A part where his story somehow didn't sit quite right. It felt like he was talking about someone else. Someone bad. Someone who wasn't me.

But I couldn't dispute the evidence. I still bore the faint scar on my forehead from the rock Hannah had fought me off with. I still remembered standing at the edge of the arch, watching her fall, with my arms outstretched. Instinctively I knew I hadn't been trying to save her. Which left only one explanation.

I'd pushed her.

'You could ask him.'

Rebecca's statement was so simple. So obvious. Tom was back in my life now; I could ask him.

Why hadn't I already?

But even as I asked myself the question, I knew the answer. 'Knowing Tom's plan would just make me feel worse. It would make everything we lost even more real. The possibility of what we could have had together. That life. That happiness. I destroyed it all.' My shoulders slumped. 'I didn't even deserve it. Not after what I'd done.'

'Is that why you dropped out? You just gave up?'

Rebecca's question cut into me. It felt like a criticism. She was right of course. I'd been weak. I'd abandoned my dream. Myself.

'It wasn't that simple,' I protested. 'It happened slowly at first. I skipped a few classes, or left early, not feeling well. I tried to keep going; to get over it. But in the end it was all consuming.'

'How so?'

I paused, unsure how to explain. It wasn't something that could fully be put into words. To someone who hadn't experienced it, any description I gave would lack the magnitude of how it actually felt.

'Lizzie?' Rebecca urged softly. She wanted to know. To understand.

Didn't I, at least, owe her the chance to try?

'I guess it's a bit like claustrophobia. At least, that's how it feels to me. The walls start closing in and there are too many people around. I get hot, shaky, dizzy and can't breathe. I get this over-whelming urge to escape, to run away before I collapse. But every time I do it makes it harder to ride it out next time. In the end I couldn't even make it through a single class without fleeing. Eventually I couldn't leave the house.'

I kept my gaze lowered I knew if I saw her expression – her disdain; her disappointment – I wouldn't be able to continue.

And I needed to continue.

It was no longer about Rebecca. At least not just about her. My need for her to understand had been unexpectedly overridden by one thing I'd never anticipated: my own need to voice the turmoil that raged inside me.

I no longer wanted to carry this secret.

I no longer wanted to be alone.

'I tried to avoid going to the doctors. I thought it would pass. That I would just get over it; get back to normal. But I didn't. I couldn't. It was like I was trapped. The old me was gone. Locked away. Unreachable. Time slipped by and I barely even noticed.'

I took a deep breath. 'Eventually we found a medication that kind of worked, I guess. I mean it's not like the pills are a magic cure. They're only part of the solution.'

'And the rest was...?'

'Me.'

As hard as it had been to find the right balance with the medication, finding my own internal balance had been even harder.

'It's all a blur to me now. Lost time. Undefined. Muddled. It's as though each day ran into the next. Maybe it was the medication. Maybe it was my illness.' Even as I said it, it felt wrong. It wasn't a real illness.

It was just weakness.

Cowardliness.

I wanted to run away because reality was too hard. I couldn't live with the guilt of what I'd done. But my fear kept me silenced.

'Talking to the therapist helped, though?'

'Yeah.' I nodded. 'Over time.'

Yet even as I spoke I wondered just how true my words actually were. At the time, everyone had thought it had helped: my parents, my GP, the therapist, even me.

As the months passed I made slow steps back to normality. At least, on the surface. I laughed at TV programmes. I took more care over how I dressed. I ventured out of the house.

And yet, if I was honest with myself, none of it was easy. None of it was natural; I did things because I was supposed to. Because they were expected.

Because it made the people around me happy.

The anguish in my parents' expressions eased a little more every time I set foot outside the house. They didn't hover over me as much, checking I was okay, asking if I was happy, if I was well.

But for my part it was never instinctive. Never genuine. Never me.

I hadn't recovered. I'd just learnt to grit my teeth and get through each day. It was the only way to make the relentless questions stop. The only way to deflect attention before I couldn't bear it any more and shared too much. I had to protect my secret. Even at the expense of myself.

'That's why you disappeared for the rest of that year,' Rebecca nodded slowly. She understood my absence now. 'I was so thrilled when you said you were going back to uni in September. I was disappointed you didn't come back to AUB, but after all that had happened, I could understand you wanting a change of scenery. But changing degree never made sense to me.'

'Mum and Dad wanted me to go back to university. They were adamant I should get a degree. It's what they'd always dreamed of for me. They wanted me to have the chances and opportunities they'd never had. But this time I took their advice and studied something more serious. More sensible. Dad worked in IT, so it just seemed natural to follow in his footsteps.'

Rebecca pulled a face. 'But you always said that was dull.'

'I was wrong. It was the smart choice. It gave me the foundations for a more stable, long term career than I would ever have had with writing. That part of my life was over and I knew it. The only way to get back on my feet was to let that dream go and start again.'

I was trying to be the girl that Tom would want. The kind of girl he would come back for. But the reality was, I was the girl that he'd left.

'But you didn't just start again, Lizzie. It's like you became someone entirely different. Someone that wasn't you.'

I wanted to deny it. I wanted to tell her she was wrong. I was still the same person; the same girl I'd always been. But she was right. I'd reinvented myself. I wasn't the same as before. I couldn't be. Too much had changed in me to go back. Part of me had died along with Hannah.

49

'Oh, my ice cream is melting,' I said as a cold sticky green trickle ran down my wrist.

'Here hold this, and I'll get you a tissue,' Rebecca said as she thrust her ice cream into my other hand and delved inside her bag. She pulled a tissue out and started dabbing it against my hand.

'I can do it,' I said, trying to back away.

'I've got it, don't wor—' I watched as tiny creases formed across her forehead. 'What's this?'

I followed her gaze to my outstretched hand and realised my long sleeved shirt had risen up, leaving my wrist exposed. Below it, angry red streaks peeked out from the cuff.

I jerked my hand back, causing my ice cream to topple from the cone and land with a splat in the sand.

'Lizzie, what happened to you?'

I shoved her ice cream back into her hand, before tugging my sleeve down. Panic welled inside me. 'It's nothing.'

'*That* is not nothing,' she said, staring at my wrist as though my sleeve was transparent.

'It's just a scratch.' Why couldn't she let it go? Why did she have to pry? To question?

'From what?'

I shrugged. 'I don't remember now.' The lie was weak. I knew it wouldn't be enough to deter her. But she'd caught me off guard. I wasn't prepared for her questions. I wasn't prepared for that look of pity and fear that was etched into her features.

She was scared.

But was she scared of me? Or for me?

'Lizzie?'

'It's nothing.' It wouldn't be fair to burden her with my secret. She'd look at me with revulsion and condemnation. And how would she feel about being asked to keep this secret?

I started to stand but Rebecca put her hand on my shoulder.

'It's not nothing. Lizzie, did you...?'

She didn't need to finish her question, we both knew what she was asking.

I wanted to deny it. But I knew it was pointless. She'd never believe my excuses.

She knew.

'Why do you do it?'

'It helps.'

'How?'

I shrugged. I felt cornered. Trapped. My secret was out on display. It was being assessed. Analysed.

'I'd like to understand,' Rebecca said softly. 'If you don't mind telling me.'

I studied her expression. There was no judgement or condescension in her eyes. Just interest and compassion.

I wanted to tell her to leave me alone and mind her own business. I wanted to tell her that it was private and I didn't want to talk about it.

And yet, at the same time, I wanted someone to share this secret with. Someone to confide in. Someone to understand. To tell me it was okay. That *I* was okay.

'Sometimes I get so...' I searched for the right word. 'Overwhelmed.'

Rebecca nodded, encouraging me to go on.

'It's like this frustration and desperation builds up inside me, and feeling pain, something physical, something real, is the only escape.' The words spilled from my lips. Unplanned. Uncensored. 'It's a release. Like screaming and letting go, but more powerful. More intense.' I searched for the words that would make her understand the magnitude of the relief it could bring. 'I feel calmer. In control.' I sighed. 'At least for a moment. But then I feel bad.'

'From the pain?'

I shook my head. 'From the shame.' I shuffled uncomfortably. 'I feel so stupid. Useless. Weak. A failure. And then the pain I've caused no longer feels good. It hurts in a bad way. It's just a shameful reminder that I've done that to myself.'

'But you still do it?'

'Sometimes it's the only way I can cope. The only way I can regain control. But now it feels more like it controls me. Whenever things are difficult, I...' I couldn't say the words. Even though Rebecca knew my secret now, I still couldn't say it aloud.

'You hurt yourself,' she finished for me.

'I always promise myself that it will be the last time; that next time I'll be stronger. But I never am.'

There was something addictive about it. It was more than a coping mechanism. More than a habit. It was a need. Desperate and overpowering.

'I need that release. That calmness. That distraction from the spiralling going on in my head. Something bad or stressful happens, or I'll just feel overwhelmed again, and it feels like the only way out. The only way to cope.

I swallowed, waiting for Rebecca's reaction. I'd never told anyone before. Never allowed them to see that part of me. That failing. I was afraid of what they would think. How could anyone understand it? I didn't even understand it. It wasn't normal. It wasn't right.

* * *

'Do you ever think about harming yourself?' the therapist had asked me once.

'No, of course not.' I shook my head vigorously. 'I could never do that.'

She paused for a moment. Her gaze locked with mine, no doubt trying to assess the truthfulness of my words. Did she believe me? Was I convincing enough?

I glanced down at my long sleeved shirt, resisting the urge to tug the cuffs down lower. Could she tell? Did my choice of clothing betray me to her trained eye? Or did my scars show at my wrists?

Perhaps I shouldn't be convincing. Perhaps I should confide in her. Even the things that were too scary to admit to myself.

But my injuries were never serious. I never cut myself deeply. I never needed medical treatment. A bruise that could be explained away. Scratch marks that I could keep hidden. It was just a coping mechanism. Some people needed a glass of wine or a cigarette. I needed this. It was my secret. My weakness. But also my strength.

I couldn't tell her. I couldn't tell anyone. They wouldn't understand. It would just scare them. They'd worry for my safety. They'd tell me it was a foolish thing to do. They'd want to talk about it. Analyse it. Analyse me.

I didn't need that. It was bad enough being here already. The prying questions, the silent judgements, the overriding knowledge that I couldn't cope. She'd never said it, of course. Her training wouldn't allow it. But we both knew it. It hung in the air between us. Never mentioned. Never acknowledged.

I didn't need anyone else's scorn to add to my own.

But mostly I knew I had to keep my mouth shut, because if I didn't, if I confided in anyone, they'd tell me to stop. They wouldn't understand that I couldn't. No one would understand that. I couldn't understand it myself.

I wanted to stop. I desperately wanted to.

But I didn't.

I deserved to feel pain. I deserved to suffer. It felt justified. Right. And yet mostly what I wanted was a release from the crushing panic that consumed me.

Inflicting pain was impulsive. It wasn't planned. I was driven by a need stronger than anything I had ever known before. And yet, at the same time, it was something controlled.

I told myself I didn't have a choice. Something came over me, something stronger than me. But I did. I always had a choice.

I chose physical pain, because in a weird way it was a release from the mental pain I was constantly in.

* * *

'It's a difficult burden to carry,' Rebecca said.

They weren't the words of comfort and understanding that I'd hoped to hear. But at least it wasn't condescension.

I bit my lip. 'It's not the hardest burden I've carried. It's not even the worst.'

My eyes met hers. 'Is that why you do it?'

'Maybe. Probably.'

'Does Tom know?'

I shook my head. 'I've never told anyone else. I was always

afraid that if I did then they would think I was crazy or maybe even suicidal.'

'Were you? Are you?' Her words were etched in fear.

'No!' I shook my head. 'It's the opposite.'

'Really?'

'I don't want to die. I'm not trying to kill myself. I'm trying to cope. To live.'

She stared at me. Studying me. I could practically feel her questions simmering beneath the surface. The confusion. The doubt.

I couldn't blame her. What I was saying sounded contradictory. How could hurting myself help me to live?

'I want to stop,' I told her as I lowered my gaze. 'I just don't know how to.'

'You'll stop when the time is right for you.'

I jerked my head up and stared at her, speechless. She wasn't criticising. She wasn't telling me not to do it again. She was trusting me to find a way through it.

'What if I don't? What if I can't?'

'I'll be here for you, whatever you need. We can talk, or sit in silence. Anything. Everything.'

'But you can't fix it for me.'

'I wish I could. I really do.'

I nodded slowly. I wished she could too.

'The thing is, you don't need me to save you. You don't need anyone to save you. You can solve this yourself.'

I was about to object, to tell her she was wrong. I did need saving. I needed saving from myself. But something stopped me.

The desire for someone else to step in and solve things for me wasn't new. I'd always needed Tom to be my saviour, even before I'd screwed our lives up. I needed him to tell me what I should do; where I should go. I needed that guidance. That control.

Then again, had I needed him to control me, or had I simply let him?

'But the decision has to come from you, Lizzie,' Rebecca continued. 'And it will, when you're ready. But...'

'But what?' My stomach tightened, waiting for her response.

'Maybe you should speak to your GP about going back to counselling.'

'I don't need to. I'm fine.'

Except I wasn't.

I knew it.

And so did Rebecca.

I'd made a new life for myself. A successful one. But I still wasn't free of my demons. They were my constant companions, always tormenting me.

I'd learnt to survive. I thought that was enough. But since Tom's return it felt like the past was growing in strength. It was as though his presence had revived the memories that had lay buried for so long.

Rebecca was right, the past still had a hold over me. Its grip was unrelenting.

'It would be better to do it now, Lizzie. While the decision is still in your control.' Rebecca hesitated. 'Before you push yourself too much and have a breakdown.'

'There are some things you do once and vow never to do again. You learn from them. Grow from them.' I shrugged feebly. 'That was the plan anyway.'

'And seeing a therapist is one of those things?'

I nodded.

'Is that why you haven't gone back to your GP?'

It felt like an accusation. As though it was something I should have done. It didn't make sense. 'Why would I?'

'You're struggling.' Rebecca said the words slowly.

'I've always been struggling. The therapist I saw before knew about the panic attacks when I was at uni. She knew I had to force myself to catch the bus and go to class. But she discharged me anyway.' I shrugged. 'I was better than I had been.'

'And that seemed good enough?'

'It seemed like it was all that was possible.'

'It wasn't. It isn't.'

'You don't know that.'

'True, but it's what I believe. Therapy only works if you work at it, Lizzie. It's not a one-off thing that can't be repeated. It can be. And sometimes it should be.'

Tears streamed down my checks. I quickly wiped them away with the back of my hand. I couldn't cry here. But the tears kept flowing. They wouldn't stop.

I fought to regain control. I didn't want to see the doctor. I was afraid that she would agree with Rebecca and send me back to counselling. I would have failed again.

But I was also scared that she wouldn't and I would have to continue as I was.

I wasn't sure which was more terrifying.

50

'Can I give you a ride home?' Rebecca asked as we walked through the lower gardens.

'Erm...' I glanced at my watch. It was early. Tom wouldn't be expecting me for a while yet. But if I didn't go home, where else could I go?

'Is something wrong?'

'No, it's just...' I hesitated. 'I didn't tell Tom that we were meeting.' Guilt weighed heavily against me. I'd lied. To Tom.

'You thought he'd disapprove?'

I raised my eyebrows.

'Yeah, okay. Fair enough. He would definitely disapprove. But why does that matter? He's entitled to his opinion, but that doesn't mean it should stop you.'

'It didn't. I'm here, aren't I?' I replied defiantly. I hadn't let Tom dissuade me from coming. I'd made my own choice.

'And where does he think you are?'

I tried not to cringe. 'At work.' I knew what she would think. What she would say. I'd been a coward. I hadn't been truthful with him because I knew he would deter me.

But then, why would he? Because he didn't like Rebecca? Because he'd guess that we would be talking about him? Or because he'd be hurt that I was taking the afternoon off to see her and yet I'd chosen to keep working during his stay.

That thought whirled in my head. Why hadn't I taken a day or two off to spend with him? Why hadn't that idea even occurred to me until now?

'Is this really how you want it to be?' Rebecca asked, saving me from answering the questions I wasn't ready to face. Not that her questions were any better. 'Didn't you get tired of all the lies last time? He's only been back a few days and you're already lying to each other.'

'It's only a little lie,' I told her indignantly. 'And he hasn't lied to me.'

'Right.' Rebecca nodded. 'And why did he say he was back again?'

'Because he missed me.' I frowned as I realised her implication. 'That's not a lie,' I said adamantly before doubt snuck back into my thoughts. 'I don't think.'

I held my breath as I realised my slip. I shouldn't have admitted that. Not aloud. Not to Rebecca. I waited for her to seize upon my hesitation, but she stared straight ahead, seemingly lost in her own thoughts.

'I can't help thinking that we shouldn't have listened to Tom. We shouldn't have let him convince us to lie. I think you would have been better off if we'd told the truth that day.'

'You can't be serious?' The mere suggestion tore into my heart. How could she wish she'd turned me in? She was my friend. Or, at least, she was supposed to be. 'You know what would have happened if we had.'

'You'd have risked your degree, your career? You don't have either anyway. You'd have lost Tom? Well, that happened too. He left you.' Her words were blunt and harsh.

I stared at her. 'You're missing the biggest thing. I'd have been arrested. I'd have been charged. I might—' I swallowed. I couldn't say the words. I couldn't confess my worst fear. If the truth had been revealed, if it ever was revealed, I'd be locked away in a prison cell.

'Tell me what really happened that night, Lizzie.'

'You already know.'

She shook her head. 'I know what Tom told us.'

'What he saw—'

'What he thought he saw,' Rebecca corrected. 'We'd all been drinking too much that night.'

'How can you defend me?'

'Because it never felt right. Not then. Not now.'

'You said it yourself, we were drunk. I was drunk.'

'So you pushed her?'

'We were arguing. She grabbed me and I—'

'Do you remember pushing her?'

'I see it in my nightmares.' I'd lost count of how many times I'd woken in the middle of the night, sweat dripping from me, my pulse racing. I'd flick the light switch on, plunging the room into brightness as I tried to block out that image of my hands pressed against Hannah's shoulders, driving her backwards off the top of Durdle Door.

'Because you remember? Or because you remember what Tom told you?'

'It's the same thing.'

'No, it's not.'

I pondered her words. Was she right?

A story Mum told about me getting lost in Marks and Spencer's when I was about five, came into my mind. I could practically see the store and feel the panic I must have felt back then, but the memory wasn't real. It was constructed from the details that she had told me. It matched her description perfectly. I couldn't recall any of the details beyond those that she had recounted.

Had I done the same with Hannah's death? Were the images I saw in my nightmares really memories? Or just my subconscious reconstructing Tom's words?

'Somebody who's capable of committing murder wouldn't feel the need to punish themselves, not the way you do,' Rebecca said softly. 'I didn't trust Tom. Not when I saw how he treated you.'

Rebecca's distrust of Tom made her more loyal to me. More eager to overlook my flaws. But there was one fact even she couldn't dispute. 'Hannah wouldn't have even been up there if it wasn't for me.'

'What are you talking about?'

'I dared Hannah to climb to the top of Durdle Door. I mean, what was I thinking? Why would I do that?'

'You didn't.'

'Yes, I did.'

Rebecca grabbed my hand. 'No. It wasn't you. It was Tom.'

I shook my head. 'No, he told me—'

'Tom told you it was you?' Rebecca cut through my words.

'Well, yeah.'

'So, you don't actually remember daring Hannah?'

'No, but—' I tried to focus on the memories that whirled in my head, but they were like wisps of candyfloss dissolving away as I tried to catch them. 'Everything's foggy. I was so drunk.'

'So the only version of events you've been relying on all these years, is Tom's?'

'He wouldn't lie to me.'

'But he did, don't you see? I *know* you didn't dare Hannah. And I know you didn't push her. It wasn't possible.'

My grip tightened on the strap of my handbag as I tried to cling on to something solid. Something certain. 'You weren't up on that arch, Rebecca. You don't know what happened.'

But Tom was there. He knew.

'I know you. Or, at least, I did back then. I knew what you were like. Quiet. Considerate. You cared about people. You weren't the kind of person to go around pushing people off arches.'

I felt hot and dizzy. There was something disconcerting about hearing Rebecca voice aloud the doubts that had circled in my own mind for years.

I'd written them off as desperation and wishful thinking. I hadn't wanted to believe the truth. I hadn't wanted to be that kind of person.

But I was.

'It wasn't just anyone. It was Hannah.'

'So you think you have morals, just not where Hannah was concerned?'

'I had an affair with her boyfriend.' I wasn't sure that I had any morals left. But then, was it really an affair? We'd held hands a few times, kissed, and talked about our future together. But beyond that...

'That's a lot different to killing her.'

Rebecca was right, of course. There was a big gap between kissing someone else's boyfriend and killing his girlfriend. They were both bad. Both things I would never have believed I would do. But the two weren't comparable. Just because I was guilty of the one, it didn't mean I was automatically guilty of the other.

In fact, the only reason I even believed it at all was because Tom told me it was the case.

But what if he was wrong?

What if he'd lied?

51

I could see them as I walked up the road from where I'd got Rebecca to drop me off, out of sight. Kate was standing on my driveway, twisting her long brown hair around her fingertips, while her other hand rested on Tom's forearm. Their laughter carried to me on the early evening breeze.

You can't trust him.

Rebecca's caution replayed in my ears.

What if she was right?

'What are you two up to?' I asked as I walked up the driveway, my smile fixed in place. I wouldn't let jealousy get the better of me.

Not this time.

Kate's hand fell from his arm instantly and she raised it in an awkward semi wave.

'Nothing.' Tom winked at Kate. 'Just getting to know our neighbour.'

Our neighbour.

'I spotted Tom coming back from his walk and just popped out to say hi,' Kate explained.

Spotted.

What did that really mean?

Was she looking for him? Waiting for him?

'I thought we could go out for dinner tonight,' Tom said, interrupting my thoughts.

'Well, er—'

'Perfect. I'll just call and make a reservation. I thought we could try that little Italian place up the road.'

I watched, speechless, as Tom jogged up the drive towards the house. I'd been too slow. Too distracted. It was too late to say no now.

'It must be nice having Tom back in your life,' Kate said.

My gaze shifted to her face, and I realised that she was also watching Tom retreat into the house. 'Yeah, it's just like old times,' I replied, feeling a familiar prickle of jealousy.

She turned towards me. 'Well, if you ever get tired of him,' she winked, 'send him my way.'

I ground my teeth together. Why did everyone always want to take him from me?

'I'd better get going,' I said, smiling sweetly. 'Tom's taking *me* out to dinner.'

I flicked my hair over my shoulder as I flounced into the house. But the lightness of my step was fake and forced, as annoyance weighed down on me. I was tired of having to fight for what was mine.

I hesitated as I reached the front door. Was I being too harsh? Was I judging her by my own standards? Tom being in a relationship with someone else hadn't stopped me. But was Kate the same?

Or, like Hannah, was she better than me too?

'Great, thanks very much,' Tom said into his phone as I closed the front door behind me. 'The restaurant is booked,' he said, turning to me.

'Won't a Friday night be a little bit busy to go out?'

'It'll be fun.'

'Yeah.' I hesitated. 'I guess.'

'Unless you don't want to go to dinner with me?' I could see from Tom's hurt expression that he'd expected more enthusiasm from me.

Was it just the thought of going out that made me apprehensive? Or was there more to it?

Seeing Kate flirting with Tom had distracted me from the doubts that Rebecca had raised. But that didn't mean they had dissipated.

Had I dared Hannah, or had Tom? Who should I believe?

Tom had told me it was me that day, whereas Rebecca's memory had had ten years to blur and distort the facts. Was her recollection reliable after all this time?

But if Rebecca was right, then it cast doubt on everything about that night. Was I not the villain that Tom had portrayed me as?

And if I wasn't, then what did that mean about Tom...? I studied him, searching his face for any trace of deception. But he seemed the same as he always had. Just Tom. My Tom.

I was so close to getting everything I'd ever wanted. If I allowed Rebecca's dislike of Tom to jade my view of him, it would be the undoing of everything. Not just our fledgling relationship, but of me too.

I couldn't let that happen.

I wouldn't.

I banished Rebecca's comments to the back of my mind, along with my own anxieties about going out. Having Tom in my life meant things would be different. Day trips and nights out. New foods. New routines.

It was normal.

It was what other people did.

And I wanted all of it.

'No, you're right, it will be good,' I added, forcing my voice to sound more upbeat.

Tom wrapped his arms around my waist and pulled me close. His lips met mine and I knew I'd made the right decision.

'Hmm, I could get used to coming home to this.'

'Me too,' Tom murmured as he nuzzled my neck. 'What could be better than going out on a Friday night, knowing I have the weekend to spend with my girlfriend?'

'Girlfriend?'

The word caught me by surprise. Tom hadn't even been back in my life a week and he was already calling me his girlfriend.

He pulled back, his gaze boring into me. 'Yeah, that's what you are, isn't it?'

He was right. That name fitted. It felt like clarity. We weren't just friends any more. We were partners. Boyfriend and girlfriend. A couple.

I belonged. For the first time in so long, I actually belonged.

I was his girlfriend.

And this time, I was the only one.

'Yes, of course.' My voice wavered.

'You don't sound very sure.'

'No, I am. I'm just slightly nervous.' I shook my head. Why had I admitted that? He didn't need to know.

'Really? Why?'

'I don't know,' I said. But it was a lie. I did know.

I was playing it safe, keeping him at a distance, afraid to risk the connection that still existed by taking our relationship further. I was in denial about how much I felt for him because I was afraid I couldn't keep him. Afraid that despite my defence of him and my determination to believe in him, there was still a chance, albeit a tiny one, that Tom might not be entirely trustworthy.

'Don't be nervous. We're going to be great together.'

'Yeah, absolutely. Really great.'

'Are you trying to convince yourself?'

I laughed. 'Possibly.' My laughter died away. 'It's just, I got hurt once before.'

'Things are different now, Lizzie. We're different.' He paused. 'I promise.'

I nodded. Things were different. We were different. This time it was just us. I'd waited ten years for this moment. I wasn't about to throw it all away because of a little fear.

'Okay.' I let out a deep breath. My response felt too short, too simple for the significance it carried. I'd just agreed to be his girlfriend. That one word had the power to change everything. For the better. Or possibly for the worse.

52

'Do you miss London?' I asked Tom as we walked along the beach watching the sun set. It had been Tom's idea after we'd left the restaurant.

'Where did that come from?'

I shrugged. 'I was just wondering. I love Bournemouth, but I know it's not what you're used to any more.' I tried to pass my question off as idle curiosity, but the reality was I was worried that Bournemouth didn't hold enough allure to keep him here.

That I didn't hold enough allure.

'Bournemouth is amazing. I love just being able to walk a little and be at the beach.'

'Yeah, it's pretty cool, isn't it?' I agreed, watching the orange glow on the horizon. I was so lucky to live so close. And yet, I'd been to the beach more times today than I had in months. I was so locked in my own world, in my own home, that I didn't fully appreciate what I had on my doorstep.

I took a deep breath of the salty air and resolved to come here more often. It would do me good to get out more. And today was proof that I could do it. I just had to keep the momentum going and not slide back into my comfortable old reclusive ways.

'People in London think of the beach only as somewhere you go for summer holidays,' Tom said, laughing. 'It's nice to live here again.'

'Live here?' My head jolted to the left to stare at him as we walked side by side.

He shrugged. 'You know what I mean, it's good to visit.'

'But you said live.' My heart rate quickened.

'Just a slip, it didn't mean anything.'

'Are you sure? You called Kate *our* neighbour earlier. And you don't seem to be in any hurry to go home.'

Why was I questioning him? Why didn't I give him space and let things develop naturally? It was good that he liked Bournemouth enough to talk about living here, even if it was unintentional. I wanted him to stay, not just in Bournemouth, but with me.

And yet, even though I wanted it, there was still a lingering seed of doubt that Rebecca had planted.

What if he'd lied?

'I'm between places at the moment.'

I frowned. 'What does that mean?'

'My lease ended and I haven't got around to finding somewhere new.'

'You haven't got around to finding somewhere to live?' I stared at him, my jaw hanging open. Somewhere to live was a basic need. It was important. Critically. It wasn't something you simply didn't get around to. It was a priority. *The* priority.

'The thing is, I travel so much that my apartment never really felt like home anyway. It was just somewhere I stayed occasionally. So when the lease ended it felt like a good opportunity to cut my ties for a little while.'

I swallowed and lowered my eyes. Was I a tie? One he would cut loose when he got bored?

'But that was before.'

My gaze darted up and our eyes met.

Tom reached for my hand. His thumb stroked my palm. 'I never had anything to stay in one place for. Until now.'

I smiled as my heart raced. I was a reason to stay. But despite my excitement, fear niggled at me. It was too soon.

Wasn't it?

He hadn't even been back a week and he was already calling me his girlfriend and talking about us as though we had a future together.

It was what I wanted. What I'd always wanted. But shouldn't we take our time? Get to know each other again?

'Maybe we should think about getting a place together.'

I halted abruptly. 'Together?' He said it so lightly, as though discussing which takeout to order. But what he was suggesting was huge.

It was one thing to tolerate him in my home, my space, for a few days, but if we bought a place together it would be permanent. He would always be present.

I'd spent ten years wishing for this very outcome, but now that it was here, I felt cornered. Trapped. I was fighting against myself. My desires conflicted with my fears. I couldn't resolve both. One way or another I was going to lose. Tom turned back. 'Don't you want that?'

'I... I already have a house.' I didn't need to move. I didn't want to. My home was my haven from the world around me. I was safe there. I could cope.

He chuckled. 'You have your parents' house.'

There was something patronising about the way he said it. 'I own it, Tom. It's mine,' I said defensively. I resented his implication that my home wasn't good enough.

'That doesn't really make it better. You need your own place. *Our* own place.'

Ours.

There was something appealing about that. I was part of something. An us.

And yet at the same time the idea of it made me nauseous. Perhaps it was just because his suggestion was so unexpected. So sudden. It always took me a while to adjust to any changes. I was a creature of habit. There was safety in the known; the familiar.

I just needed time for the idea to soak in.

But somehow that didn't quieten the voice in my head that was telling me it was too soon.

'A new place would be a fresh start,' Tom continued. 'Away from all the memories and mistakes.'

A vice gripped my stomach at the reminder of the past. For a moment, I had actually forgotten about my mistake and what it had led to.

'Somewhere new. Somewhere exciting.'

'N-new?' My breathing quickened. Even if I was able to find the courage to sell my home and buy somewhere new, I didn't want to leave Bournemouth.

I couldn't.

'It's a fresh start, remember? We can't do that here with Hannah's memory constantly haunting us.'

He said her name so casually. So dismissively. As though she hadn't mattered. Her death hadn't mattered.

'She should haunt us. We treated her so badly,' I reminded him.

'Some of us worse than others.' Tom's words were like a punch to my stomach. He was right, of course. He'd cheated on her, whereas I'd killed her.

Our betrayal, our guilt, wasn't in the same league.

'But that was ten years ago, Lizzie. We can't live in the past forever. Hannah wouldn't want us to.'

I stared at him silently. What would Hannah want? Not this surely? Not Tom and I reunited. Not me moving on; being happy.

I didn't deserve it.

Not when I'd stolen it all from her.

53

I slid my key into the lock and pushed open the front door. I was home.

I stepped inside and paused, waiting for that familiar sensation of safety and calmness to wash over me.

But it didn't come.

'What are you dawdling there for?' Tom asked behind me, giving me a gentle nudge out of the way.

Was Tom the reason why my home didn't feel the same? Why it didn't feel safe. Comforting.

I kicked off my shoes and walked into the kitchen, unable to look at him. I couldn't risk him seeing my expression and reading my thoughts. I couldn't let him see my doubts. My fears.

I picked up the broom and started sweeping the kitchen floor. It wasn't even dirty. I knew it, but I couldn't stop. I didn't want to stop. The therapist had called my cleaning habits a safe behaviour, something I defaulted to when I was stressed. An attempt to make me feel more in control. More secure. I could cope with stress better if everything around me was calm and orderly.

I needed that now: the calmness, the clarity. Tom's suggestion for us to move in together had destabilised me. I needed to regain my balance. My centre.

'You're cleaning again?'

I heard the disapproval in his voice.

'I like it. It's soothing.'

'Soothing?'

He didn't get it. He couldn't. To him, cleaning was a chore. Something to be put off until absolutely necessary. It was tedious and inconvenient. He didn't understand the therapeutic feel of it. The sense of control that came with bringing order to chaos.

'It makes me feel safe.'

Tom stared at me. 'You don't feel safe normally?'

'I'm always on edge.' I swallowed. Had I just said that aloud? My eyes met Tom's and I could see from his stunned expression that I had. 'It's like my body and mind are constantly on high alert.' Why was I still talking? Trying to explain it was only making it worse. I was making myself sound crazier.

My shoulders slumped. I was crazy.

I'd wanted to help him understand, but instead I'd revealed too much.

'Even with me?'

There was a quiet undertone to his voice; I'd hurt him.

Deny it.

The command sprang into my head, forceful and loud. I couldn't let him know how confused and afraid he made me. It would crush him. It would ruin everything that we were starting to rebuild.

'Sometimes.' The confession slipped out. Despite my intention to lie, the truth was stronger. It was Rebecca's fault.

Didn't you get tired of all the lies last time?

Her voice was my conscience.

This time I would do better.

I would *be* better.

'I didn't realise you felt that way.' I could feel the disappointment radiating from him. He'd thought we were in a good place. That we were connected and strong.

I'd let him think that.

'It's not you,' I told him quickly. I couldn't let him think it was his fault. 'It's just me. How I am. How I've become.'

Tom snorted. 'Isn't that what people say when they are dumping someone? It's not you, it's me.'

'I'm not dumping you.' Despite my doubts, my fears, the one thing I knew for certain was that I didn't want to lose him.

I couldn't.

I needed him too much.

'I have agoraphobia.' I lowered my gaze, unable to meet his eyes while I waited for his reaction. The truth was out there now.

'Isn't that a fear of open spaces? But we were just walking on the beach and you were fine.' I could hear his confusion. What I was telling him didn't add up against what he thought he knew.

I shook my head. 'No, agoraphobia isn't just about open spaces. It's about feeling like you need to escape.'

Tom shrugged. 'Isn't there like treatment or something for that kind of stuff?'

I flinched.

That kind of stuff.

His wording felt dismissive. He didn't understand the magnitude. He didn't understand how it felt. How *I* felt.

It had been foolish of me to hope that he would. It wasn't fair to expect that from him. He'd never been there. Never experienced it.

I shouldn't have told him.

'I saw a therapist for it when it first started.'

Perhaps Rebecca was right. Perhaps I should go back to the therapist. But how could I? It would be like going backwards.

Admitting that no matter how far I pretended I'd come in the last ten years, I hadn't really gone anywhere at all.

Besides, the therapist I'd seen before had done all she could for me. I would just be wasting everyone's time.

'It's not as bad now. It's manageable. I can keep it in check. I can go out.' I was downplaying it. Trying to make it sound like it was no big deal.

But it was a big deal.

It was my life.

My being.

The anxiety was always with me. Always present.

Even when I felt okay, I would find myself checking for signs of it. The absence of anxiety didn't make me feel better; if anything, it made me more anxious. It meant I'd missed something. The anxiety kept me safe. I needed it. It was like an addiction. One I wanted to give up, but one I couldn't live without. I was trapped in an unending loop. Not even therapy could break me free from it.

Therapy only works if you work at it.

Rebecca's words sprang to mind. Was that what I'd done wrong before? I hadn't really committed. I hadn't really tried. I'd skirted around the details of what had happened to trigger the panic attacks. I'd been so desperate to keep my secrets that I hadn't let the therapist know the whole story. I hadn't told her how bad it felt. How desperate it made me. And yet, I'd still expected her to cure me.

'This is why I'm here, why I came back. Because you need me,' Tom said.

My head jolted up and I stared at him. 'But how could you know that?'

'Because I know you.'

My heart soared. He did know me. He wasn't judging me for what I'd told him. He might not fully understand it, but he'd accepted it. Accepted me. Despite what I'd done in the past and who I'd become in the present, he still wanted to be with me.

'You've always been fragile. You always needed me to look out for you,' Tom said.

His words caught me off guard. Was he right? Had I always been weak? I thought it was repercussions of carrying the guilt of what I'd done. But was there more to it?

Perhaps so. Maybe that was why I'd done what I did. My weakness. My fear.

'But you don't need to worry now. I'm back and everything is going to be okay.'

He wrapped his arms around me and I clung to him. He was right. He was here now. I was safe. Everything was going to be okay. *I* was going to be okay.

I'd done the right thing by telling Tom. He didn't need to know everything. But enough for him to understand. We were moving in together, starting a life together; he needed to know what he was getting into. It was right to be honest with him.

There was hope now. Recovery. Normality.

'Lizzie?' Tom whispered in my ear. 'Let's get married.'

54

'M-married?' I must have misheard him. Tom couldn't have just asked me to marry him.

'Yes.' He was so certain. So adamant.

I pulled back to look at him. 'We can't.'

'Why not?'

'Because...' A thousand reasons raced through my mind, but they were all drowned out by one thought. Tom would be mine.

'I guess I can't blame you for hesitating,' Tom said sadly. 'I let you down before. It was my fault. I should have been stronger. Braver. I should have ended it with Hannah. I should never have let you feel like you were second place to her. I should have shown you that you were the one I wanted; that you had nothing to be jealous of Hannah for; that you didn't need to do what you did.'

'I didn't mean to.' My voice wobbled. Rebecca had made me start to question it, to doubt if I could really have hurt Hannah, but hearing Tom confess his sorrow at knowing he was the reason behind it made me more certain. Tom knew what he'd seen. He knew what I'd done.

'It took me a long time to find the courage to come back and face you, to look you in the eyes; knowing that what you'd done, you did because of me. You did it *for* me. To be loved that strongly, that much, it was,' Tom hesitated, 'overpowering. I was afraid for you. Afraid that I was no good for you. That I didn't deserve you.'

He thought he didn't deserve me? No, he had it backwards. It was me who had never deserved him. Wasn't it?

'But being apart from you wasn't the solution. Not for me. And not for you either. It's tough to live a life where you're not happy, but maybe it's also a way of protecting yourself.'

My eyes widened as I stared at him. 'How can being unhappy be a way of protecting myself?'

'You keep yourself stuck to avoid taking chances. You stay in a bad situation because at least you know how to handle that.'

'That's...' I wanted to object, but I couldn't find an argument.

'Different is scary. Different means you have to make a decision for yourself. Take a chance. Risk failure.' Tom shrugged. 'It's easier to tell yourself that you're not good enough. Not strong enough. Not well enough. It would fail. You would fail. So you're better off staying where you are. Unhappy but safe.'

I drew back.

Could he actually be right?

Perseverance and determination were my strengths, but perhaps they were also my weaknesses. I tackled every obstacle, so desperate not to fail that I worked like mad to succeed. But what if they were the wrong obstacles? What if the reason they were so difficult was because I was focusing my energy on the wrong things?

My solution to everything had always been to keep going and get over it. Until Tom had come back into my life. He'd been my circuit breaker. He'd made me think differently and opened my eyes. He'd given me hope.

'But now I'm with you. You're not alone any more.'

It sounded so simple. So easy. Like flicking a switch and making everything okay again. Could it be?

'I love you.'

My heart raced. They were the words I'd waited more than ten years to hear. I'd longed for him to love me, even before we'd kissed. Those words were everything. And yet... 'How can you? After what I've done. How I've become.'

Why was I trying to chase him away? Why didn't I just stay quiet? He didn't need to know what my life had become. What I had become. I should have just said 'I love you too'. It was the truth. It had always been the truth. No matter what else had changed, what else I'd lost, I'd always loved Tom.

'I've seen you at your best and at your worse. And I've loved you through all of it.'

I fought to keep my balance as the room swayed around me.

He loved me. He really loved me.

That was enough.

Wasn't it?

'So, what do you say? Will you marry me?' Tom asked again.

He was waiting for an answer. I owed him that. He'd put his heart out there. He was vulnerable and exposed. All he needed from me was one little word: yes.

I opened my mouth, intending to say it. But the word wouldn't come.

I'd spent years missing him. Wishing he was here. With me. It was my dream. My hope. My fantasy. I'd have given anything to achieve it.

And now, it was my reality.

Tom was here. He was part of my world. My life.

So why wasn't I happy? Why, of all things, did I crave space from him? Time alone? Independence?

I wanted to reclaim my home. My life. I wanted to feel free. I wanted space to move. To stretch. To breathe.

And yet, I was never free. Even before Tom's arrival my home had been more of a cage than a retreat. So what made me think him leaving would make it revert to something it had never been in the first place?

It was illogical.

How could I ever find happiness, if the one thing that should bring me joy, only brought me more turmoil and more anxiety?

Was the dream broken, or was I?

'We'd be great together,' Tom said, taking my hand in his. 'We are great together. Don't you feel it?'

I nodded instinctively. It was what he expected. What he needed from me.

But if I was honest, I didn't feel it.

I wanted to. I should. But I didn't.

Was I that incapable of love? Of togetherness? Of commitment? Had I fallen too far for even Tom to save me?

I'd thought he was my chance. My only chance. He knew my darkness. He knew my crime. But he'd protected me. He'd come back for me. But even he wasn't enough.

He was here. The future I'd dreamed of was back within reach. More so than it had ever been in the past. We were closer now. There was no Hannah to come between us. No one to share his attention with. No one to distract him. To take him away from me.

I should be relieved.

I should be happy.

Instead, I just felt restless. Wrong.

Was it the anxiety playing tricks on my mind again? Making me search for a danger that didn't exist? Making me doubt? Making me scared?

Or was happiness out of reach? Was I too broken to feel it? To know it?

Perhaps it was the way it should be. I didn't deserve it. It shouldn't be mine. It should have been Hannah's.

I'd learnt to wear a smile on my face as though it was part of my makeup. If I smiled enough, no one looked deeper. No one questioned it.

But I knew better than anyone, that appearances could be deceptive.

I hid what I'd done. Who I'd become. I was so far from the girl I used to be.

I'd thought having Tom back in my life could help me find her again. Help me to be her.

But then, had she been real, either?

Maybe at one point, when I was younger. When I'd known my own mind, had my own dreams. But somewhere along the way, my dreams had merged with Tom's. He'd chosen our uni. He'd chosen our path. We were an 'us' before ever being a couple.

I sought his approval. I trusted his opinion. I relied on him. Had he become too strong, or had I become weak?

It wasn't as though he'd forced me to comply. He never raised his voice, never threatened me. And yet, somehow there never seemed to be an option. Tom was always right. It was as simple as that.

But there were moments when I doubted him. Moments when my fragmented memories showed details that conflicted with his version of events. But out of the two of us I was hardly the most reliable one.

'Can I think about it?'

Tom's expression changed. It was as though his emotions shut down. That happy gaze, full of admiration, dulled in an instant. 'Of course. Take all the time you need.' His words were right. Appropriate. They were what I needed to hear. But they sounded wrong. Flat. Empty.

He hadn't expected that response from me.

I could tell from his demeanour that he'd been confident I would say yes. After all, when had I ever said no to Tom before?

55

'We're out of milk,' Tom said as he drained the last few drops into his cereal bowl on Saturday morning.

'I'll pop it on the grocery order,' I told him as I reached for the remaining slices of the loaf of bread. I'd have toast for my breakfast then.

'But the delivery isn't coming until Monday evening.'

'We can manage,' I said with a shrug.

Tom drummed his fingers on the table. 'You're just trying to avoid going to the supermarket.'

I froze.

Perhaps it had been foolish to confide in him after all. Now that he knew about my agoraphobia, he knew when I was hiding.

'You should go.'

You.

My stomach somersaulted and I set the bread down on the worktop, my appetite instantly evaporating.

'We could go together.' I heard the hope in my voice. If he came with me it would be easier. We could chat on the bus ride. I wouldn't feel so isolated in the crowded store. He could distract me as we stood in the long queue, waiting to pay.

'Come on, Lizzie. You're a grown woman. You can handle going to the supermarket by yourself.' He paused. 'Can't you?'

It felt as if there was a taunt to his question. To say no would be to admit my weakness. My failure.

I nodded. 'Of course I can. I just didn't want to waste any of our precious time together by spending Saturday morning apart.'

'Hmm.' From his tone I could tell Tom knew I was lying. 'You'd best make a list of everything you need then.' He picked up his spoon and scooped up his Shreddies, the conversation clearly closed.

I swallowed. He knew how scared I was, but he was still going to make me do this. Alone.

I opened the fridge, obediently checking to see what else we were short of, but my gaze had no focus. My mind was racing. Going out to the Italian restaurant last night had been difficult, being with Tom was the only thing that made it possible. But now he wanted me to go out without him. Alone.

Any time I went out it was carefully planned. I allowed myself time to prepare. To psych myself up.

Until today.

Tom had caught me off guard. I wasn't spontaneous. I didn't go out unscheduled.

And yet, what choice did I have?

* * *

I hitched my shopping bag higher up on my shoulder and quickened my pace, eager to catch the bus so I could get home to Tom. Asda had been quieter than I'd expected for a Saturday morning and I'd managed to get in and out remarkably quickly. I cast a sideways glance at the half empty bag on my shoulder. Admittedly, part of my speed might also be due to the tiny amount of shopping I'd actually done.

Once I'd stepped into the store I'd felt so overwhelmed by its sheer size that I'd simply grabbed the essentials and hadn't even bothered to check my list to see what else I needed. Not that it mattered. Anything I'd missed could be added to the delivery for Monday. This wasn't really about doing a full grocery shop. This was about going to the store by myself. If I thought about it like that, then my feeble purchases were a complete success.

I smiled as I approached the bus stop. I felt calmer than I had when I'd left the house.

And then it hit me. That familiar wave of anxiety, like being doused in icy cold water. My excitement and optimism were instantly extinguished, replaced with an unnerving feeling of something being wrong.

But what?

I mentally scanned my senses, searching for the danger. My chest felt tight, but it wasn't too bad. I didn't feel nauseous. I wasn't freaking out. I was okay. I was...

My eyes widened as realisation dawned on me. That was it. It wasn't that something was wrong, it was that something was missing.

The anxiety welled up inside me, causing my heart to race and my palms to sweat. *Just keep walking*, I told myself. I had to keep walking. But each step was like wading through syrup, as my body fought against itself.

I'd be home soon. Everything would be fine. But every cell in my body screamed at me that something bad was about to happen. It was like a premonition, that unexplainable sense of danger. Like the sensation of knowing someone was watching me before I'd even seen them. I could sense it; the unseen; the unknown; the danger.

The anxiety that accompanied me in virtually every moment had been temporarily suspended. I hadn't been planning my journey. I hadn't been talking myself through it, persuading myself that I could do it.

And yet, now I felt it.

The absence of the anxiety itself was what was making me anxious.

It didn't make sense. I should be glad, elated even. It was a good thing. It was what I'd wanted for so long: to be normal, to be free.

But it felt ominous. I couldn't let my guard down. I couldn't forget. That was when things went wrong. The anxiety wasn't my enemy; it kept me safe, it protected me. It kept me away from bad situations. It kept me cautious, alert, controlled.

Yet even as I thought it, doubt crept into my mind. Did the anxiety keep me safe? Or did it just keep me trapped?

I knew what the therapist thought.

* * *

'The panic attacks are a signal that your body is on high alert. It's trying to protect you from danger. But often that danger doesn't really exist.'

'So how do I make them stop?'

'You have to teach your body to ignore the false signals. When you feel a panic attack coming on don't indulge it. Don't focus on it. Don't analyse your situation, your feelings, trying to identify the threat. Every thought you have that focuses on it simply feeds the anxiety. You're effectively telling your brain that it's right, that there is something wrong, something dangerous.'

'But how do I know that there isn't?'

'You have to have trust yourself to learn the difference. If there's no fire, no one chasing you, no speeding car hurtling towards you, you're probably just receiving false signals.'

'Trust myself?'

Those were two words that didn't belong together. They weren't compatible. They weren't achievable.

I was the one person who I absolutely couldn't trust.

* * *

I forced myself back into motion. I reached the bus stop and lingered away from the queue. By standing apart I still had options. I had an escape.

I watched the bus pull up in front of us and the queue of people shuffled forwards, congregating on top of each other, as though they were afraid of being left behind.

I waited until the last person was just about to step onto the bus. Decision time.

I couldn't delay it any longer. On or off. Stay or go.

I took a deep breath, pushed my shoulders back and stepped forwards. There had never been any doubt really. Not because I was stronger than my fear, but because there wasn't any other choice. To give in was a slippery slope. One I had been down before.

I tapped my phone to the terminal and found an empty row. I shuffled gratefully into the window seat.

Maybe it was a good thing that Tom hadn't come with me. He hadn't been here to witness my internal meltdown.

But then, if he'd been with me, maybe it wouldn't have happened at all.

56

'Everything's fine, Dad,' I heard Tom say as I pushed open the front door.

I bit back my hello, which I would usually call out, and crept in quietly. I didn't want to disturb him.

'It's just a job. I'll get another. I hated it anyway.'

I heard him sigh as I put my bag on the floor and started to close the door slowly.

'It'll all blow over. You know Davis has made a mistake. He's just looking for someone to blame. I'm gonna lay low for a litt—'

Tom stopped mid-sentence as the latch clicked.

'Hi,' I called automatically, feeling as though I was doing something bad, sneaking into my own home.

'Lizzie?'

'Yes, it's me.'

'I gotta go, Dad.' I heard his footsteps approaching from the kitchen before the door swung open. 'Why are you home so soon?' There was an edge to his voice. His question almost sounded like a demand.

'Sorry, I...' I hesitated. Had I just apologised for coming home early? To my own home? I shook my head. 'I finished my shopping so I came home.'

'Hmm,' Tom grunted. 'You could have called.'

'Why?' My voice reflected my bewilderment. Why would I call to let him know I was coming home earlier than expected? Later, maybe. But even then, it wasn't as though he actually lived here. I didn't owe him an explanation of my movements and my schedule.

Except I couldn't help wondering if my objection was really about his prying, or the fact I was feeling guilty about having come back without half the groceries. I might think of my shopping trip as a success, but would Tom?

'I-I,' Tom stuttered. 'I could have met you at the bus stop. I could have given you a hand with your bags.' His words were rambling and stumbling into each other.

Now he wanted to help me with the shopping? He hadn't seemed bothered about me carrying it when he sent me off alone.

The unsettled feeling that had been weighing on me since my conversation with Rebecca intensified.

Something was off.

Bile rose in my throat. I'd been here before. This uncertainty. This doubt. This fear.

I'm going to leave her, just give me a little more time.

I'd felt it then too. That fear that he was lying. That he wouldn't leave her. That he wouldn't pick me.

Perhaps that was why I hadn't waited. Why I'd taken matters into my own hands.

I have a plan. A way for us to be together. Just you and me.

'What was your plan?'

Deep lines ceased Tom's brow. 'What plan?'

There was a nervousness to his voice. Tiny, almost unnoticeable, but it was there.

'The day before Hannah died, you said you had a plan. A way to leave her but keep your job, your career. What was it?'

'Oh, that.' His frown passed instantly. He looked almost relieved.

My chest tightened. Why would he look relieved? 'What plan did you think I meant?'

Tom chuckled. 'If you must know, I was on the phone planning a surprise for you.'

'For me?'

'Of course for you. Who else would it be for?'

Kate.

Her name sprang into my mind and I shook my head, trying to shake it away. I hadn't heard much of his conversation, but I knew there was no surprise. Not for me, not for Kate. And yet, she niggled in my thoughts.

Just as Hannah used to.

Present.

Lingering.

Ominous.

'So, what was it?'

'The plan at uni?'

I nodded.

'It was, er...' Tom shrugged. 'It was ten years ago. I can't remember every tiny thing I thought about doing ten years ago.'

'But this wasn't a tiny thing. It was important. It was the key to us being together. That's what you said.'

'Yeah, it was. But it's irrelevant now. You were so jealous. You didn't want to wait any longer. Your impatience destroyed us. It destroyed everything.'

The air felt heavy as my breathing quickened.

My jealousy was a side of myself that I feared. I had no control over it. It made me impulsive. Reckless. Dangerous.

I could feel it tingling inside me even now. Hannah was gone but I was still jealous of the hold she'd had over Tom. She'd captivated him in a way that I never had. Never would.

Seeing him with Kate had reignited that part of me. That voice in my head that told me I would never be good enough for Tom. There would always be someone else. Someone like Hannah.

Like Kate...?

He was right, my jealousy had cost us. It had ruined everything once before. I had to get it under control, or it might do so again.

'I'll make us a cup of tea,' Tom said as he turned and walked away.

I stared after him. He'd avoided the question. I still didn't know what his plan had been.

Cold dread seeped thought my veins. Had there ever really been a plan? Or had he just been stalling? Lying to me?

If Tom had lied about that, what else had he lied about?

Was Rebecca right? Was it Tom who'd dared Hannah to climb Durdle Door? Had he made a mistake? Or had he lied?

We'd all lied about so much that day. How could I be sure what was true any more?

* * *

'And you didn't notice that Hannah was missing?'

I sat on the sofa between Tom and Rebecca, my hands clenched together in my lap as the police officer studied us one by one.

'We didn't wake up until quite late this morning. We'd had a bit to drink last night,' Tom said. 'When I got up, I just thought Hannah must have gone for a walk on the beach.'

I dug my nails into my flesh, praying that the police officer believed his explanation.

'So you don't know what time she left?' the second officer behind him asked.

Tom shook his head.

'And when you did realise she was gone, were you concerned about her going off alone?'

'Hannah's a free spirit. She's very independent. Very capable.'

'Even when she's been drinking?'

'She's a bigger drinker than us,' Rebecca added. 'We were pretty wasted last night, but she seemed fine. Just the same as she always was.'

'Do you know what happened to her?' Luke asked from where he was standing by the window, a little removed from the rest of us.

From our lie.

'Her injuries are consistent with impact, typically from falling from some height.'

I turned away as my stomach lurched.

'We've had a few instances of people tombstoning off the top of Durdle Door.'

'What's that?' Luke asked.

'Thrill seekers jumping from something high into the water. It often results in substantial injuries. If not death. Were any of you thinking about doing that? Was Hannah?'

We shook our heads in unison. It was the first honest response we'd made. None of us had planned to jump. Not even Hannah.

'She never mentioned it. But she's adventurous. She loves a challenge,' Tom said. I could hear the pride in his words. He admired her. More than he'd ever admired me.

'I mean, she loved a challenge.' Tom's voice cracked as he corrected the present tense to the past.

Hannah was gone. I had to keep reminding myself of that too. It still didn't seem possible.

One minute she was here and then next she wasn't.

'Any thoughts on what else she might have been doing up there?'

None of us spoke.

'Did she seem troubled at all?'

'You think she could have jumped on purpose?' I surprised myself with my question. I hadn't intended to speak. I hadn't dared to. But his questions gave me hope. Tombstoning. Suicide. There were other possibilities. Other explanations.

Besides the truth.

'We're just trying to get a full picture of what she was like. What might have been going through her mind. Why she might have climbed up the rocks while all of you slept.'

'She was so vibrant. So full of life,' Tom said wistfully. 'It doesn't seem possible to think of her choosing to take her own life. But,' he sucked in a deep breath, 'I know she was troubled.'

'In what way?'

'Things with her family were complicated,' I replied, seizing on this train of thought. 'I don't think she really wanted to be at uni, at least, not doing event management. That was her dad's dream for her. Not her own.'

I caught Tom's surprised expression. He hadn't expected me to be so observant, at least, not about Hannah. He didn't know that in my own quiet way I noticed things. Understood things. He'd underestimated me.

Perhaps we all had.

57

'I'll be right back,' I said before climbing the stairs to the bathroom. I closed the door, shutting out the sound of the kettle boiling in the kitchen.

My thoughts whirled chaotically.

Tom had avoided answering my question. But was it realistic that he could have forgotten what his plan was? Surely, the plan that had been so crucial to everything was too important to slip from his mind.

Unless there had never been a plan.

I kept coming back to that thought. That fear. I tried to block it out. To banish it from my mind. But I couldn't.

It felt disloyal to doubt Tom. Because I knew I wasn't just doubting his memory, I was doubting everything.

Had he ever really wanted to be with me?

Memories from ten years ago bubbled to the surface, fighting for attention.

* * *

'I'll come with you,' I said to Tom as we followed Luke and Rebecca to the cars. The journey back to home would give us time to talk. Time to plan what was going to happen next.

Things hadn't gone the way they were supposed to, but, at least, he was finally free of Hannah. Free to be with me.

'It's not a good idea,' Tom said, shaking his head.

'Why not?'

'We can't be seen together right now. It's too risky,' he said. 'For you,' he added quickly.

'He's right, Lizzie. You'd be better off coming back with Luke and I,' Rebecca said, linking her arm through mine.

'But I want to be with Tom.'

'We don't always get what we want, Lizzie.' There was a patronising tone to Tom's voice. He reminded me of Hannah. Condescending. Belittling. 'We'll need to take some time apart. I need to focus on cleaning up your mess.'

I flinched and drew closer to Rebecca.

'It's the only way to keep you safe,' Tom added, his tone softer this time. 'We have to be careful. We have to keep quiet about Hannah. About us.' He shrugged slightly. 'No one can know.'

* * *

Had he been trying to keep me safe, or had he been lying to me?

Tom's version of events conflicted with Rebecca's. How could I know who to believe? Who to trust? The simplest explanation was that Rebecca was mistaken. Ten years was a long time to remember things exactly. Especially such a small detail.

I should let it go. It didn't matter.

Except, for some reason, it did.

There was one other person who knew what had happened: Luke.

He was impartial and independent. He was the deciding vote.

I rummaged in my pocket for my phone and called Rebecca. 'I need Luke's phone number,' I said, as soon as she answered.

'Er, hello to you too.' She laughed.

'Sorry, hi,' I apologised for my rudeness. 'But it's important.' I kept my voice low. I couldn't risk being overheard.

'I don't have it.'

No, that couldn't be right. 'You still talk, though. You knew he'd moved to Winchester.'

'We're part of the same Facebook group. I see his posts sometimes.'

'That's all?'

'We haven't spoken since we broke up. Why the sudden eagerness to talk to him all of a sudden?'

I hesitated. Would Rebecca be offended that I wanted to check her story with him? That I didn't just trust her? 'I, er, wanted to ask him about the dare.'

'You mean who dared Hannah?'

'Yes.' There was no point denying it. It wasn't as though I had any other reason to contact Luke after all these years.

'So, you admit it's possible that I might be right?'

I blinked. She didn't sound offended. In fact, she sounded kind of smug. 'Maybe.'

'Well, this is new.'

'What do you mean?'

'You're finally starting to doubt Tom.'

'No, I'm...' My objection died on my lips. I was doubting him. If I was honest with myself, part of me always had. I'd never fully believed he would leave Hannah for me. I'd never completely trusted his sudden reappearance. But I wanted to. I wanted to so badly that I'd tried to bury my doubts, just like I'd tried to bury my mistakes.

If I ignored them for long enough, maybe they would disappear. Maybe they wouldn't be real.

'I wish I could help,' Rebecca said. 'But truthfully, even if I had his number, I don't think he'd actually talk to you.'

My shoulders sagged. 'Possibly not.' I'd got so caught up in the idea, that I hadn't fully thought it through. Rebecca was right. Luke was hardly likely to talk to me. Not when he blamed me for the way things had turned out.

And yet, despite that, I knew I still had to try.

Ten years of gritting my teeth to get through each day had taught me one thing: determination. I didn't give in at the first hurdle. I couldn't.

I said a hasty goodbye to Rebecca and opened Facebook. I typed Luke's name into the search box and scrolled through the results. I perched on the side of the bath as I squinted at one of the tiny images. Could it be him?

I opened the profile and smiled as I scrolled through the photos he had uploaded. He always did love selfies.

I checked his about info.

Studied at Arts University Bournemouth.

My right knee bounced up and down as I studied the screen. Finding Luke had been the easy part. Getting him to talk to me was going to be much trickier.

There wasn't a phone number or email address in his about info. That left me with only one option. I clicked the message button and stared at the empty message box.

I drew in a deep breath and held it for a moment before releasing it. We hadn't spoken since our trip to Durdle Door.

* * *

'I can't believe I actually agreed to go along with this,' Luke grumbled as he drove Rebecca and me back towards Bournemouth.

I stared out of the window, watching the passing cars. I wished I was in one of those cars. It didn't matter where they were coming from, or going to. Anywhere was better than where I was.

'Hannah's dead, Luke. It makes no difference if we tell the police we were there,' Rebecca said.

'It does if it wasn't an accident.' I could hear the fear buried beneath his anger.

'Hannah fell,' Rebecca insisted.

'We don't know that.' I turned back and my gaze met his as Luke glared at me through the rear-view mirror. 'You heard what Tom said,' Luke added.

I turned away. He thought I could have pushed her. He thought I could have killed her.

I wished Tom was with me. I needed him here. I needed to feel his hand wrapped around mine. I needed to know that we were going to be okay.

'Just 'cause Lizzie and Hannah were arguing, it doesn't mean Lizzie pushed her off the top of an arch. She wouldn't. She couldn't.'

Silence engulfed us.

'What did Tom say to you to make you change your mind?' I asked Luke.

'Nothing.'

Rebecca twisted in her seat, pulling her seat belt out of the way, so she could face him. 'Lizzie's right, you were ready tell the police everything, until Tom whispered something to you. What did he say?'

'It was just some rubbish about friends sticking together.'

'That's it?'

'It's Tom. He can be persuasive.'

Rebecca grunted an agreement.

We all knew it was true. Tom could be very persuasive when he *wanted something. But although Luke's words made sense, something about his manner still felt off.*

I'd seen his face as Tom whispered to him before the police came to ask us questions. Luke's expression hadn't shown grudging acceptance and solidarity. He'd looked scared.

It was almost as though he was more afraid of Tom than the police.

* * *

I drummed my fingers against the phone. Rebecca was right, Luke wouldn't want me back in his life. A message from me would be easy to block. I was too much of a threat to him for him to view me as a friend.

Or perhaps, that was exactly what I needed him to think. I needed him to be too scared to ignore me. I needed him to want to talk to me to find out what I was going to do.

We need to talk. I've being thinking a lot about that night.

Remembering it.

Reliving it.

It's time the truth finally came out.

I hit send.

That should get his attention.

58

I walked back into the kitchen and lingered by the door.

'Your cup of tea's ready,' Tom said, nodding to the mug on the kitchen table.

'Thanks.' I picked it up and held it in my hands, clinging to its warming comfort. I wasn't sure what to say, or how to act. How could I pretend that everything was normal between us when I'd just sent a message to Luke?

Guilt chafed against me. I was checking up on Tom. Checking his version of events. I was doubting him.

'Are you okay?' he asked, eyeing me dubiously.

'I'm fine.'

He shook his head, and I knew that he hadn't fallen for the lie.

'No, you're not. And I know why.'

My stomach lurched.

'I thought me coming back would be enough to help you, but now I realise that it's not. The past is too big for that. Its burden is too heavy.'

'What are you saying?' Was he going to leave? Did he think that was what I wanted? Or had he given up on me? Was I beyond help? Beyond redemption?

'We all have to accept responsibility for our actions. We have to face our own demons or they will eat away at us. Never allowing us to truly move forward.'

He was right. I had carried the secret for too long. It had chipped away at me for years, eating into my life, my soul.

'I can see how much the past still weighs on you, Lizzie,' Tom continued. 'It's like you stopped living. You're frozen here in this time warp. Living in your parents' house. Abandoning your dreams. Yourself.'

I swallowed. 'How can you see me so clearly?'

'I've always seen you, Lizzie. I see the amazing person that you are: tender, kind, smart and beautiful.'

Tears welled up in my eyes before trickling down my cheeks. I didn't even try to stop them. I couldn't. He was telling me all the things I longed to hear, but I didn't deserve them. Not from him. Not when I had so many doubts about him. About us.

'I know the last few years have been hard on you.'

I swallowed. 'Y-you do?'

He nodded slowly. 'I want us to be together. I want us to have a future together. But...'

I edged towards him. 'But what?' He'd changed his mind. Yesterday he'd asked me to marry him and today he'd given up on me.

I might not be ready to say yes, but did I really want him to leave?

'I'm not sure you're ready for that. I'm not sure you will ever be ready until you face the past. Face what you did.'

'What are you saying?'

'I was wrong that day. I thought I was doing the best thing for you. I thought I was protecting you. But all our lie did was trap you in the past. You'll never be free of your guilt until you face your demons.' He reached for my hand and clasped it in his. 'You need to confess, Lizzie. It's time.'

'W-what?' I stared at Tom. He couldn't have said what I thought. It wasn't possible. Didn't he realise what that would mean? It would destroy me.

The room began to dip and sway and I struggled to breathe.

He was supposed to protect me. To love me. Not lock me away.

'I understand what I'm suggesting is hard. But that doesn't mean that you can't do it. You are so strong, Lizzie. You always have been. You've carried this secret alone for all these years, but it was too much. The only way to be free of it is to finally confess.'

'I can't.' I pulled my hand free from his. Didn't he realise what he was asking me to do? What it meant? 'We only just found each other again, and now you want to send me away?'

'I'm going to help you. I'll never leave you again, Lizzie.'

'If I confess, you wouldn't have a choice. We would be torn apart. They would lock me away. I'd lose everything.'

'You'd gain your self-respect. You'd be able to look at yourself in the mirror and recognise the woman you see.'

His words dug into my heart. It had been so long since I had liked the woman who stared back at me from the mirror. So long since I had felt like myself. Since I had felt good. Worthy.

'You won't be the only one who is hurt by the truth. I will lose too. But I'll willingly give up everything for you.'

'You lied to protect me, that's not the same as what I did.'

'Once my family know that I covered up your part in Hannah's death, they will never look at me the same way. And Davis,' Tom shook his head, 'he will make sure I never work in event management again. My career will be ruined. I'll be ruined. But I'll still have you.'

My head spun. He was willing to sacrifice everything for me. But his plan was flawed. 'I'll be in prison.'

'I'll hire the best lawyer money can buy. They'll make sure the court knows you weren't in your right mind. You were drunk. Desperate. It was a mistake. A momentary lapse of judgement. You would never hurt anyone intentionally.'

My fingers instinctively traced the scars on my left arm. Tom was wrong. I did have the capacity to hurt someone intentionally. All these years I'd told myself that it didn't matter. That I didn't matter. But perhaps it did.

Perhaps it was a sign that the darkness was still within me. I channelled it at myself. At least for now. But what if someone else crossed me one day? What if someone took a little too much interest in Tom? Someone like Kate...?

I could change my career, my address, my life, but no matter what I did I would never outrun the source of my problems. The past was like a ghost at my back, always with me but never really there. It gnawed at me like a dog at a bone, persistent, unwavering and undeterred.

I'd tried to ignore it; to sidestep it; to become someone new. But the one thing I had never done was face it. My past. My ghosts. My crime.

* * *

'You need to start practising self-care,' the therapist said.

I rolled my eyes at the term. It sounded so fluffy and self-indulgent.

'Self-care isn't all relaxation and pampering,' she said. "Yes, it can be a day at the spa, or getting your nails done. But it can also be about making tough choices, staying strong and not giving in to negative impulses. It can mean getting out of bed when you want to hide under the covers,

leaving the house when your body's telling you not to, not harming yourself even when the temptation is so strong.'

I tugged at my sleeves, instinctively protecting my scars. If she noticed, she didn't comment.

'Self-care isn't always easy and it won't always feel good. Making the right choice can be difficult and painful. The key is to learn to manage the destructive behaviours that can control your life.'

What she was suggesting was impossible. The darkness in me couldn't be managed. It couldn't be controlled. I wasn't strong enough.

'Sometimes the changes that take place over time, like a new job or finishing exams, help recovery. The sense of moving on can be enough to help some people stop. When that particular trigger and source of stress is removed, some people find that they don't need to self-harm as a coping method.'

* * *

I'd thought she was wrong. After all, I'd finished my exams, I'd left university, got a job, bought my own home, and nothing had changed.

But then those things weren't the source of my anxiety. They were just a symptom.

The source was Hannah.

It always came back to her.

'You're not alone. I'm here for you,' Tom said. 'I'll always be here for you. We will face it together. Whatever happens.'

No one can know.

Tom's command reverberated through me.

It had been my lifelong companion, my guiding light. Keeping me safe. Keeping me alone. Isolated.

Keeping me trapped.

Perhaps Tom was right. It was finally time.

59

'The train is now approaching Winchester.'

My grip tightened on the strap of my bag that rested on my lap, as the guard's voice boomed through the tannoy system.

I was here.

Winchester.

It was only an hour away but it was the farthest I'd been in years.

I hadn't expected Luke to demand that we meet in person. A phone call would have been easier. But he'd refused.

My boss had been surprised at my request to take another day of leave, especially at such short notice. But he'd obliged. Perhaps he could tell from my tone how desperate I was.

I glanced down at my phone and reread Luke's last message. It was only brief; just the time and place to meet. Perhaps it was crazy to make this trip based on so little. Especially when I had already decided to turn myself in.

Tom had arranged a meeting with the lawyer he'd found. Once I met with him, once I finally said the truth out loud, everything would change.

And yet for some reason, instead of spending my last few days of freedom organising my affairs and talking to my parents, I was making my first train trip in years just to ask one stupid question: Who dared Hannah to climb Durdle Door?

I wasn't even sure why it mattered. The dare wasn't what killed her. I was.

But there was something about the question that niggled at me. Maybe it was Rebecca's certainty that it was Tom. Or perhaps it was because it had never sat right with me that I would have even thought of the idea, let alone actually dared someone to do it.

Either way, I needed answers.

The passengers around me started to gather up their belongings and congregate in the narrow aisle.

I turned away and stared out of the window, unable to watch.

I'd done it. I'd caught the train. I'd stayed on it until my destination. In a few moments I'd finally be able to get off.

I'd be able to breathe.

At least momentarily.

Something told me the train journey wasn't going to be the hardest part of this trip.

The train pulled to a stop and the doors pinged. The crowd shuffled forwards, spilling out onto the already crowded platform beside us.

A space opened up in the aisle as the remaining passengers dwindled. I shuffled out of my seat and followed the queue.

I hesitated in the doorway as my gaze fell upon the swarm of people before me. I took a shaky breath and merged into the crowd. I was surrounded. Engulfed. They swept me along like the tide. I couldn't escape now. I would only be free when I reached my destination and the wave dissipated.

I pulled up the e-ticket on my phone as the crowd jostled me on our way to the platform exit. I scanned the image on the little screen and hurried through as the gates opened.

My gaze darted left and right, frantically searching for the way out. I didn't care which exit I took. I could figure out directions later. I just needed air. I needed space.

I spotted an arrow marked 'way out' and walked towards it as though it had an invisible pull over me. I was oblivious to everything else around me. I couldn't focus on the crowd. I felt dazed and disorientated, almost as though I was in a trance.

I was here. I was present.

But I wasn't.

Finally, I stepped outside. A sharp wind whipped around me, but I relished the feel of it against my skin. Cold. Fresh.

The crowd thinned out as everyone split off into different directions.

I opened Google Maps on my phone and typed in Chococo. I tapped for directions and a little blue route appeared. Thirteen minutes, the screen informed me.

I glanced at the clock even though I already knew I was early.

I'd caught an early enough train to allow myself plenty of time. But I still hurried down the busy streets, eager to reach my destination and grateful that at least it wasn't the weekend, when it would undoubtedly be even worse.

I paced back and forth outside the café, aware that I was starting to attract attention from the customers who were seated outside. I didn't need their curious stares watching my every move. I was already nervous enough as it was.

All the outdoor tables were taken, but through the window I could see an empty table just by the door. It would have to do. I felt too conspicuous to linger out here now, and I couldn't wander off further away and run the risk of missing Luke.

I joined the short queue and stared at the menu board above the counter. It had been a while since I'd been to a café.

'What can I get you?' the girl by the till asked me with a smile.

'Erm, a hot chocolate, please.'

'I'll bring it over,' she said as I paid.

I thanked her and retreated to my table in the window, to resume scanning all the faces that passed, searching for Luke.

'Here you go,' the waitress said as she placed the hot chocolate on the table in front of me. 'And there's one of our handcrafted sea salt caramel chocolates for you to try as well,' she added, indicating to the chocolate perched on the saucer beside my drink.

'Thank you,' I said, surprised by the extra little touch. I'd been eyeing the display of chocolates in the glass cabinet as I'd waited in the queue to be served. It was quite an unexpected treat to get to sample one.

I took a sip of the rich chocolate, and closed my eyes, savouring the flavour. It was delicious. I'd have to come here again, another time, when I wasn't so nervous about meeting Luke.

My eyes flew open. Had I really just thought that? Was I actually planning to come back?

Could I?

Coming here today had been a one-time thing. Hadn't it? I was on a mission to find out the truth from Luke. If he hadn't been so insistent that we meet in person, I would never have left Bournemouth.

And yet...

My knee jigged up and down as I checked my watch again. Luke was ten minutes late now. What if he'd changed his mind? What if he'd decided meeting me was too risky? What if I'd come all way for nothing?

What was I going to do? I couldn't wait around here all day. But how could I go home without any answers?

How would I even manage to get back on the train?

The only thing that had got me through the journey here was the simple fact that my fear of not uncovering the truth about Tom outweighed my fear of being on the train. But now...

The swoosh of the door opening caught my attention and I looked up to see a guy in his late twenties, wearing a tailored suit, surveying the tables.

His eyes met mine and I knew in an instant, despite all the years, that it was Luke.

'Lizzie?' Luke asked, and I nodded mutely.

He pulled the chair out opposite me.

'Do you want something to drink?' I asked, finding my voice and my manners.

'In a minute.' His voice was terse. 'First, I want to know what you're up to.'

I flinched, caught off guard by his hostility. Perhaps my message had been too forceful. But then it wasn't as though it was him who'd pushed Hannah. I was the one with the most to lose here.

Wasn't I?

'I'm not up to anything,' I said calmly. 'But I need your help.'

'Seriously? You as well?'

I frowned. 'As well as who?'

'Look, I'll tell you the same thing that I told Tom. I've—'

'Tom?' I cut through his words. 'Tom asked you for help?' My hot chocolate lay heavily in my stomach. Something felt wrong. Why would Tom ask Luke for help? What kind of help?

Luke sighed. 'Like I was saying; I told him I've moved on. I've made a life for myself. No thanks to any of you.'

'I know I screwed up, Luke. And I know I put you all in an

impossible situation covering for me. I never got a chance to tell you how grateful I was. How grateful I still am.'

'I didn't do it for you.'

'Then why did you do it?' It was a question that had circled in my brain for years. Luke had been so against the cover up. He'd wanted to turn me in. He'd believed I should be punished for what I'd done. And yet, he hadn't said anything. He'd gone along with the lie just like the rest of us.

'I did it because I was scared. We were drunk and stupid and getting caught up in that mess would have got us kicked out of AUB. It would have ruined our lives. Hannah was gone and us dealing with the fallout wasn't going to change that. But what we did was wrong and I've had to live with that every single day.'

I drew back as he hurled his words at me like rapid fire.

Luke leaned in across the table. 'So, like I said to Tom, stay away from me.'

'When did you tell him that?'

'What does it matter?'

'It just does, Luke. Please.'

'About a week ago. He showed up on my doorstep. I mean, can you believe the nerve of the guy? I haven't even seen him in years, and he just turns up at my house on a Sunday afternoon, uninvited.'

I gripped the table, desperate to hold on to something solid. 'S-Sunday?' my voice shook. 'A w-week ago?' Luke must be wrong. Tom arrived at my house that Sunday. He said I was his first stop. His priority.

But he didn't reach me until the late afternoon.

'Yeah, does that matter?'

I shook my head. But it did matter. It mattered a lot.

It meant Tom had lied.

'At least you had the decency to message. Not that there was anything decent about the wording of your message.'

'I needed to be sure you'd talk to me.'

Luke snorted. 'You always were good with words, weren't you?'

'Why did Tom come to see you?' I asked, moving the topic back. If Tom had lied to me about visiting Luke then there had to be a reason.

'He wanted a place to stay. He practically invited himself in, or, at least, he tried to.'

My heart raced as my temperature climbed.

'But you said no?'

'Of course I said no.'

The truth hit me like a punch in the gut. Tom had wanted to stay with Luke. I wasn't his first thought. I wasn't his plan. His priority. I was Tom's fall back. A place for him to stay when Luke had turned him away.

Was that all I'd ever been?

'His financial problems aren't my concern.'

I blinked. 'What financial problems?'

Luke snorted. 'His risky lifestyle finally caught up with him. He's broke, from what I gathered. Even had to hand his apartment over to pay off some of his debt.'

'But he rents his apartment. The lease ended. That's why he doesn't have anywhere right now.'

Luke studied me. 'Let me guess, that's what he told you?'

I nodded mutely.

'And you believed him?'

I heard the scorn in his voice. He thought I was foolish. Gullible.

Perhaps I was.

'Anyway, it's not my problem. I don't want anything to do with him, or any of you, for that matter,' Luke continued.

'Then why did you agree to meet me? Why in person? You could have just told me to leave you alone over the phone.'

'This isn't the kind of conversation you can have over the phone. You were talking about the truth coming out. That won't just affect you. That affects all of us.'

'I won't reveal your part in it.'

Luke laughed. 'You really think once you start talking that the whole story won't unravel?' He scoffed. 'Just because you've suddenly grown a conscience, you want to destroy all our lives.'

He pushed his chair back and stood up.

'Luke, wait.' I sprang to my feet. He couldn't leave yet. I still hadn't got the answer I had come here for. 'Just one more question and then I'll leave you alone, I swear.'

Luke sighed, and lowered himself back into his seat. 'Fine, one question.'

'Who dared Hannah to climb to the top of Durdle Door?' I asked as I perched on the edge of my chair.

'What?'

'Who dar—'

'I heard you. I just can't believe you messaged me to ask me that.'

'It's important.'

He rolled his eyes.

'Do you remember?'

'Yeah, I remember. It was Tom.'

'Y-you're sure?'

'Positive. He knew she'd accept. Hannah was fearless.' His brow creased as his gaze drifted over my shoulder. 'No, not fearless. It's more like she was determined to prove herself. To never back down. Never show weakness.' Luke shook his head as his gaze refocused on me. 'I guess she learnt that from her dad. He was a tough boss and a harder father, from what I saw of their encounters.'

A faded memory stirred in the recesses of my mind.

* * *

'I have a dare for you,' Tom said, nuzzling Hannah's neck. 'If you're not too scared.'

Hannah pushed him back and glared at him. 'You know I'm not scared of anything.'

'True,' Tom conceded. 'In that case, I dare you to climb up there.' Tom lifted his hand and pointed to the top of Durdle Door.

I gasped. He had to be joking. No one in their right mind would climb that.

* * *

And yet we had.

60

'It *was* Tom.' I could see it now. I remembered. I sank back into my chair. 'How had I forgotten that?'

'You were so drunk. I'd never seen you that wasted before.'

'I never had been. I wish I hadn't chosen that night to start.'

'I wish I hadn't taken all that wine with us.'

We sat in silence for a moment before Luke sucked in a deep breath. 'Well, what's done is done. None of it matters any more.'

I shook my head. Luke was wrong. It did matter. It all mattered.

'Why did you go along with the lie? Why didn't you turn me in? I know you wanted to.'

'You said one question.' He snorted. 'I guess the lies never end with you, do they?'

'Please, Luke.'

'Like Tom said; we needed to stick together.'

'But you didn't want to. You were so against it. The cover up. The guilt. You hated it. It came between you and Rebecca. It destroyed your relationship. *I* destroyed your relationship.'

'Is that what you thought? That we broke up because of you?'

'Rebecca defended me, but you—'

'Wanted to turn you in? Yeah, I did. But I couldn't.'

'Couldn't?' A large knot formed in the pit of my stomach. 'What do you mean, you couldn't?'

'Leave the past where it belongs, Lizzie.'

'I can't. Tom wants me to come forward. To confess. And I've agreed.' It felt strange to say aloud. There was a part of me that wasn't sure if I would really do it. But telling Luke made it seem more definite. More real.

Luke's eyes widened. 'Why would he want you to do that?'

'He thinks I need to; for my conscience; my peace of mind.' Tom was right. He knew what was best for me. He always had.

And yet, somewhere inside me a little niggling doubt was growing. Did Tom want what was best for me? I'd tried to pass it off as Rebecca's distrust invading my thoughts, but truthfully I knew that doubt had been ever present since I opened the door to find Tom on my doorstep.

I'd pushed it aside, determined to ignore it. But like so many things it still haunted me.

The only way to deal with it was to address it head on. That was why I was here after all. Why I was asking Luke questions.

The deeper I dug the more that doubt grew.

'That doesn't make sense.'

'You don't know how hard it has been to live with myself, knowing what I did—'

'I get that. I get why you might want to clear your conscience. But it doesn't make sense for the idea to come from Tom.'

My shoulders tensed. 'Why not?'

'Because you aren't the only one with a secret.'

'What are you talking about?' My heart thudded. Who else had a secret? Tom? The idea no longer seemed as impossible as it once would have done. He'd lied to me about coming to see me first.

He'd lied about who'd dared Hannah to climb Durdle Door. What other secrets could he have?

'It doesn't matter. Just remind Tom that he has a lot to lose.' Luke pushed his chair back. 'Don't contact me again,' he said as he stood up again. 'And make sure Tom doesn't either.'

'What do you mean, Tom has a lot to lose?' I leapt to my feet. He couldn't leave without explaining that statement.

'He'll know.'

Luke started to step away but I grabbed his arm. '*I* want to know.'

He shook my hand off. 'Leave it alone, Lizzie,' he hissed, as he glanced around the café and I realised that people were looking at us.

'What does he have over you?'

The colour drained from Luke's face. 'I don't know what you're talking about.' He turned away and marched to the door.

I grabbed my bag off the back of the chair and hurried after him. 'Luke!' I called as I followed him outside.

He turned back to face me.

'I know there's something. I knew it that morning as we drove home from Durdle Door.' Even as I confronted him I wondered if maybe Luke was right. Maybe I should leave it alone. If I angered Luke he could go to the police. I might be about to turn myself in, but I needed to do it on my terms, not his.

And yet, even though Luke had wanted to tell the police everything at the time, he hadn't. Something told me he couldn't. Not then. And probably not now.

'Tom persuaded you to go along with his plan, even though you didn't want to.'

'Lizzie...' Luke shook his head.

'How?' My voice was steely. I'd spent ten years wondering what had really happened that night. I wasn't going to let the answers slip away from me again. Not when I was so close.

'Tom uses people, it's what he's good at. He used me. He used Hannah.'

'To get the job at DEM. That's why he wouldn't leave her.'

'Not just for the job.'

'What else?'

'Tom talked Hannah into getting her dad to hire me too. We were only first year uni students, so we started at the bottom. Making coffee, filing papers, carrying boxes, that kind of stuff. We were kept well away from the clients. It sucked, but it made sense. I figured we'd prove our worth and gradually we'd move up the ranks. But Tom hated it. He wanted more. And he didn't want to wait. He was like that, though, always looking for the easy way to get ahead.'

'I thought he loved his job. He was so proud to be working there.'

'He wanted everyone to think he was more important to Davis than he really was. It didn't matter either way to me; he was my mate, so I just went along with it. But that still wasn't enough for Tom.'

'What do you mean?'

'He persuaded Hannah to get us into her dad's office one night after everyone had gone home. He said he wanted to get some info on potential clients off Davis's computer. He reckoned if he had access to their files he could come up with the perfect events for them and win Davis over.'

'Did it work?'

'I was just there to keep watch by the door. That's all I did. But...'

'But?' I stepped back. 'What did Tom do?' I felt a queasy sense of foreboding. Part of me didn't want to know, but another part knew that I had to. It was the only way to understand everything that had happened. To finally know the truth.

'He stole from the company.'

'No, that can't be right.' Tom may have told a few lies, but he wasn't a thief. 'How would that even be possible?'

'Hannah. She was the boss's daughter. She helped with the accounts. She had access. They set up a fake supplier, one linked to his own bank account and then Hannah approved the invoices.'

'That's what Tom had over you, how he got you to keep quiet about Hannah's death?'

'He reminded me that a police investigation would not be ideal. If it became known that Tom had been up on the top of Durdle Door with her, and that you and he were having an affair, it was possible that the police might start to question if her death was premeditated.'

An affair.

The term jarred against me. It sounded so distasteful. So wrong.

'But Tom didn't push her. I did. So he was protecting me.'

'Maybe. But it wasn't just about you. Think about it, Lizzie. By keeping your relationship a secret, Tom played the broken hearted grieving boyfriend. Davis welcomed him into the company as though he was family. Whereas if his betrayal had become known he ran the risk that the police would think he had a motive for killing Hannah. Which, in turn, could have run the risk that the theft could have come to light.'

'So he blackmailed you to ensure your silence. But was he protecting me? Or himself?'

'Do you really not know the answer?'

61

I took a deep breath and pushed open the front door. It felt backwards. Usually, I needed courage to go out of my house, not in.

'Hi,' I called, forcing my voice to sound normal as I stepped inside.

'Hey,' Tom said, as he poked his head round the living room door. 'Welcome home.'

There was something so normal about his greeting, so welcoming and caring, that it made me wish I could forget everything I'd learnt. I wanted the Tom I'd thought he was. The one I believed. The one I trusted.

But he wasn't that man.

Perhaps he never had been.

And yet I still missed him...

'How was work?' he asked as he walked towards me.

I swallowed. He wasn't the only one who couldn't be trusted. I'd let him think I was at work all day, when in reality I'd been investigating him.

'Are you okay? You seem distracted,' he said when I didn't respond.

'It's just been a long day.'

He hugged me tightly and I felt my body tense. His touch didn't bring me comfort now.

'How about we go out for dinner tonight?'

'No.' My tone was sharper and more adamant than I'd intended, but the thought of going back out again filled me with fear. I'd barely got through the day and was finally home. I didn't have the energy to go anywhere else.

'O-k-ay.' Tom drew the word out as he gazed at me nervously. 'But the groceries won't arrive until later though, so...'

'We can order in.'

'Sure.' Tom backed away and turned towards the kitchen. 'I'll check what's available down here.'

I nodded, but my mind was preoccupied. We needed to talk. I needed to confront him. I needed to tell him what I knew. But I couldn't work out how to start.

Or, perhaps more accurately, I was afraid to start. Because once my accusations were out there, there would be no going back. Everything we had would wither and die.

I knew his lies now. There would be no need for pretence any longer. Had anything he'd said since his return been real? Was anything about *him* real?

But I was done being afraid; of running away and hiding from things that were difficult to face.

I knew more now than I ever had before, but there were still gaps. Still questions.

I pushed my shoulders back and followed him into the kitchen. 'Tom? Why did you make us leave the beach? Why wouldn't you let Luke and Rebecca call for help? Why did you lie to the police?' The questions that had circled in my brain since Tom's return tumbled out.

A flicker of anger passed across his face, before he smiled reassuringly. 'I did it for you.'

'Did you?'

'Of course I did. What kind of a question is that?' There was a tone to his voice that I couldn't distinguish. Was it hurt? Or exasperation?

He thought we had a neat little plan to resolve everything. I would turn myself in. I would make peace with my actions. We would move forward. And yet, here I was, picking at the scab again.

'Luke told me that you had your own reasons for lying to the police.' My voice was steely as I fought to keep my emotions in check. I wouldn't be weak. Not this time.

'When did he tell you that?' Was it my imagination or had I seen a flash of fear in Tom's eyes?

'What did he mean?' I persisted, ignoring his question.

'I don't know.'

'Then why did you cover for me?'

'Because I love you. I wanted to protect you.'

You can't trust him.

Rebecca's words replayed in my mind.

She was right. There was so much he had lied to me about. But was this another lie? Or could it be the truth?

The breakfast dishes stacked beside the sink caught my attention. Tom had promised to put them in the dishwasher when I left this morning. I sighed, marched to the dishwasher and opened the door.

'Why are you doing that now?'

'Because you didn't,' I told him as I picked up the dishes and stacked them in the dishwasher.

'I would have done.'

'When?'

Tom shrugged. 'When I got round to it.'

I closed the door and my gaze fell upon the plug socket where the sandwich press was switched on. Tom must have used it for his lunch. I gritted my teeth and flicked the switch off.

I heard Tom approach behind me. I ignored him and turned to the toaster, but he beat me to it. He peered at it, exaggerating his movements as he ran his fingers across the empty socket, as if proving to himself that it was unplugged.

He chuckled as he moved to the fridge and leaned his weight against the door.

I scowled at him. 'Don't do that.'

'What?'

'Don't mock me.'

'I'm not. I'm just checking the kitchen.'

I shook my head. 'No, you're make a big performance of it, laughing at me and making me feel stupid.'

'I d—'

'But the thing is, it's not stupid.' My words picked up speed. 'It's perfectly sensible to want to check the hob is off and not going to cause a fire. Or that the freezer door is shut properly, so I don't have to mop up a flood of water in the morning and throw away defrosted food because the door was ajar all night.'

I was rambling, I knew it, but I didn't care. I was tired of feeling stupid. Of trying to hide my desire to check things. My desire for order. Routine. I was tired of the disapproval. The condescension. But was it his that frustrated me? Or my own?

I viewed myself as broken. Flawed. My routines were excessive. A sign of my weakness. But at their foundation they were rational and sound. It was wise to be cautious.

People stayed safe that way.

I just needed to find a balance. A way to be satisfied with checking something once.

The repetition was my comfort. But it was also my downfall. It kept me stuck in a loop.

But Tom's mockery wasn't the way to free me from it. Instead, it made it worse. It made me feel bad. Foolish. Broken.

Unlovable.

My heart pounded at that thought. I'd be alone. Forever.

I couldn't count on him. I no longer knew if he would be around. I wasn't even sure that I wanted him to be.

I could feel my anxiety ramping up inside me. It was like a fire that burned continuously within. It required constant attention and supervision. I had to keep it restrained. Controlled. It drained my energy. It made it harder to focus on anything else, do anything else. If I took my eyes off it, if I looked away, it would grow stronger. Wilder. Out of control.

Tom's teasing made it worse. It stoked the fire.

It made me seek comfort. The kind I got from my routines. From checking.

It made the need stronger.

I needed to start again now. I needed to do it myself. To do it properly. Tom's way was wrong. Incomplete. Exaggerated. Ineffective.

'I can't rely on you,' I snapped. 'I couldn't when we were kids and I can't now.'

'That's not fair.' He drew back, as though stung by the sharpness of my words.

'You're right, it's not. Because I deserved to be treated like I mattered. I deserved to be a priority.' The anger that had been building inside me since I'd met with Luke couldn't be restrained any longer.

His brow furrowed and he studied me silently. I could practically see him debating how to handle the situation. How to handle me.

'I'll do better.'

I paused. I wanted to believe him. I always had before. But this time was different. This time I knew better.

I knew he'd lied.

'Your words are meaningless. Just empty promises.' I snorted. 'But then you were always good at those.'

I'd spent years believing in him. Waiting for him. I couldn't do it any more.

I marched back into the hall. 'I'm going for a walk,' I said as I slid my feet into my pumps.

'What? Now?' Tom asked from the kitchen.

'Yep.'

I heard his footsteps approaching. 'I'll come wi—'

'Bye,' I called as I slipped out of the door. It was the fastest I'd opened the door and left the house in years.

I strode down the driveway and turned right onto the pavement. I didn't linger. Not today. I didn't want company. I just wanted escape.

Escape.

The word circled in my brain.

That was new.

Not the idea of escape. That need for escape, of constantly checking for exits and ways out, was always with me. But home was usually where I ran to. Home was my escape. Out was a place I never went willingly.

Until now.

The sea came into view ahead of me and my pace quickened. I hadn't even thought about where I was going. It was as though my feet were on a mission. It was instinctive. Determined.

They'd led me here.

I made my way down the chine, dodging the tourists as they headed back to their cars and hotels for the evening, laden with picnic bags and deckchairs. Their lives seemed so idyllic. To them Bournemouth was an escape from their day to day lives. For me it was a just another part of the trap of my own making.

It was time to break free from it.

I knew Tom's solution.

But now I also knew his motives were questionable. He'd told too many lies for me to believe that he was acting in my best interests. There was another side to him. One I hadn't seen before. One I could no longer ignore.

62

I froze as the doorbell chimed.

It was a sound I dreaded. A disruption to my carefully planned life. An intrusion. But this time it wasn't unscheduled. It was necessary.

It was overdue.

'Do you want me to answer that?' Tom asked as we sat at the kitchen table, half eaten sandwiches on our plates in front of us. He'd been overly attentive and helpful since I'd returned from my walk on the beach last night.

We hadn't discussed it. We'd simply carried on as though nothing had changed.

But I knew that everything had.

I shook my head. 'No, I'll get it.' I strode through the hall, full of purpose, and swung the door open.

'Lizzie Green?' the man in his late fifties asked from my doorstep.

I nodded and stepped back to allow him to enter. I didn't need to ask his name. I recognised him from his photos online. Tom wasn't the only person I had stalked over the years. Tom's wasn't the only life my actions had derailed.

'A-Alan!' I heard the shock in Tom's voice as it carried from the kitchen behind me.

'Tom?' Mr Davis froze in the doorway.

I glanced back and forth between them as they stared at each other in stunned silence.

'W-what are you doing here?' Tom finally asked.

'I called him,' I said as I lifted my chin, attempting to portray a courage I didn't feel. 'I asked him to come.'

Mr Davis stepped forward and I started to shut the door behind him, but I paused. I gazed down the driveway. There was still time to call this off. To tell him I'd made a mistake. There was still time to escape.

But then again, as long as the past hung over me, would I ever really escape? My shoulders sagged. The last ten years were proof that I wouldn't. I couldn't.

It wasn't only Mr Davis that needed closure.

'Y-you did?'

I couldn't blame Tom for his bewilderment. Hannah's father was the last person he'd expect to see in my home. He was the last person I would have ever thought I would invite. But Tom's return had taught me that despite my best efforts, life was not something that could be hidden from and it was finally time that I faced that.

I sucked in a deep breath and clicked the door closed. 'Let's go and sit in the living room,' I said to Mr Davis as I nodded down the hall. 'Are you coming?' I asked Tom, who was still sitting at the kitchen table as though frozen in place.

'Er, yeah,' he replied, casting me a bewildered look as I passed. It was the first time I'd ever seen Tom shaken. He was always so in control. So confident. So certain.

I heard him follow behind me as I joined Mr Davis in the living room.

'Are you sure this is the best way to do this, Lizzie?' Tom asked as he crossed his arms in the doorway, blocking me in.

I was trapped.

'It's time for the truth to come out. Just like you said,' I told him, fighting to keep my voice steady. There had been too many secrets. Too many lies. It was time they all came out. Mine. And Tom's.

I saw the corner of Tom's lips lift for a second before his concerned expression fell back into place. 'Don't you want to talk to a lawyer first?'

I shook my head. 'I have nothing to hide.' Not any more. I was done hiding from life. From the truth. From who I was.

'You said you had something to tell me about my daughter?' Mr Davis said, impatiently. I couldn't blame him. I'd been cryptic on my call, dragging him all the way to Bournemouth to sit in my living room.

I inhaled slowly, searching for how to begin. 'Why did Tom leave DEM?'

I watched the colour drain from Tom's face. He hadn't expected me to know that piece of information. Not that it was hard to figure out after overhearing his call with his dad. 'That's not relevant—'

'Everything is relevant,' I told him firmly. I wouldn't allow him to talk me out of this. I wouldn't allow him to make me lose my focus. Not this time.

'I fired him,' Mr Davis answered flatly.

I nodded. 'You uncovered the fraud?'

'Lizzie!' Tom hissed from across the living room.

I tried not to recoil. I couldn't show weakness. Not now.

'You knew?' Mr Davis's eyes narrowed as he stared at me. I could practically feel him assessing me, trying to determine if I had been part of it. Involved. Complicit.

'I figured it out.' He still looked sceptical, but I wasn't about to reveal how I knew. Luke didn't deserve the scrutiny that could follow. 'They set up a fake company, didn't they? And used that to charge DEM for supplies that never existed?'

'They?' Mr Davis edged forwards. 'There were others involved?'

'Hannah.'

Mr Davis's expression hardened. 'My daughter is dead, Miss Green. Something I am sure you are aware of considering you claimed to be her friend.'

'But she was involved ten years ago. They started it together.'

He inhaled sharply. 'Hannah wouldn't steal from me.' His tone was harsh. He didn't like me accusing Hannah. I couldn't blame him. She was his daughter. And she was gone. But there was too much at stake to sidestep around his feelings.

'Wouldn't she?'

Mr Davis flinched. It was only a tiny movement, but it was enough to confirm my suspicions. 'She admired you. But she...' I fought to summon the courage to continue. I was treading on dangerous ground. One wrong word... One accusation too far... 'She resented how much you favoured your business over her. She felt like you loved it more than you loved her.'

'I was building it for *her*.' His head dropped. 'I was training her to take over. To be in charge. To have something that was hers.'

'She didn't need it. All she wanted was you.' I glanced at Tom. I understood how Hannah had felt now. How far she had been driven to try and win back affection from the person she needed the most. And how far she had sunk when she'd failed.

'I heard Tom and Hannah arguing the night that she died.' Mr Davis's head jerked back, his attention fixed on me.

The fragmented memories which had tumbled through my thoughts for years had finally started to take shape since Tom's return. Perhaps it was his presence sparking clarity. Or perhaps the truths that I had learnt from Rebecca and Luke meant I was no longer blinded by Tom's version of events. Or perhaps I was finally strong enough to focus on them and allow them to flow uninterrupted, without my fear of recalling what I believed I had done causing me to shut them away.

* * *

'She knows too much,' Hannah snapped at Tom.

'She doesn't know anything. And even if she did, it doesn't matter. Your dad won't do anything. He'd be mad. He'd yell. But nothing would happen. Not as long as we stick together. You're his daughter. He'd never let the police arrest you, which means he can't come after me either.'

'Why would I stick with you? You talked me into this. You used me. You needed my access to my father's office. You needed me to create the fake supplier and approve it on the system.'

'You could have said no. But you didn't, because you wanted to take his precious money. You wanted to take something that mattered from him.'

'But it's not just his money we stole. We stole from his clients too.'

'We had to cover our tracks. Your dad would have noticed if he was losing money.'

* * *

'When we upgraded our finance system a couple of months ago we discovered additional charges embedded in the formulae which we used to charge clients,' Mr Davis said, his voice also holding a touch of admiration. 'It was clever. A tiny tweak, small enough not to be noticed. We probably still wouldn't have caught it if we hadn't changed the software.'

He looked across the room at Tom. 'Of course, we started an

investigation as soon as it was discovered. Tom had been quite vocal in his recommendations against the upgrade. He was adamant that it wasn't necessary. My suspicions were raised, but—'

'You didn't think Tom would betray you like that.'

Mr Davis shook his head slowly. 'Tom seemed so dedicated and earnest. I actually felt bad for doubting him for even a second. But as we dug deeper we found a supplier who didn't exist. The bank account led us back to Tom.'

I glanced at Tom, expecting to see some sign of remorse, but his expression was hard. He didn't appear to be sorry for his crime, just angry that he'd been caught.

'Are the police aware?'

'Of course. Tom was arrested. His family bailed him out pending the trial. They are quite convinced that he has been set up, but the evidence is solid. Hannah's access was used to create the fake supplier but the money trail leads directly to Tom.'

'So you already knew she was involved.'

He shook his head. 'Hannah's involvement might not have been done knowingly or even willingly. Tom could have used his relationship with her to steal her password, he could have coerced her or even forced her to participate.'

Mr Davis looked across the room at Tom. 'I'm surprised to find you back in Bournemouth. I know your family moved away years ago. Given your current situation I expected you to be staying with them. And yet, here you are, back in the region where Hannah died.'

'I was visiting an old *friend*.' I heard the hostility he placed on that word and I knew that a friend was the one thing he no longer considered me to be.

It was inevitable. And yet, it still hurt.

'I assume it has something to do with the investigation into Hannah's death?'

'You're investigating?' I tried to keep the fear out of my voice. An investigation into the death that I had caused.

'We can see from the dates on the falsified records that this took place six weeks before Hannah's death. Given what we now know, the timing is suspicious.'

'You think Tom killed her?'

'Don't you dare try and pin this on me,' Tom said, his voice raised as he stepped towards me.

Mr Davis leapt to his feet. 'Tom!' His command caused Tom to freeze instantly. 'Back away.'

Tom hesitated for a moment before complying and returning to his spot by the door.

I let out a deep breath. I hadn't seen that anger in Tom's eyes before. It was a side of him I didn't know. A side I didn't want to know.

'In answer to your question, Miss Green, yes, I think it's possible. Tom, however, strongly protested his innocence.' Mr Davis shrugged. 'Hardly surprising. But we did reach an agreement.'

'I-I don't understand.' His statement unbalanced me. I'd thought I was in control here. Yet Tom was a step ahead. Again. 'Tom stole from you for years, you think he was involved with your daughter's death, what kind of agreement could you possibly make with him?'

'I agreed to drop all charges, in exchange for evidence about what really happened to Hannah that night.'

63

The temperature in the room seemed to rapidly increase as I fought that familiar fuzzy feeling that warned me I was just about to faint. I clenched my fists, digging my nails into my palms.

'That's why you're here,' I said, staring at Tom.

I finally understood why he had come back to Bournemouth. To me.

It had never been because he missed me.

He was going to turn me in to save himself.

'I promised Alan I would bring him answers.' Tom sounded calmer now, more in control.

And yet, I hadn't been arrested. Tom hadn't even called Mr Davis. I had.

Tom couldn't just accuse me. To do so would reveal his own lie. It would be his word against mine. He had motive now. If he admitted his involvement he risked being charged as an accessory.

There was no physical evidence to incriminate me. If there had been, the police would have found it ten years ago. I would already be in prison.

Tom needed evidence. The realisation stuck me like a blow to the chest, sucking the air from my lungs.

It was the one piece that was missing. There was nothing to tie me to Hannah's death. The rain that morning had washed away any evidence that we were ever up on the arch with Hannah. His accusation alone would be meaningless, especially given his own crime.

Tom needed my confession.

He had nothing without it.

I want us to be together. I want us to have a future together.

Tom's words repeated in my memory. All he had was my love for him. My need to be loved by him in return. My willingness to do anything to keep him.

He knew how to manipulate me. How to use me. He always had.

'Lizzie, it's time.'

By willpower alone the room started to come back into focus and I turned to face Tom, wondering if the inner battle I was fighting was displayed on my face.

I didn't need to ask him what it was time for. I already knew.

It was time to confess.

Now was my chance to face the demons that I had carried for too long. To finally admit my mistake. My crime.

My thoughts drifted back to that night.

* * *

'I can't.' Tom's voice floated into my thoughts as I teetered on the edge of consciousness. 'I won't.'

'You have to,' Hannah insisted. 'She's a liability.'

I forced my eyelids open and found myself staring at Tom's trainers. Why was I lying on the ground.

I raised my hand to my head, trying to ease the pounding that reverberated through me as I fought to focus on their words. Who was a liability? What were they talking about?

'She doesn't know anything,' Tom insisted.

I felt a drop of rain on the back of my hand, and I peered up at the grey sky. That was all we needed right now. I staggered to my feet, pushing aside the nausea that swelled inside me. 'We should head back down,' I stuttered, struggling to form the words.

'I don't believe you,' Hannah snapped at Tom, oblivious to my presence.

'Okay, but even if she does, she wouldn't talk.'

'She will when you end it.'

'End what?' They both turned to face me then. Tom looked so guilty. Like when he was a child and got caught stealing chocolates.

As I gazed at Tom I knew that the nausea I felt wasn't all attributable to the unaccustomed volume of alcohol I had drunk. Something was wrong. Very wrong.

'You owe me,' Hannah said, glancing back at Tom.

He shook his head. 'Not this. It's too much.'

'You need me, Tom.'

'We need each other. You have the access, but I'm the one that made it work.'

'What's going on?' What was all this talk about needing each other? Tom didn't need Hannah. He needed me.

He was breaking up with her.

I glanced back and forth from one to the other.

Wasn't he?

'Fine, if you won't do it then I will.' Hannah charged at me.

I saw her coming, but my brain couldn't compute it. 'What are you—'
She collided into me, her hands pushing against my shoulders, causing me to stagger backwards as she drove me towards the edge.

'Tom!' I screamed. His eyes met mine but he didn't move. He stood there motionless, watching.

'He was never going to choose you,' Hannah hissed as she leaned her weight into me. 'You never meant anything to him. Not like me.'

I bent my knees, trying to find a solid stance as I wedged my feet against the rocks to give me more resistance. 'Fine, you win. I don't want him.' I wanted someone who would put me first. Someone who didn't expect me to share. Someone who came to my aid when I needed him.

'It's too late for that. You know too much.'

I twisted my shoulders to the right, dislodging her hands and then swung my left elbow back at her. I heard a whoosh of air as it connected with her stomach. 'I know too much about what?'

My head felt fuzzy. What she was saying didn't make sense. What did I know?

'Don't play dumb. Tom's too conceited not to have told you. He's so impressed with himself for coming up with the idea, for outsmarting my father.'

'I don't understand.'

Hannah's focus seemed to clear as she stared at me. 'Huh, maybe you don't. Perhaps Tom was telling the truth after all. At least about that.' She snorted. 'Not that it matters. Even if you didn't know anything before, you know too much now.'

She lunged at me again, her slender fingers wrapping themselves around my arms as she pushed me backwards towards the edge.

'No!' I screamed. I didn't want to die. I had too much to live for. Despite my exhaustion and drunkenness, from somewhere deep within I summoned the final reserves of my strength. I pushed her back as hard as I could as I twisted my body, desperately trying to get away from the edge.

I felt her body buckle as her ankle seemed to collapse underneath her. I seized the opportunity and broke free from her grasp. My sudden movement threw her further off balance and she tottered backwards.

Her eyes widened with panic as her arms flailed, desperately trying to grab hold of me. Some instinct inside me told me to help her, but I didn't. I just watched, frozen, unable to move, as she tumbled backwards over the edge of the arch.

64

'I remember.' After all these years, all the guilt, the self-hatred, I finally knew what had happened.

Hannah had tried to kill me.

'Miss Green?'

I blinked as Mr Davis came back into focus.

'What do you remember, Miss Green?'

Tom was right. I had pushed her. Hannah had fallen because of me. But it wasn't in the way that I thought, the way that he'd said. I hadn't attacked her in drunken jealous rage. I'd merely defended myself.

'I...' My confession evaporated from my lips.

I'd been prepared to face the consequences for my actions. I'd brought Mr Davis here to tell him what I'd done. But I'd wanted him to know the whole story. Not just my part. But Tom and Hannah's too. I wanted the truth about all of us to finally come out. The cheating. The stealing. The murder.

But it wasn't what I'd thought. *I* wasn't what I thought.

To tell the truth now would be to unravel all of our lives. I would have to admit to my presence on the top of Durdle Door. Admit to my lie. Our lie. Rebecca and Luke had already lost enough because of me. I wouldn't make them lose more.

Hannah had tried to kill me. And Tom had been willing to stand by and do nothing to prevent it. I didn't owe them anything. Not any more. Maybe I never had at all.

'Hannah...' I searched for the right words. I wanted to tell him that Hannah had tried to kill me. I wanted to tell everyone. But that was a truth no father needed to hear. 'Hannah was so drunk that night. She was happy to be surrounded by friends. To be part of our group.'

'Lizzie, stop this. You're just playing for time. But you have to face the consequences. You have to confess.'

'Confess?' Mr Davis's eyes narrowed as he glared at me.

'To what?' I asked, widening my eyes as though I was surprised. I'd spent ten years learning how to play a role. My life was an act. I pretended to be normal; to belong; to be happy. I realised now that it had all just been preparation for this moment. The final performance of the lie that had become my life.

Tom stared at me, stunned. 'To pushing Hannah off Durdle Door.'

'What?' I shook my head. 'I wouldn't climb up there. That would be an insane thing to do. You and Hannah were always the brave ones. You two were fearless. Always challenging each other. Daring each other.'

I saw a flash of uncertainty pass across Tom's face. He didn't know I knew about the dare. He didn't know I knew it had been his dare, not mine, that had triggered all that had followed.

'But she taunted you. She pressured you into going with her,' Tom urged, as though hoping to jog my memory.

'Why would she do that? She was my friend.' I turned to her father. 'Hannah and I would chat about uni, Tom, even you. She admired you so much. She was such a strong personality. At least on the surface.' I blinked away the tears that had formed in my eyes. 'Beneath the act, though, there was a kind of fragility to her. A fear that she wasn't good enough. Wasn't accepted.'

'You saw that?'

I smiled slightly. 'Like I said, she was my friend.' My voice cracked as I spoke. I wished my words had been true. Maybe if I'd known her better. Maybe I could have helped her. Or maybe without me she wouldn't have needed help. No matter who she was at her core, I knew that I had contributed to the path that she had chosen.

Mr Davis sniffed. 'She didn't let many people see that side of her. She thought it made her look weak. Vulnerable.'

'I know.'

He nodded. 'I'm glad she had a friend like you.' There was a gravelly tone to his voice and I knew that whilst he might not always have done the right thing for his daughter, he had loved her.

'I just wish I could have saved her.' My words were filled with conviction and I realised I meant it. Despite trying to kill me, I wished that she hadn't died. I didn't hate her any more. She had no power over me now. Neither did Tom. I'd given them their power. Now I was choosing to take it back.

'This was your plan?' Mr Davis asked with hostility as he turned back to glare at Tom. 'To accuse Hannah's friend? You thought if you gave me another suspect, I would drop the charges against you and stop investigating you?'

'B-but...' Tom stuttered.

I shook my head. 'There's nothing to investigate.'

'She wouldn't be so reckless. She wouldn't go up there. Not alone. Not without a reason,' Mr Davis insisted. 'And before you say it, I will never believe the police's theory that she was suicidal. I know she was troubled. She acted out. She drank too much. Partied too hard. But that didn't mean she wanted to die.'

'I—' Tom started to protest but I cut through him.

'No, it doesn't,' I agreed. I knew better than anyone that taking risks, punishing my body, myself, wasn't necessarily a sign that I didn't want to be here. I finally understood that side of Hannah. 'It was just her way of coping. Of living.'

'Then what are you saying?'

'The Hannah I knew would have climbed that limestone arch because it was there. Because she could. Not because she was fearless or reckless. Not because she wanted to die. But because she was trying to find herself. Prove herself. Her strength. Her worth. Because she wanted to live. Really live.' I shrugged. 'That's my theory anyway.'

Silence engulfed us.

I could feel Tom's gaze boring into me, but I refused to look at him. I didn't need his approval, his encouragement.

I could imagine his confusion, his anger. I'd ruined his plan. I'd confused him. He was unusually quiet. Presumably because whilst I wasn't confessing my guilt, I wasn't blaming him either.

He was stuck. For once he was completely and utterly reliant on me.

Mr Davis stared at me. 'But then why all the drama? Why did you bring me here to tell me what the police had assumed ten years ago; that there had been no foul play? What did you mean by your big proclamation about it being time for the truth to come out?'

I swallowed. I couldn't blame Mr Davis for his doubts. I had planned a bigger reveal. I'd planned to expose a murderer; me.

Because of Tom, I'd believed it.

'It was always about Tom,' I replied, knowing that the full meaning of my words would be lost to Mr Davis. Everything had always been about Tom. 'I wanted you to know what he'd done. I knew how close the two of you had become after Hannah's death. I was furious when I learned that he'd been manipulating you. Using your grief. Your trust. But I also know how good he can be at sweet-talking his way out of things, avoiding responsibility, avoiding blame.'

'So you wanted to make sure he had to face me? Face his crimes?'

I nodded, unable to think of anything further to say. My words were true. I just hoped that was enough to convince Mr Davis.

He turned to Tom. 'But if you weren't responsible for Hannah's death, why did you accuse Miss Green? If there was no crime, why accuse anyone?'

Tom blinked. 'I, er...' He glanced at me and took a deep breath. 'I was scared.' His shoulders slumped and I knew that for the first time he was speaking the truth. 'Once you knew about the embezzlement, and you'd expressed your doubts about Hannah's death, I knew I was the prime suspect in your eyes. I thought the only way out was to cast doubt on someone else.' He licked his lips, his eyes pleading with mine. 'I'm sorry, Lizzie. I was so desperate. I didn't know what else to do.'

I turned away. His apology was too late. If it was even sincere.

'So it was just...' Mr Davis's voice cracked and he swallowed, unable to continue.

'An accident,' I replied firmly. I knew the truth now. I hadn't meant to hurt her; to kill her. I'd been defending myself. There was no premeditation. No intent. No murder.

65

'I'm sorry,' I said as I opened the door.

Mr Davis looked weary as he arched his eyebrows. 'For what?'

'If we hadn't gone away that weekend; if we hadn't drunk so much; if—'

'If onlys are a lonely, futile game, Miss Green. Believe me, *I* know.'

I nodded. But the list of ifs continued in my head. If I hadn't kissed Tom. If we hadn't cheated. If I hadn't been so jealous. Hannah wouldn't have taunted me into doing something reckless and stupid.

Despite knowing that I hadn't murdered his daughter, I still knew that I was responsible for what had happened. Not solely. Not totally. But it was enough.

Maybe without my interference, Hannah would still have climbed Durdle Door that day. Maybe she would still have fallen. Or maybe she and Tom would have spent the last ten years happily together.

I would never know.

Mr Davis was right. There would always be if onlys. But they could never change what was.

'What will you do about Tom?' I asked.

'I'm not sure.'

'He kept his word.'

'True,' Mr Davis agreed. 'He brought me closure. Not in the way I expected. But then Hannah never believed in doing what was expected. She lived by her own rules. I never told her, but I always rather admired her for that.'

'Yeah, me too.' I smiled slightly.

'He still needs to repay what he stole, though. Every penny. He may have signed the deeds for his apartment over to me, but that doesn't cover what he took.'

I nodded. 'That's only fair.'

'Thank you, Miss Green,' Mr Davis said as he stepped out into the bright sunshine.

I watched him walk to his car. It felt wrong to be thanked. I'd lied. Again. But this time my lie wasn't to protect me. I'd given him closure and peace. More than the truth would have done.

'Well done,' Tom said behind me, clapping in applause. 'That was quite a performance. You got both of us off the hook.'

I closed the door and turned to face him, rage simmering inside me. 'I should never have been on the hook for anything, Tom.'

'You pushed her.'

'I defended myself.'

'N-no, you—'

'I remember,' I said as I walked towards him. 'I remember everything now.'

'You can't be sure that what you think you remember is actually real, though. Not after all this time. It's just your mind creating—'

'I remember,' I repeated firmly.

I was no longer blind to Tom's manipulation. I didn't need him to recount what had happened. His version of events had always jarred against me. It had never seemed like me. That was the scariest part of all. That I could do something so out of character; so inconceivable; so awful.

And yet, I'd never thought to doubt Tom's word.

'If anyone else had accused me of killing Hannah in a drunken jealous rage, I would have denied it, disputed it. It was only because it was you that I believed it. I believed *you*. I trusted you more than I even trusted myself.' I shook my head slowly. 'That was my biggest mistake of all.' Without that trust, that infatuation, I would never have become entangled in his relationship, his life. I wouldn't have been the other woman, the other girlfriend. And Hannah wouldn't have died.

It was an implication I could never have foreseen, but a mistake I would never make again.

'I guess I could have made a mistake. I mean, I'd been drinking too. Maybe—'

'Or maybe you just lied,' I cut through his feeble attempts to worm his way out of trouble, to excuse his actions, his deception.

'At least I know why you came back. You were going to sell me out. Pin everything on me, so you could walk away from your fraud without charge. I guess that's why you went to Luke first.'

'He'd never wanted to go along with the cover up.'

'You blackmailed him into it.'

'It was the only way to keep him quiet. I thought he'd be relieved to finally come clean, to clear his conscience. But he wouldn't even hear me out.'

'So you came to me. You used the opportunity to go through my stuff, didn't you? Were you hoping I would have confessed my guilt in one of my stories? Or were you just looking for more ways to manipulate me?'

'I just wanted to be with you. We were always so close, we had such a powerful connection. We still do,' he added, reaching his hand out towards me.

'Do you really think you can still charm me? You tried to get me to confess to murder.'

His hand dropped back to his side. 'If you were truly mad about it, if there wasn't some part of you that didn't still love me, you wouldn't have got Davis to drop the charges.'

'You think I did that for you?'

'Who else could it be for?'

'Everyone else,' I replied. 'Mr Davis gets to hold on to the illusion that his daughter was innocent. Rebecca and Luke don't have to admit to their part in the lie that you manipulated us into. And Luke is free from your threats to claim he was involved in your fraud. I know you well enough to know that you have no qualms about blaming your so-called friends to get you out of trouble. As long as you were in danger, so was he.'

Tom smiled. 'When did you get so smart?'

'When I finally woke up and saw you for who you really are.' I turned and strode up the stairs.

He grabbed my arm and twisted me back to face him. 'You need me, Lizzie.'

I stared at him, assessing him. Did I need him? I'd thought I did. I'd spent years convinced of it. Certain that all my problems would disappear if he was with me.

His return hadn't been the instant cure that I'd hoped for, but it had helped. Things were better than they had been, I was better. I went out more often. I travelled further. But was he the reason, or was I?

I'd made it through every panic attack I'd ever had. I'd survived them. I'd kept going to uni, to work, despite them. I always chalked it up to something else; because I'd followed my routines, because my writing distracted me, because I kept water and mints at hand, because Tom was back.

I thought I was weak because I experienced panic attacks at things that normal people did every day without a second thought. But maybe I wasn't weak. Maybe I was strong.

Strong enough to keep going. Strong enough to survive.

Strong enough to live.

Maybe it was time I stopped giving Tom credit for something that I was already doing without him.

The only thing he had really done, was make me realise that no matter what we both had thought, it turned out that I really didn't need him at all.

I jerked my arm free and continued up the stairs. 'I thought I needed you to remind me of who I was. I thought I needed you to give me confidence and courage, to be able to help me cope.' I heard a step creak and I knew Tom was following me. 'But everything I needed was already within me. You weren't helping me to uncover it, you were the one who'd buried it in the first place.'

'That's not true,' Tom objected behind me.

'Your actions, your lies, they are what caused me to doubt myself. Not just about Hannah's death. I can see now that wasn't the beginning; that was just the grand finale. Your deception and manipulation had started long before then. I was just too infatuated with you to see it. Mum did. She tried to warn me. Rebecca too. But I didn't listen. I thought I knew better. I thought I knew *you* better.'

I marched into the guest room, picked up Tom's case from the corner of the room and flung it onto the bed. I didn't even care that its mud-encrusted wheels were resting on the cream duvet cover. Somehow it didn't seem so significant any more.

'What are you doing?' Tom asked as he stood in the doorway.

'Packing.' I unzipped the case and flipped it open. 'All this time I was afraid that you wouldn't like who I am now, this new version of me, withdrawn and afraid, full of darkness and guilt.' I opened the wardrobe and began pulling his clothes out and tossing them into the open case. 'But that just made me more pliable, didn't it? You could feed me more lies and I would never question them because I was so in love with you, and so afraid of myself.'

'You could at least fold them,' Tom said as he tried to tidy the heap of clothes.

I turned and studied the crumpled clothes for a moment, before shrugging and carrying on. 'Instead of worrying about whether I was acceptable to you, I should have focused on whether you were acceptable to me. Because I'm not sure that the version of you I fell in love with ever really existed outside my own imagination.'

I finished my rant and turned, my eyes scanning the room for any further traces of Tom.

'Oh, the bathroom.' I pivoted, marched to the bathroom, scooped up his toiletries from the shelf and dumped them into the case as well.

'What happened to you needing everything to be ordered and tidy?'

'I still do. But it turns out my need for you to be gone is even stronger.'

Tom grunted and zipped his case shut.

'You know, a moment of your attention made me feel so important, so loved, but your neglect made me unravel like a loose thread. That was part of the game though, wasn't it? Part of your power. Your strength. You fed off my need. You relied on the fact that I would always be here waiting. Always adaptable. Always compliant. Because I needed you. Whereas you just needed to be needed. To be wanted. Desired. To be a little out of reach. Uncommitted. Distant. Yet always welcomed back, even after ten years.'

'And I was welcomed back. We were going to get married.'

'I never said yes.' I smiled slightly. Perhaps I wasn't as gullible as he'd thought. 'I'm guessing your proposal had an ulterior motive. If we were married you would gain access to the house and my savings while I was in prison for a murder I didn't commit, right?'

'You think I would do that to you? I'm hurt that you could think so little off me.'

'Are you hoping for sympathy? Because you won't find it here. Not any more.'

'You're right. I don't deserve it. I don't deserve you. I screwed up.' Tom caught hold of my hand in his. 'But Lizzie, I can change. I can be better. You make me want to be better.'

'Seriously?' I twisted away from him and marched across the landing towards the stairs.

'Don't give up on us so easily, Lizzie. You still need me, just as much as I need you. It's how we work.'

'It may have been how Lizzie worked. But as I told you before, I'm Beth now. Lizzie represents a part of my life that is well and truly over. And so do you.'

I saw it then; the same flash of anger in his eyes that I had witnessed earlier. This was him. The real him. Beneath the sweet words and promises. This was who he really was.

'You screwed it all up, Lizzie,' he hissed at me. 'I had a plan. A perfect plan.'

'Just like last time.'

'No, last time you did exactly what you were supposed to.'

I reached for the banister as the meaning of his words ricocheted against me. I knew then that he hadn't lied. There had been a plan to leave Hannah.

I was the plan.

'You intended for us to be at the top of Durdle Door, didn't you? You set us both up. You knew which buttons to press to make us do exactly what you wanted.'

A smile tugged at the corners of Tom's lips. The anger had faded from his eyes now, replaced with a smug gleam.

'Rebecca was right. Hannah did know about us. But she knew because you told her, didn't you? You needed her to know. To be jealous. To see me as a rival. You provoked her.'

Tom edged towards me and I realised my mistake. I was alone. Trapped in my home.

With him.

'I was never interested in Hannah. She was just a way to get to Davis. It worked better than I ever imagined. Her resentment of him gave me more opportunities than I could have dreamed of. She was only too happy to steal from him, to take the one thing that mattered most to him. His money.'

'So why didn't you want to stay together? If she was so useful to you, why did you want to end it?'

'You saw her. You knew what she was like. Demanding. Showy. Everything was a performance with her. Until she tired of it.'

'You thought she'd tire of you? And when she did, you would have been left with nothing.' It made sense now. Tom had always adapted to what people wanted, what they expected from him. He knew how to be everything to everyone.

I'd envied him that. That ability to fit in. To be liked. To be noticed.

But none of it was real.

It was all as fake as he was.

'Everything was dependent on her. She controlled what we took and when. She could make me rich. Or she could destroy me. I knew she was only using me to help her get back at her dad. Once she got tired of me, there was nothing stopping her turning me in. She could pin it all on me. Maybe by catching a thief she could even earn a little of the respect she so desperately craved from her father.'

'You don't know that she would have done that.'

'I couldn't take that risk.'

'You set us both up. You provoked her. Made her angry and jealous. She could have killed me.'

'It was a possibility.'

I felt cold as I gasped for air. 'You didn't really care which one of us died, did you? Either way you were going to win.'

'Hannah would either be gone, or she'd be back under my control. She wouldn't have been able to risk turning me in for the embezzlement without me exposing her role in your death.'

I shook my head. 'How did I misjudge you so much?'

'Because you saw what you wanted to. What you needed to.'

'Not any more. Now I finally see you for what you really are.'

'Hmm,' Tom murmured. 'And what are we going to do about that?'

My body tensed at his ominous tone.

'Thanks to you I owe Davis the rest of the money I stole.'

I edged backwards, pressing my body against the wall. 'But he no longer sees you as a suspect in his daughter's death.'

'True, but then I was never planning on taking the fall for that, was I?'

I gritted my teeth.

His gaze drifted around the landing. 'This house was going to pay Davis off. I'm sure there's a way it still can.'

All I'd ever been to Tom was a safety net. A way to solve his problems ten years ago and again now. It was time that changed.

I straightened my back. 'You're on your own with that one. I won't help you.'

'Are you sure you're in a position to argue?' Tom asked as he leaned towards me.

'Do you really think I haven't learnt enough to take precautions?'

Tom drew back. Doubt crossed his brow. He wasn't sure of the answer. The Lizzie he knew before had been pliable and controllable.

But I wasn't her.

'It wasn't just me there that night, Tom. It wasn't just my life your scheming derailed. We all have a grudge against you. We all want our revenge. Just give us a reason.' I channelled the resentment I felt for him into my words. He'd tried to take everything from me. I wouldn't let him take any more.

'Rebecca and Luke don't know anything.'

I pulled my phone from my pocket and showed him the screen with the open WhatsApp call. 'They've been listening to every word. Recording every word.'

'B-but you didn't know. You couldn't have known.'

'We knew enough to know we couldn't trust you.' Rebecca had agreed instantly when I'd called her from the beach on Monday evening. Luke had been less enthusiastic, but once he'd listened to my plan, even he was willing to participate. It was the only way any of us would be free from Tom, and we all knew it. 'If you ever step out of line, that recording goes to the police.'

'You wouldn't. You all have too much to lose. You were still part of the lie. Part of the cover up.'

'We're prepared for that. The question is: are you?'

I pivoted and strode down the stairs. There was silence for a moment, and then I heard him following behind me. I wasn't afraid. Not now. Tom couldn't touch me. He couldn't hurt me any more. His instinct for self-preservation would keep us all safe.

I reached the front door and pulled it open. 'It's time to go, Tom. And this time don't come back.'

He hesitated in front of me. 'I guess I underestimated you, Lizzie.'

I nodded. 'We both did.'

I leaned against the open door as I watched him walk down the driveway. He didn't look back. There was no reason for him to. There was nothing here for him now.

All these years I'd thought I had nothing without Tom. I *was* nothing without him. I'd thought he was the way out of the rut I had got stuck in. The way back to the person I'd once been. Before the darkness had consumed me. Changed me.

I hadn't been able to see that he was just another trap. Or maybe I had. Maybe I saw it, but just didn't care. I thought I could cope with him by my side. I thought I could be happy with him.

We were happy. At times.

Even that was more than I'd known in so long.

But I realised now that Tom had broken me. His lie ten years ago broke the part of me that believed in myself. The part that believed I deserved to be happy. The part that hoped. That dreamed.

He left a shell of an existence. All I had left to keep me going was routine. Structure. I knew how to clean, tidy, organise, work hard, follow rules, and obey. But I didn't know myself. I denied my feelings, my opinions, my needs. Something inside me died the same day as Hannah. Or maybe even before.

Was it possible to live now? To love? To hope? To dream? Was I strong enough to recognise what I wanted or needed and believe in myself enough to go after it?

66

'You're moving?' Rebecca asked, as she nodded to the 'for sale' sign in the front garden.

'I think it's time.' I smiled ruefully. 'Actually, I think it's well overdue.'

I'd stayed in this house, even after my parents had moved away, because it felt safe. Known.

But it wasn't.

It was my home, but it was also my prison.

I realised now I would never heal in the same place that had broken me. As long as I stayed in this house, this county, some part of me would always be living in the past.

A new place wouldn't be an instant cure, even I knew that. But it would be a clean slate, a fresh start.

I couldn't recreate myself by burying the parts I didn't like. I'd tried that before. It didn't work. I was my past. My choices. My guilt. My fears.

But I was also more than that.

Or at least, I could be.

'Where will you go?'

'Anywhere.' I grinned. 'Everywhere.'

'Do you, er...' She hesitated. 'Do you think you'll be able to?'

'Because of the panic attacks?'

She nodded.

'Honestly, I'm not sure. I'll start small and take it one step at a time. I have support from my parents and therapist.'

'And friends,' she added.

I smiled and squeezed her hand.

'The one thing I learnt from Tom being back here, was that I am capable of much more than I thought I was.'

She tipped her head to the side. 'I never thought I'd be one to say anything positive about Tom, but in a weird way he helped you to find yourself again.'

'He gave me hope. A reason to look forward, to be excited, to daydream, to want to do things and go places.'

I lowered my gaze, unable to meet her eye. 'I used to think the only way to cope with the panic attacks was to grit my teeth, refuse to give in and just white knuckle my way through the day.'

'That sounds so hard.'

I chuckled at her understatement. 'It was beyond hard. It was hell.' Few people knew what my life had really been like. It wasn't something I'd shared. I'd never known how to before. The difficulty I encountered felt like a failure in itself. Catching a bus or sitting in a meeting was something so trivial to everyone else. I thought it meant I was broken or weak because I wasn't like them.

But I knew now that the sadness I heard in Rebecca's tone wasn't pity for my weakness, but sympathy because she cared.

'Every day was a battle I faced alone, with no end in sight. The only thing I knew was that I couldn't give up. I wouldn't.'

'And now?'

'It turns out it makes a difference if I'm going somewhere or doing something I want to do, rather than something I feel like I have to do.'

'It's that simple?'

I laughed. 'No, but it's a start.'

'Do you think maybe the panic attacks were a sign that you weren't on the right path?'

'Maybe. At least partially. By not facing what I thought I'd done, I'd gone against who I was. I'd tried to force myself down a road that didn't feel right to me. The lies. The secrets. The guilt.'

'Your body rebelled.'

'Dramatically.' I snorted. 'But even then I didn't listen. I tried to become someone else. Someone I thought was more acceptable. A different degree. A different career. A different life. I couldn't see there was another way. A better way.'

'So where to first?'

'I thought I'd visit my parents in Spain. I've never actually seen their place out there.'

'You're going on a plane?'

I lifted my head and straightened my back. 'I am.'

'Wow, you sound so certain.'

'Hmm, just because I'm certain, doesn't mean I'm not still scared. But the difference is I want to do this. No one is making me. There are no obligations. No time pressures. No judgement if I don't go. It's my choice and I'll do it when I'm ready. I'll have music to listen to, mints and water in my bag and my writing to help keep me occupied. And maybe a friend for company?' I added hesitantly.

'Absolutely!'

We grinned at each other. It was good to have her back in my life. I knew that I couldn't allow myself to rely on her in order to cope. I wouldn't let her become a crutch as I had with Tom. I needed to learn to be independent. To not rely on someone else, or something else, to get me through the day. And I would. In time.

'Sounds like you have it all worked out,' Rebecca said.

'I have a plan, but I also know that life rarely goes to plan.'

'And you're okay with that?'

I paused as I contemplated her question. There was a time when I couldn't cope without control, or, at least, the illusion of it. But now...

I smiled. 'I'm learning to be okay with it. And right now, that's good enough for me.'

ACKNOWLEDGMENTS

To my wonderful boyfriend, Ahl – your belief in me kept me going even on the days when this book didn't want to be written.

Thanks to my parents for your continued support and encouragement. I'm grateful to Mum for all the feedback on the early drafts.

To my incredible editor, Emily Ruston, thank you for your phenomenal patience, and for helping me get this book back on track. And to my mentor, Jonathan Eyres, and my fantastic friend, Ellie Henshaw, for your invaluable input. We did it!

Thank you to the incredible team at Boldwood Books for all their exceptional work behind the scenes. And to Stuart Gibbon, for answering all my crime related questions.

Thank you to my fantastic colleagues and everyone in the RNA for your amazing friendship and support. Thanks for sticking with me, even when I neglected you through the seemingly endless days of writing and editing.

And finally, thanks to all the wonderful readers who have been so supportive of my first book, *The Perfect Daughter*. Your reviews, social media posts and lovely messages, have meant the world to me. Special thanks to Diane Saxon, Sheryl Browne, Lisa Philips, Erin Green, Kath McGurl, Josie Bonham, Katie, Vicky, Yvonne, Lucy and Sonia.

MORE FROM ALEX STONE

We hope you enjoyed reading *The Other Girlfriend*. If you did, please leave a review.

If you'd like to gift a copy, this book is also available as an ebook, digital audio download and audiobook CD.

Sign up to Alex Stone's mailing list for news, competitions and updates on future books.

https://bit.ly/AlexStoneNewsletter

The Perfect Daughter, another gripping read from Alex Stone is available to order now.

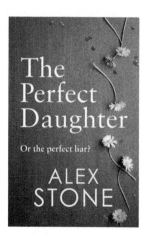

ABOUT THE AUTHOR

Alex Stone, originally an accountant from the West Midlands, is now a psychological suspense writer based in Dorset. This beautiful and dramatic coastline is the inspiration and setting for her novels. She was awarded the Katie Fforde Bursary in 2019.

Follow Alex on social media:

 twitter.com/AlexStoneAuthor

 instagram.com/AlexStoneAuthor

 facebook.com/AlexStoneWriter

Boldw∞d

Boldwood Books is an award-winning fiction publishing company seeking out the best stories from around the world.

Find out more at www.boldwoodbooks.com

Join our reader community for brilliant books, competitions and offers!

Follow us
@BoldwoodBooks
@BookandTonic

Sign up to our weekly deals newsletter

https://bit.ly/BoldwoodBNewsletter